Urgon watched as his mother invoked her magic. She began by closing her eyes and taking a few deep breaths, then the words of power issued from her mouth. Entranced, he sat still as her fingers, glowing with magical energy, were placed over his wound. The colour flowed into him, completing the spell as warmth enveloped his hand.

Kurghal shook her head. "You cleanse the wound with magic but refuse to heal the flesh. Where is the logic in that?"

"The scar will be a constant reminder of his foolishness. Would you want me to remove the evidence?" She turned to her son. "Now go outside, Urgon, and fetch wood for the fire."

The young Orc rose, feeling the strange tugging sensation as he flexed his hand.

"Be quick about it," she urged, "or we will need to start another fire from scratch."

He paused by the doorway, long enough to throw a fur over his shoulders, then stepped outside, the cold taking his breath away.

The village lay spread out before him. As a shamaness, his mother commanded a prominent position amongst the huts, living in one close to the chieftain's. Around this central structure, all the other dwellings were arrayed in concentric circles. Single hunters were clustered together in longhouses that held anywhere from twelve to twenty Orcs. Those already bonded or who held a position of influence, were allowed their own.

Urgon made his way to the log pile behind their hut, only to discover their stores depleted. He cursed, for the snow was deep and the wind much too cold to set out into the woods for more. His first thought was of the great firepit in front of the chieftain's hut—they must have wood to spare. He had gone only fifteen paces when a familiar voice called out.

"Urgon, what brings you out in weather like this?"

He smiled, for his friend Kraloch was of a similar age. "I am on the hunt for firewood," he replied. "Have you any extra, by any chance?"

"I regret I do not." Kraloch noted Urgon's hand. "What has happened here?"

"Only a minor cut. One day soon, I will bear a scar to boast of."

"Yes, and no doubt you will embellish the story, the better to sound heroic. How did you truly get it?"

Urgon laughed. "I was cutting wood for an arrow, and my knife slipped."

# Also by Paul J Bennett

**HEIR TO THE CROWN SERIES**

SERVANT OF THE CROWN

SWORD OF THE CROWN

MERCERIAN TALES: STORIES OF THE PAST

HEART OF THE CROWN

SHADOW OF THE CROWN

MERCERIAN TALES: THE CALL OF MAGIC

FATE OF THE CROWN

BURDEN OF THE CROWN

MERCERIAN TALES: THE MAKING OF A MAN

DEFENDER OF THE CROWN

FURY OF THE CROWN

MERCERIAN TALES: HONOUR THY ANCESTORS

WAR OF THE CROWN

TRIUMPH OF THE CROWN

MERCERIAN TALES: INTO THE FORGE

GUARDIAN OF THE CROWN

ENEMY OF THE CROWN

PERIL OF THE CROWN

**THE FROZEN FLAME SERIES**

AWAKENING | ASHES | EMBERS | FLAMES | INFERNO

MAELSTROM | VORTEX | TORRENT | CATACLYSM

**POWER ASCENDING SERIES**

TEMPERED STEEL | TEMPLE KNIGHT | WARRIOR KNIGHT |TEMPLE CAPTAIN |
WARRIOR LORD | TEMPLE COMMANDER

**THE CHRONICLES OF CYRIC**

# MERCERIAN TALES: HONOUR THY ANCESTORS

## THY ANCESTORS

Heir to the Crown: Book 8.5

PAUL J BENNETT

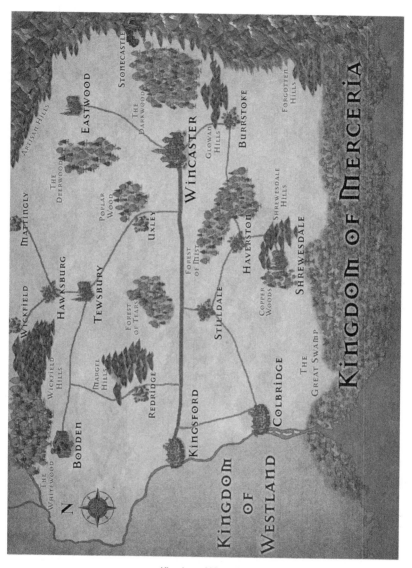

Kingdom of Merceria

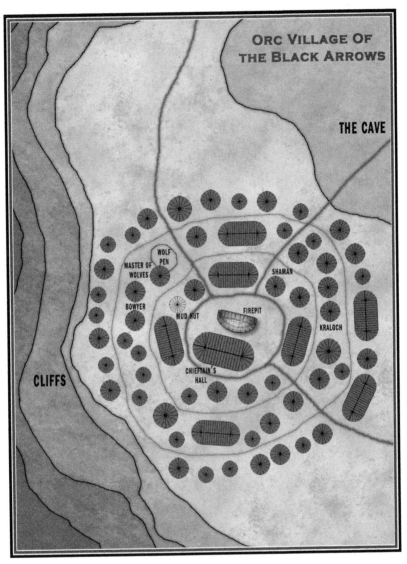

Orc Village of the Black Arrows

# Dedication

*For Jeffrey Parker*

*1962 - 2021*

*Forever a friend and a part of our gaming group.*

# ONE

## Winter

WINTER 946/947 MC (MERCERIAN CALENDAR)

"You injured your hand," said Shular. "How did you come to do this?"

"With my knife, Mother. I was trying to cut wood for an arrow."

She looked down at the small green hand held within her own. "You should take more care, Urgon. Such an accident shows a lack of concentration. Most unbefitting for one of your age."

"You are a healer. Can you not fix it?"

"Of course, but if I were to do that every time you injured yourself, what lessons would you learn?"

"That my mother is the greatest of all Orc healers?"

"Do not be impertinent. Now sit still while I stitch the wound."

"Will it hurt?" the youngling asked.

"Yes, as it should. The cut hurt when you acquired it. Does it not make sense it would do likewise when repaired?"

The hide that covered the door to their hut was pushed aside as Kurghal entered, bringing the icy grasp of winter with her.

"What is this?" she asked. "Has my brother injured himself again? One would think that after twelve winters of living, he would be able to handle a knife."

"It was not my fault," insisted Urgon. "My hands were numb."

"Then you should know better than to attempt something like that." She turned towards Shular, who had withdrawn a bone needle and was pulling forth a collection of hair with which to sew up the wound. "The weather is getting worse, Mother."

Shular held up the needle, threading it with ease. "As I suspected it would."

"And the hunters returned empty-handed again!"

"It is not their fault. All the game fled these hills long ago."

"How can you be so calm? We are starving. Another few ten-days, and we shall all perish."

"Calm yourself," said Shular. "Urdar will not fail us."

"Urdar is a fool," said Kurghal. "He will perish in the cold."

"Mind your words, Daughter. He is your brother's father."

"Yes, but not mine. I see no reason to honour him."

Shular gave her a withering stare. "You should honour him because he is my bondmate. Either that or you can choose to live elsewhere. I might remind you that you are full grown now and, as such, are not required to grace this hut with your presence."

"But I am a shamaness, like you."

"No, you are not," her mother replied. "You are still learning, and are yet to master your first spell. As such, I expect you to behave appropriately when in my company."

Kurghal bowed. "Sorry, Mother. I will not speak ill of him again."

Shular grabbed Urgon's hand and drove the needle in, eliciting a shout of pain from the young Orc.

"Be still," she ordered, "or I shall make a mess of it."

Urgon, trying to keep his mind off his mother's ministrations, turned and watched his sister as she sat down amongst the furs. She lifted the lid off the large clay pot that lay on the coals and gave it a tentative sniff, then wrinkled her nose.

"Have we no meat?" she asked.

"Only a little," said Shular, "and that will go to Urgon."

"Why does he get it?"

"Were you the youngest, it would be yours, but as you saw fit to be born several winters before him, you are forced to make the sacrifice."

"So we must go hungry while he eats?"

"If you cannot abide by my rules, you are free to eat elsewhere."

Kurghal frowned. "I am sorry, Mother. Hunger drives me to harsh words."

"We are all hungry, Daughter, but we must make sacrifices if the tribe is to persevere. It has always been this way amongst our people, and it will continue to be so."

"Kurghal can have my food," said Urgon.

"That is not for you to decide. You are still a youngling." She tied off the hair and held his hand closer to the fire to examine her work. "There, it is as good as new. Now, hold still while I cast a spell. We cannot allow the flesh to turn rancid."

Urgon watched as his mother invoked her magic. She began by closing her eyes and taking a few deep breaths, then the words of power issued from her mouth. Entranced, he sat still as her fingers, glowing with magical energy, were placed over his wound. The colour flowed into him, completing the spell as warmth enveloped his hand.

Kurghal shook her head. "You cleanse the wound with magic but refuse to heal the flesh. Where is the logic in that?"

"The scar will be a constant reminder of his foolishness. Would you want me to remove the evidence?" She turned to her son. "Now go outside, Urgon, and fetch wood for the fire."

The young Orc rose, feeling the strange tugging sensation as he flexed his hand.

"Be quick about it," she urged, "or we will need to start another fire from scratch."

He paused by the doorway, long enough to throw a fur over his shoulders, then stepped outside, the cold taking his breath away.

The village lay spread out before him. As a shamaness, his mother commanded a prominent position amongst the huts, living in one close to the chieftain's. Around this central structure, all the other dwellings were arrayed in concentric circles. Single hunters were clustered together in longhouses that held anywhere from twelve to twenty Orcs. Those already bonded or who held a position of influence, were allowed their own.

Urgon made his way to the log pile behind their hut, only to discover their stores depleted. He cursed, for the snow was deep and the wind much too cold to set out into the woods for more. Instead, he must now rely on the generosity of others. His first thought was of the great firepit in front of the chieftain's hut—they must have wood to spare. He had gone only fifteen paces when a familiar voice called out.

"Urgon, what brings you out in weather like this?"

He smiled, for his friend Kraloch was of a similar age. "I am on the hunt for firewood," he replied. "Have you any extra, by any chance?"

"I regret I do not." Kraloch noted Urgon's hand. "What has happened here?"

"Only a minor cut. One day soon, I will bear a scar to boast of."

"Yes, and no doubt you will embellish the story, the better to sound heroic. How did you truly get it?"

Urgon laughed. "I was cutting wood for an arrow, and my knife slipped."

"It is fine stitching. Did you do that yourself?"

"No, it is my mother's work."

Kraloch's face looked at him in surprise. "And she did not heal your flesh?"

"No, she told me it was an important lesson."

"What? That she refuses to do her job as shamaness? Someone needs to look at it before the cut begins to seep."

"Not to worry," said Urgon. "She used her magic to prevent that."

"Yet she still insisted on stitching the wound? That is very odd."

"You describe my mother perfectly, but of more import at the moment is where can I find some wood. Our fire is low, and we have none."

"Let us seek out the master of wolves," suggested Kraloch. "I am sure he would have plenty to spare."

"A good idea. It is getting colder even as we speak, and I wish to warm myself by a fire."

Past the chieftain's hall they went, then turned north, towards the outskirts of the village. Here they found what they sought—a woodpile stacked as high as their chins. Kraloch examined the timber, but Urgon's attention was on the wolves that prowled around their enclosure. He leaned on the waist-high fence, gazing at them as they paced.

"They are magnificent beasts."

"So they are," agreed Kraloch, "and invaluable on the hunt."

"I wish I could take one with me when it comes time to face my ordeal."

Kraloch laughed. "That is still nearly two winters away, Urgon. By then, you shall be more than ready for the hunt."

"Still, it would help to have someone to protect me while I slept."

"They say that on the ordeal, one does not sleep."

"Of course you sleep," said Urgon. "It is ridiculous to believe an Orc could go a ten-day without resting."

"Resting is not the same as sleeping, and during that time, survival will be utmost in your thoughts. Do you not remember Malanag? She died on her ordeal."

"True, but she encountered a hill cat."

"So she did," said Kraloch, "but had she not been sleeping, she would have been alerted to its presence."

Urgon waved away the idea. "And had she not slept, she could just as easily fallen down a cliff as she staggered around in her exhaustion. Her fate is no lesson."

"The Ancestors say—"

"Please," said Urgon, holding up his hand. "I have heard enough lecturing about the Ancestors. Sometimes I think that is all my mother ever talks of."

"She IS the shaman of the tribe," said Kraloch. "Do you forget that?"

"Forget it? No, most assuredly not, for she would never permit me to."

Latuhl, a large, elderly Orc, stepped into the wolf den, a wooden bowl in hand. From it, he withdrew scraps of raw meat, tossing them to the ground where the wolves circled, eager to fill their bellies. After snatching up the morsels, they then lay down, gnawing away at the sinewy meal. Finished, the old Orc looked to where the two younglings stood watching.

"Have you nothing better to do?" he called out, his voice gruff, but his face wearing a smile.

"We are here seeking wood," said Kraloch. "The shamaness's fire grows cold."

"Then take what you need from the pile," the elder replied.

"I cannot," said Urgon.

Latuhl moved closer, leaning on the fence. "Oh? And why not?"

"You spent your energy collecting this wood. It is not right that I should take it."

"If you feel that way, then you can replace it once the weather clears. Would that be acceptable?"

"It would," said Urgon.

"Then take what you need and be quick about it, or the entire village shall hear of how you let our shamaness freeze to death."

Urgon turned to his companion. "Hold still, Kraloch, and I will fill your arms. Once I am done, I can then gather my own stack."

He knelt, retrieving half a dozen pieces, and was placing them in Kraloch's arms when a bit of bark caught on his stitches, tearing them loose. Urgon pulled his hand back quickly, watching as his black blood rose to the surface anew.

Kraloch stared at Urgon's wound. "You reinjured yourself."

"It is nothing."

"The stitches have parted," said Kraloch. "We must take you to your mother so she can repair it."

"No!" insisted Urgon. "She will be furious with me."

"But the bleeding must be stopped!"

"Then you can stitch up my hand."

"Me? Why would you even suggest such a thing?"

"You are good with your hands," said Urgon. "I have seen how deftly you handle a spear."

"A spear is a far cry from a needle."

"Nonsense. It is the same—a needle is just smaller."

"Much smaller."

Urgon grinned. "Of course, it has to be. You cannot sew up a wound with a spear!"

"True enough," said Kraloch. "Let us seek out my cousin Urzath. She will have a needle and sinew."

"Sinew? Why not hair?"

"We must make do with the tools at hand. Now, come. She is in the hunters' longhouse."

"Which one?" said Urgon. "There are many."

"The one closest, as it happens."

"Are you sure it is all right to enter? We are not yet hunters."

"True," said Kraloch, "but as I said, Urzath is my cousin. And as well you know, visitors are not forbidden." He led Urgon across the pathway, then entered the longhouse, pushing aside the hide that kept winter at bay.

The building consisted of a series of logs connected to create a framework. To this, smaller sticks were attached, then the whole assembly was covered in bark.

Urgon had never set foot in a hunters' longhouse, yet he had lived beside one his entire life. Inside, the place held several small firepits, with shelves of wood on either side, large enough to sleep upon. There were at least two dozen hunters here, although exact numbers were hard to tally because of the relatively dark interior. He let his eyes adjust as Kraloch moved ahead, searching for his cousin.

"Here she is," he called out.

Urgon advanced, coming to rest before Urzath. Kraloch's cousin was tall for an Orc and towered over them.

"What have we here?" she asked.

"Urgon has injured himself," said Kraloch, rushing to get the words out. "His mother sewed it closed, but it has reopened."

"Should you not simply let her resew the wound?"

"No!" spat out Urgon.

"Why not? She is the shamaness after all."

Urgon felt his ears burn. "I would prefer not to trouble her, for she has much to occupy her mind."

"And you expect me to do it? I am no healer."

"No," said Kraloch. "I would ask only to borrow a needle and some sinew that I might repair the wound myself."

"You?" said Urzath. "You have not even passed your ordeal."

"I am more than capable, I promise you."

"It is not I who you must promise, but Urgon here. It takes trust to let someone sew up your hand and is not something to be considered lightly."

"I trust Kraloch," insisted Urgon.

Urzath stared into his eyes for a moment. "The choice is yours. Let me see what I can find amongst my belongings." She crawled to the back of her sleeping shelf, digging through a pile of furs. The younger Orcs waited patiently as she tossed things aside, then emerged with a look of triumph.

"I have it," she said, producing a fine bone needle and a small wrapped skin.

"Thank you, Cousin," said Kraloch. He took the items, then opened the skin, picking through the remains to extract the sinew.

"As you can see," said Urzath, "I already pulled it into fibres. Be sure you do not use them all. I still have clothing that needs repairs."

"I shall only use a portion, Cousin. Thank you."

She smiled, showing her ivory teeth. "Good. Now you had best get to work. Your friend is bleeding all over the mat."

They moved nearer the fire, and then Kraloch got to work threading the needle. Urgon stared into the flames, holding out his hand when his companion indicated he was ready.

The needle dug in, and Urgon winced, but he was determined not to show any pain. Much to his surprise, the whole procedure was complete within moments. He examined his hand, marvelling at the precision of the work.

"You have a gift for this type of thing," he said.

"Possibly," said Kraloch, "but if we do not get those logs to your mother soon, she may come looking for us, and you know how that worked out last time."

"True," said Urgon, "but this time, I shall take greater care with the wood."

Shular stirred the pot. "Where is that brother of yours?"

"Getting into trouble, I would imagine," said Kurghal. "And I might remind you he is only my half-brother."

As if summoned by the mere mention of him, Urgon stepped through the doorway.

"I brought wood, Mother," he announced.

"You should have been back some time ago," said his sister. "Instead, you went off to Hraka knows where and left us to freeze!"

"Now, now," said Shular. "Let us be thankful he has at least returned before the fire turned to ash." Logs fell against the side of the hut, the sound echoing in the cramped interior.

"And who is that?" asked Kurghal.

"Kraloch," said Urgon. "Who else would it be?"

"Then, for the Ancestors' sake," said Shular, "invite him in before he freezes. This is not the weather to remain outside."

Kurghal moved to the door, calling in the visitor. Urgon, meanwhile, carefully placed logs on the fire. His mother suddenly reached out, grabbing his injured hand and holding it before her eyes.

"What is this?" she demanded.

"It is nothing."

"Nothing? You reinjured your hand, Urgon. Who did this?"

"No one. I caught it on some bark."

"No, I mean who sewed your wound?"

"I did," said Kraloch as he entered. He bowed his head. "I hope I did not overstep myself, Shamaness."

"Not at all," said Shular looking up from her son's hand. "This is outstanding work, Kraloch. Have you always been so gifted?"

"Ever since I can remember. I often help my parents with sewing."

"Have you ever considered becoming a shaman?"

"Does one not need the potential for magic to become one?"

"Yes, but this"—Shular pointed at Urgon's hand—"this is a gift. I must first consult the Ancestors, but maybe once you come of age, you might consider learning the ways of magic."

"You honour me," said Kraloch, "but surely there are better candidates?" His eyes flicked over to Urgon.

"The Ancestors have seen fit to deny my son such a blessing. His future lies elsewhere."

Kraloch bowed once more. "I shall consider the offer, Shamaness. It is most generous."

Shular turned her attention back to her son. "Go and fetch water, Urgon, and make sure Kraloch's parents know of this offer."

"Yes, Mother."

Urgon took a deep breath once he and Kraloch had stepped outside.

"I must apologize, my friend," said Kraloch. "I did not intend to take what is yours."

"Do not shed tears for me. You have been given a gift. You should embrace it."

"But she is your mother, and the magic must be strong in your bloodline. After all, your sister is gifted."

"Yes," said Urgon, "but remember, we have different fathers." He noted his friend's look of concern. "I have always known magic is not in my future and am content to be just a hunter."

"I doubt you will ever be JUST a hunter, Urgon."

A frigid blast of air blew in from the west, putting a halt to their conversation. They both huddled into their furs, waiting until it dissipated.

"See, the west calls," said Kraloch. "It is a sign from the Ancestors."

"You are wrong," Urgon replied, "for the Ancestors have abandoned me."

# TWO

## Visitors

WINTER 946/947 MC

A horn sounded in the distance, and most of the tribe stopped what they were doing, rushing to grab spears and axes. Urgon emerged from his hut to thick snow descending over the village. Many were already gathering by the great firepit, their breath frosting in the chilly winter air. He soon spotted Kraloch standing off to the side, spear in hand, watching as the hunters talked amongst themselves. Urgon stomped through the snow, coming to a halt beside his friend.

"Do you know what the horn means?" asked Urgon.

"I have no idea," replied Kraloch, "but the chieftain has gathered all the hunters she can. I suspect they intend to investigate."

"Do you think we might be under attack?"

"I doubt it. After all, what enemy would announce their arrival?"

"Well, we Orcs do not use horns!"

The hunters, including Urzath, were standing around, talking amongst themselves when Shuvog emerged from the chieftain's hut, spear in hand.

"As you most likely heard," she began, "outsiders approach. I shall lead a group of hunters into the hills and intercept whoever it is. The rest of you are to remain here and guard our homes." She turned to Ruloch, one of the oldest hunters. "Bring the elderly and young to the great hall where it is easiest to protect them. Tarluk, you are with me. Select two dozen of your best hunters."

Shuvog gave them a moment to organize themselves, then set off at a jog, the hunters following closely.

Urgon grabbed Kraloch's arm. "Come," he said. "We shall follow. This is our chance to discover who approaches."

"They might be heading into danger," warned his comrade.

"Which makes it even more interesting."

"And if a fight ensues?"

Urgon grinned. "Then we can come back and warn the others."

"You convinced me," said Kraloch, "but let us proceed cautiously, for it would not do well if we were spotted. It could lead to trouble for both of us."

Urgon grinned even wider. "You are a wise Orc, my friend."

"Wise? Or foolhardy? I might remind you we are not yet full-grown and are ill-prepared for battle."

"Come now. We may be young, but that only means we can outrun any enemy that might appear."

"Can you outrun a mountain cat?" asked Kraloch.

"What mountain cat would use a horn?"

"We should wait until the snow obscures them, then follow in their wake. Their footsteps will be easy to find in this snow."

"Good idea," said Urgon, "but stay alert. I would hate to be taken by surprise."

Shuvog and her hunters disappeared into the blizzard before Urgon led Kraloch forward, navigating the deep snow as best he could. The footsteps were easy enough to follow, but he was surprised to see how quickly the view behind them became lost in the blowing snow.

"I do not like this," said Kraloch. "It is difficult to walk in the drifts, and the village is gone from sight. How, then, are we to navigate?"

"Our chieftain has marked the path by her footsteps. You should worry less, Kraloch. Might I remind you it was your idea to follow at a distance?"

"And now I am regretting the choice."

They had trudged through the snow for what felt like an eternity when shadowy figures emerged from the whiteout. Urzath led the way, using her spear as a staff. The figure behind her, however, was significantly shorter and waist-deep in the snow. Urgon stopped, gaping in fascination, causing his companion to stumble into him.

"What are you doing?" said Kraloch.

In response, Urgon pointed. "Look," he said. "If I am not mistaken, that is a Dwarf."

The hunter, Urzath, drew nearer, then spotted the younglings. "What are you two doing out here?"

"We came to see what all the commotion was about," said Urgon.

She halted before them. "This," Urzath said, "is Gambreck Ironpick. He comes to us from the mountain fortress of Stonecastle."

"Greetings," said the Dwarf, his mastery of the Orcish tongue impeccable. "I bring you the warm regards of my king."

"This is Kraloch, son of Maloch, and this is Urgon, son of Shular and Urdar."

Gambreck moved closer, then knelt before Urgon. "I honour your loss."

"I do not understand," said Urgon.

More Orcs and Dwarves appeared through the snow, and then the young Orc noted their burden. They pulled sleds piled high with supplies, but one stood apart, for on it lay what looked like a body, wrapped in coarse blankets. He felt his heart ache, then ran forward, ignoring those around him.

There could be no doubt it was the body of an Orc, for his people were broad of shoulder and significantly taller than the mountain folk. As the Dwarf's words echoed in his head, he knew with absolute certainty who lay before him. Urgon fell to his knees, the tears coming freely.

"F-Father," he stammered.

Strong arms gripped his shoulders, and Urzath's voice spoke with reverence. "He is with the Ancestors now."

Gambreck approached. "Come," he said. "Let us take him to your village, and I will relate to you the story of his bravery."

Urgon stared at the Dwarf. Gambreck looked back through a face full of hair, yet there was compassion in his eyes. Other Dwarves trundled past, pulling the sleds, but Gambreck remained.

"Your father was brave," he said, "and gave his life to save your people. Without him, we would never have learned of your plight."

Urgon felt an anger building within him, a fire that threatened to overwhelm him. "He is gone," he spat out, "and shall never tread the paths of our village again." The young Orc wanted to lash out, to destroy something, anything to overcome his feelings of helplessness. He turned back to the Dwarf. "Why do you bring his body to us?"

"Do you not bury your dead?"

"The body is but a vessel," said Urgon. "It is the spirit that lives on in the Afterlife."

"Ah. It appears our traditions differ from yours," said Gambreck. "Your father made a great sacrifice. In our culture, we honour such bravery, even if you do not. Now come, let us follow the others before we become lost in the snow."

The Dwarf began moving again, struggling through the drifts, even though those in front had forged a path.


The Orcs of the Black Arrow were scattered across multiple villages, but it was here, in Ord-Dugath, where their chieftain lived. As such, the chieftain's hut had been built large enough to house the entire village when needed. Urgon had to force his way in this day, as it was packed full, not only with Orcs but with their visitors, the Dwarves.

Along the centre of the room lay a long firepit, with the villagers arrayed around it. Shuvog, their chieftain, sat at the western end while Urgon's mother, as the senior shaman, was by her side. Kraloch waved Urgon over, and he sat on one of the woven mats that covered the floor.

"Has anything happened yet?" asked Urgon.

"Shuvog welcomed them, but there have been no announcements as yet."

"And the Dwarves, do they mean to stay?"

"We must wait and see."

Shular stood, her staff held high to get everyone's attention. All eyes turned towards her, then she sat, allowing the chieftain to take her place.

"My fellow tribemates," began Shuvog, "it has been a hard winter. The mountain deer fled from the storms that have plagued us for these last few ten-days. As a result, the tribe has suffered, so much so that we were forced to take drastic steps to survive. We all sacrificed, eating sparingly in the hopes we might live to see another day. Had we continued in this manner, we would all have surely perished, but one amongst us braved the elements to bring us hope for the future. The story of his great sacrifice is best told by those who witnessed it, and so I present to you, Gambreck Ironpick, one of the mountain people."

She sat, allowing the Dwarf to stand. The silence in the great hall continued, broken only by the crackling of the fire.

"We came here," the visitor said, "not only to bring you food but to honour the sacrifice of one of your greatest hunters. Without the efforts of Urdar, we would have remained in ignorance of your troubles. He braved the harshest of winters to find us, a trek that ultimately led to his demise. Our patrol found your heroic hunter, half-frozen and starving to death in the high hills of the stone peaks. He was near his end, but before he passed, he told us of your plight. We resolved to deliver aid as quickly as possible, and so we set out with food, blankets, and the body of this honourable Orc."

He paused, his eyes roaming the crowd. "Six sleds we brought, and more will follow for your other villages. We will not let our ancient brethren starve!"

Latuhl, the master of wolves, stood, signalling he had a question.

"Yes?" said Gambreck.

"What price do you ask in return?"

"None," said the Dwarf, looking over at Shuvog. The chieftain nodded, then rose as Gambreck sat, yielding the floor.

"Let us all honour the name Urdar," she called out. The Orcs passed around bowls containing a pale white liquid. Each was to take a sip, then hand it on, remaining silent as the ceremony unfolded.

Urgon watched as a bowl come his way. Everyone knew of the milk of life—it was used for solemn occasions between people of import. Yet he had never seen it handed out to the entire village before, nor had he ever consumed it himself. When a bowl was finally placed in his hands, he held it to his lips with trembling fingers. Taking a sip, Urgon felt a warmth engulf him, then passed it on to Kraloch. He watched his friend's face, eager to see if he experienced the same sensation, but if he did, there was no indication.

The ritual finally complete, Shuvog dismissed the assembly, and Orcs filed out of the hut. Standing up, Urgon felt light-headed and reached out, grabbing Kraloch's arm to steady himself.

"Are you unwell?" asked his friend.

"My senses are jumbled. It is as if the room is spinning."

"Close your eyes, and it should pass. I have heard that it is a not unknown for some to react strangely to the milk of life the first time they try it."

"Did you have the same sensation?"

"No," replied Kraloch, "but then again, I am not suffering a recent loss."

"I am not weak because of my father's death!"

"Perhaps not, but the news was a shock. It takes time to adjust to such things."

Urgon closed his eyes, willing away the sensation. He opened them to see Kraloch staring at him.

"Maybe you should lie down," said Kraloch. "Your eyes are acting strange."

"Strange in what way?"

"They are constricted, as they would be in bright light, yet the hut is dim. Let me take you home."

"If you insist," said Urgon, "but you had best steady me. I fear I might stumble."

Kraloch led him outside, and the moment they hit daylight, Urgon felt a stabbing pain in his eyes and fell to his knees, his hands instinctively covering his face. His actions did not go unnoticed, and his sister, Kurghal, was soon there, kneeling by his side.

"What has happened?" she asked.

"He drank the milk of life," answered Kraloch, "and now his eyes are not adjusting to the light of day. Is this normal?"

"I have heard of reactions like this before, but never have I seen it for myself. We must take Urgon home where he can rest until he is recovered."


Urgon awoke, finding himself wrapped in furs while the fire crackled away, light flickering against the hut's walls. Soft voices reached his ears, and he raised his head to see his mother, Shular, sitting by the fire, Kurghal by her side. Across from them was Gambreck, along with one of his companions.

"Your bondmate made a great sacrifice," the Dwarf was saying. "His honour is admirable."

"You talk to me of honour," said Shular, "yet I would gladly exchange it, were he to be returned to me."

"What you ask is impossible, but we shall ensure that at least his memory lives on as an inspiration to others."

"Why? Of what interest is an Orc's fate to the mountain folk?"

"Orcs we may not be," said Gambreck, "but his actions serve as an inspiration to us all." He turned to his companion and nodded, resulting in the fellow pulling something out of a large sack. "Please accept these gifts from our people as a token of our respect for what you lost."

Urgon strained to see what was being exchanged, but his sister's back blocked the view.

"These are fine gifts indeed," continued Shular, "and I thank you for them."

"There is more."

"More?"

"Yes," said the Dwarf. "We wish to build a memorial to Urdar, something that would allow his sacrifice to be recognized."

"And what form would this memorial take?"

"A stone pillar, the height of an Orc. We would inscribe it with runes to tell his story."

"Orcs do not have a written language."

"I have been told this," said Gambreck, "but the Dwarves and Orcs do share an ancient language. It has changed over the centuries, but I believe it would still have meaning to your Ancestors. I would like your permission to build it."

"My permission? Surely that is a decision for our chieftain?"

"I spoke with Shuvog, and she left it for you to decide."

Shular sat for some time, staring into the flames. The others waited patiently, but Urgon couldn't understand what was taking her so long to make up her mind. His mother finally stood, looking the Dwarf in the eyes.

"Very well," she said. "You may build your monument."

The Dwarves both stood, bowing deeply.

"Thank you," said Gambreck. "We shall leave you now and mark out a suitable location." They turned, leaving the hut in solemn silence.

Kurghal turned to her mother. "What shall I do with these?" she asked.

"Bury them," Shular replied, "just as I must bury my feelings for Urdar."

Urgon felt anger building within him. Did she not care for his father? He knew his sister had no love for his sire, but his mother's words drove a knife through his heart.

Kurghal rose, the bundle held before her. Whatever it was, it was wrapped in a blue cloth—an unusual colour amongst Orcs.

"I shall see to it," she said, making her way to the hut's entrance. She paused for a moment, looking back at her mother, then lifted the flap, departing into the cold, wintery night.

A wave of frigid air drifted across to Urgon, and he tightened his grip on the furs. He tried to guess what gift the Dwarves might have left, but he could think of nothing. Closing his eyes, he was determined to return to sleep, then heard the soft sobs of his mother as she finally mourned the loss of her bondmate.


The following day, the Dwarves set to work. Urgon and Kraloch watched them chisel stone blocks, curious as to what they were doing. The mountain folk laboured away at it for nearly a ten-day, until finally, a stone obelisk with four sides and a cap shaped like a small pyramid emerged at the edge of the village. It stood just above Urgon's head, but was thin enough he could put his arms around it, should he so desire. Once the Dwarves were done, Urgon asked them about the strange markings decorating the sides.

"Those," explained Gambreck, "are Dwarven runes. They tell the story of how your father saved your people." He pointed at a symbol. "You see this one here?"

Urgon stared at the mark. It consisted of two lines at an angle, forming an arrowhead pointing upward. Above this was a single line pointing to the sky, while between them sat a horizontal line.

"What of it?" the young Orc asked.

"This is your father. It's the symbol of a mighty hunter, for that is the true meaning of his name. Maybe one day you too will gain fame as a hunter?"

"Are your people hunters?"

"Some," said the Dwarf, "but as we live in cities, such a trade is rare."

"Then how do you feed yourselves?"

"We farm."

"We live in the foothills and can't grow anything here. How, then, do you manage to do so in the mountains?"

"We use large underground caves to grow our crops."

"It must be quite something to see," noted Urgon.

"Indeed it is. When you're old enough, you can visit Stonecastle and see it for yourself. You would be welcome there, Urgon of the Black Arrows."

"I would? What have I done to earn such a reception?"

"You carry your father's legacy."

A warmth came to Urgon's cheeks, turning him a darker green. "I am humbled by the offer." He gazed once more at the runes. "Tell me, if you would, why this symbol? All I see is a series of lines, yet you say it represents a great hunter?"

"It does. The bottom lines represent the legs of a hunter, the horizontal line his spear."

"And the line that points to the sky?"

"The upper torso and head," said Gambreck. "When we work stone, we use straight lines whenever possible."

"And this is how Dwarves communicate?"

"It is. We call it the ancient tongue. At one time, we shared it with your distant ancestors."

"They would have to be distant indeed," said Urgon, "for to my knowledge, no one here has even heard of such a thing."

"Perhaps one day your people will return to the ancient written language of your forefathers?"

"Perhaps," replied Urgon, "but I doubt it will be in my lifetime."

"You might be surprised," said Gambreck. "You are yet young, with an entire life ahead of you. Much can happen in that time."

"Yes, but my people do not live as long as Dwarves. You will still tread this land when my descendant's descendants have long since joined the Ancestors."

The Dwarf smiled. "Also true, but I've a feeling your legacy will last much longer than mine." He patted the monument. "Mark my words, your father was very brave. I think you are destined to follow in his footsteps."

"And die in the snow?"

"Hardly. There are many ways to impact the lives of your people, Urgon. You must find your own path to tread."

# THREE

## The Mud Hut

SPRING 948 MC

T he knife scraped along the whetstone, its noise echoing in the still morning air.

"If you sharpen the blade any more, there will be none left," said Kraloch.

Urgon smiled, holding up the weapon to examine the edge. "One can never be too careful with such things. A sharp knife could make the difference between life or death."

"You are nervous about your ordeal."

"I am, although it is some time yet before I must undertake the task."

"Yes, at least two seasons, yet you fret. Why?"

"I remember well the words of the Dwarf," said Urgon. "I have a lot to live up to."

"You mean your mother? It is not your fault she is the shaman of the village."

"It is my father's memory that I must live up to." He pointed to the monument. "That is a constant reminder of all he accomplished."

"You put too much pressure on yourself. Live your life to the fullest, Urgon. You should not pay attention to such things."

Kurghal exited the hut to stand in the sun for a moment, letting her eyes adjust to the brightness, and then she spotted the two friends.

"Kraloch," she called out. "Shular would have words with you."

"With me? Do you not mean Urgon?"

"Do you think I cannot tell the difference between the two of you?"

she responded. "Now come, and be quick about it. The shamaness does not like to be kept waiting."

"You had better go," said Urgon. "Kurghal called her shamaness. That makes it something important, and you know as well as I how angry my mother can get when a visitor is late."

Kraloch entered the hut while Kurghal remained outside.

"Why is he wanted?" asked Urgon.

"That is for him to discover, not you."

"And yet it must be something important."

"It is not your concern. Now begone before I tell Mother you are being difficult."

Urgon rose, his knife and whetstone in hand as he made his way across to the hunters' longhouse, then sat, his back against the wall. His sister gave him a look of disgust before disappearing back inside their home.

The knife scraped along the whetstone absently while he pondered the situation. He knew his mother considered Kraloch an excellent choice for an apprentice, but that kind of thing usually came after their ordeal. Why, then, was he needed now?

His thoughts were interrupted by the emergence of the three of them—Shular leading the way, followed closely by Kurghal, with Kraloch bringing up the rear. They headed westward, past the great outdoor firepit and over to the strange mud hut across from it. After the two females exchanged a few words, his friend remained outside while his mother and sister entered the hut. Urgon was soon on his feet, crossing the distance to close in on Kraloch.

"What is this?" he asked.

Kraloch noted the arrival of his comrade. "They are seeking guidance," he said.

"From who?"

"The Ancestors."

Urgon turned to stare at the strange hut. Of a typical construction, it was comprised of sticks and thatching. Yet it had been smeared liberally with mud over time, giving it the look of stone.

"I do not understand," Urgon said. "Why does my mother not cast the spell at home? Can the Ancestors not answer questions there as easily as here?"

"I am unsure, but she was most insistent they seek advice here."

Urgon moved closer to the hut, pressing his ear against its side. "I cannot hear anything. The walls must be too thick."

His companion shrugged. "It matters little. If we are lucky, your mother will reveal all once she emerges."

"That is not my mother's way." He stepped back, examining the wall. "What is in this place?"

"That, I am unable to answer."

"Unable or unwilling?"

"I would tell you if I knew," said Kraloch, "but such things are beyond my understanding. This hut has been here as long as I can remember."

"So it has. Hmmm, I always thought of it as a place of storage." He grinned. "It seems we have a mystery to solve."

"I should tread carefully if I were you, or you are likely to upset your mother."

The sound of a flap opening drew their attention. Kurghal was backing out of the hut, bowing as she went.

"Quick," said Kraloch. "Hide before she sees you."

Urgon ran around behind the hut, then pressed up against the wall, eager to learn more. He soon heard his mother emerge.

"Kraloch," she said, "we consulted the Ancestors, and they agree with my decision to train you. We will commence your education once you finish your ordeal."

"Thank you, Shular."

"It is not me who you should thank, but the Ancestors. They are the ones who determined your fate. The road you have been chosen to tread is a difficult one. Learning to control the forces of magic is no easy feat, and the spirit world... well, that is another matter altogether."

She paused, and Urgon crept closer, trying to peer around the hut.

"You should go home," Shular continued. "No doubt your mother will be pleased to hear of my decision."

"I shall do as you suggest," replied the young Orc.

Upon hearing their footsteps receding, Urgon emerged from his hiding place. He looked around, searching out who might be here, but the area was quiet. Resolving to get to the bottom of this mystery, he moved to the hut's entrance where two hides hung, side by side, their edges overlapping. To his amazement, when he reached forward to part them, they refused to budge, and then he noticed strange symbols upon them. Was this some sort of magic?

To Urgon's mind, finding out when the hut had been constructed was the most logical place to start. To this end, he walked over to the home of Latuhl, the master of wolves. As an elder, he had lived nigh on forty winters, an age Urgon considered quite ancient.

He called out as he approached, to be greeted by the raspy voice he knew so well. Urgon pushed aside the skins and peered into the hut where Latuhl sat in the middle of a pile of furs, sipping on a skin of water. When he saw the young Orc at the doorway, he waved him over.

"Come, join me," Latuhl said, indicating a space on the floor.

Urgon entered and sat, only to rise quickly when the furs suddenly moved, and a wolf appeared.

"Pay no attention to Rockjaw," said Latuhl. "Like me, his days of being fearsome are a thing of the past."

The young Orc lowered himself once more while the wolf gave him a sniff, then lay down at his side. Urgon reached out, petting the thick fur.

"He is tired," the young Orc said. "He looks like he wants to sleep."

"As do we all, but I doubt you came here to discuss Rockjaw. Tell me, young Urgon, what brings you to the master of wolves?"

"I would ask you a question."

"Then ask, and if it be within my power to answer, then I shall."

"It concerns the mud hut," said Urgon. "I wish to know what lies within."

"That, I am unable to tell you, for in truth, I have no idea."

"I thought you knew everything?"

The old Orc chuckled. "I am the oldest within the village, that much is true, but I am certainly no wellspring of knowledge. I can remember when it was built, but I know little else. I care for the wolves, and that is enough to keep me busy."

Urgon leaned forward. "How long ago was it built?"

Latuhl gazed up to the ceiling as his mind worked. "Fourteen winters," he said. "I can still remember the day Arshug began work on it."

"Arshug? The bowyer?"

"Yes. She had help, of course, but she was the one who oversaw its construction. Likely a visit to her hut would provide the answers you seek."

"Perhaps," mused Urgon. "But have there ever been other mud huts?"

"None I know of, but your mother would know better than I."

"My mother?"

"She is the village's shaman," said Latuhl. "And, as such, is fully aware of our tribe's history."

"And yet she has never spoken of the hut."

The old Orc grinned. "There is probably a reason for that. It is not our place to question her."

"Is it not our right to know what lies within the confines of our own village?"

"It is, but I sense there is more to these questions than idle curiosity. That hut has been with us since before you were born. What is it that has now turned your attention to it?"

"My mother and sister both entered the hut this very day. When they emerged, they informed Kraloch he was to be trained as a shaman."

"And so you reason the two events are connected?"

"What other explanation could there be?"

Latuhl nodded. "I suppose that is a reasonable assumption. But if your mother wanted you to know, would she not have informed you?"

"I will not be a full-fledged hunter for some time. My mother still sees me as little more than a youngling."

"Is that what drives you to seek answers? The desire to prove yourself?"

Urgon paused, running the idea over in his mind. Was this what he was doing? He shook his head. "No," he continued. "I must find the answer to satisfy myself, not others."

"You have a naturally inquisitive mind," said Latuhl. "That is a trait I greatly admire. In many ways, you remind me of myself at your age."

"You sought answers?"

"I did, although in my case, it concerned animals instead of huts. It is what led me to become master of wolves. I had an affinity for creatures like Rockjaw there, but at the same time, I always wanted to learn more. Keep digging, my young friend. I wish you well in unearthing this mystery. Who knows, it might lead you to your destiny?"

"My destiny?"

"Perhaps destiny is not the right word. Each of us has strengths, Urgon. The key to a happy life is finding yours and building upon them."

"And you believe the hut holds the true secret of my strength?"

"It is not the destination that teaches, but the journey."

"You sound like my mother."

"I shall take that as a compliment," said Latuhl. "Now, best you be gone from here. The sun has reached its height, and I must rest before I exercise the wolves."

Urgon rose. "Thank you, wolf master, for your words of encouragement."

"Do not thank me, thank your father. Urdar always encouraged you to speak your mind." Latuhl selected a bowl, pouring some water into it and setting it down for Rockjaw. The old wolf rose, padding across the hut to drink.

Urgon felt his chest tighten. "I miss my father."

"As you should," said Latuhl. "His loss was keenly felt by everyone, but you must find your own way, Urgon. His path does not dictate yours."

"I shall remember your words," the young Orc promised.


Urgon paused at the hut of Arshug, the bowyer. Her bows were well known throughout the Artisan Hills, and Orcs from other villages travelled days to trade for such fine weapons. The hut itself was large as far as shelters go, for not only did it house her and her foster son, Gorath, it also acted as her workshop.

"Who is there?" came a voice, breaking his reverie.

"Urgon, son of Urdar," he replied.

The flap opened, revealing the weathered countenance of the master bowyer.

"And to what do I owe this visit?" asked Arshug. "Have you come seeking a bow?"

"No," said Urgon, "only your wisdom."

"Oh? Would you have me teach you the skills to become a bowyer?"

"No, merely answer some questions, if you are willing."

"Questions I can answer," said Arshug, "but I would know to what end."

"That requires some explanation."

She held the flap aside. "Then you had best come inside."

He stepped through, looking around the interior. Like most huts, the floor was covered in skins, yet here, there were stacks of stout poles laying aside them, ready for her to work them into bows.

"Sit," said Arshug.

Urgon sat, then glanced to the side at the sound of wood striking wood.

"Ignore the noises," she said. "Gorath is practicing with his bow."

"One day he will be a skilled hunter."

"No doubt, but I gather you did not come here to talk of my son?"

"I did not."

Arshug saw the hesitation in his face. "Speak," she urged. "I would hear your words."

"I just came from the master of wolves. He informed me you oversaw the building of the mud hut."

"I did. What of it?"

"I was wondering what you could tell me of it?"

"What is there to tell? It is a hut much like any other. Is there something specific you want to know?"

"There is," said Urgon. "How was it constructed?"

"It is, in size and form, similar to others in the village. Its walls are a framework of sticks, as is your own home. The only difference is the mud that decorates its walls, instead of the skins and bark used elsewhere."

"This I understand. What I am trying to understand is why the mud?"

"I do not know."

"But you built it, did you not?"

"I did, on the explicit orders of Shular. Her instructions were quite clear on the matter."

Urgon struggled to understand. "My mother commissioned the hut? To what end?"

"I am led to believe it was built not as a home but to keep the spirits appeased. She gave little in the way of additional information. I do remember, however, it was quite warm inside once it was done. The mud serves to keep out the cold."

"Then why do we not use a similar construction on other huts?"

"The process is quite labour intensive. The dirt in these hills is not suited to such a purpose, and we had to travel into the lowlands to find suitable material to encase the walls. On the other hand, animal skins are plentiful and are easier to work with, hence why our own homes use a different technique."

"So it was a major undertaking?"

"It was," said Arshug. "Half a ten-day it took us to get the frame up, then we began the process of mudding the walls."

"And how long did that take?"

"Another ten-day, but the vast majority of that time was spent bringing dirt and straw up from the plains."

"Straw?"

"Yes, to mix with the mud, else it would flake off at the slightest touch."

"How is it you knew all this?"

"As I said, it was under Shular's direction. She consulted the Ancestors to learn what was required."

"You answered the how," said Urgon, "but I would know the why?"

"It is not my place to question the shaman."

"Did you not wonder as to the reason for such a strange construction?"

"I did," she admitted, shifting her position.

He sensed her unease but pressed on. "What lies within that hut?"

"I..."—Arshug paused a moment, struggling to remain composed—"I am not sure."

"And yet you suspect?"

"There have always been rumours, of course, but none I will dignify by repeating."

"Have you ever visited it?"

"No, of course not," the bowyer said. "That is the domain of our shamans. They alone have the right to enter."

"Why do you think that is?"

Arshug shrugged. "Perhaps that place is closer to the Ancestors?"

"Yet for many generations before, it did not exist. Why build it fourteen winters ago?"

The bowyer suddenly stood. "I am afraid our time is up. I must see to Gorath. He needs his afternoon nap."

"Have I said something to upset you?"

"If I were you, Urgon, I would cease this line of questioning. It can only lead to trouble. Now begone from my hut. There are things I must attend to."

Urgon rose, bowing respectfully. "I thank you for the information, sparse though it was. I shall trouble you no more."

He stepped outside, mustering all the dignity his thirteen-year-old self could manage. Other Orcs were strolling around the village, going about their business, heedless of the curiosity within him screaming to be let out. The mud hut stared back, mocking him with its very presence.

Fourteen winters ago, that place had been constructed, but why? Was it merely a hut of casting used by his mother? He stared at it, hoping for some type of clue as to its purpose. Arshug had indicated the mud kept the place warm. Was that its big secret? Was there something inside that needed the heat?

He shook his head. No, that was not it. The bowyer had said something about keeping the spirits appeased, leading him to wonder if something might not be imprisoned. Still, he could think of nothing that might require such a specific design.

Urgon thought of his father. Urdar had always been honest with him, plain-spoken even, in sharp contrast to his mother, who always seemed to speak in riddles. It was said younglings should cherish the time they lived at home. Yet Urgon could hardly wait to take up residence amongst the village's hunters to be free of the cloying atmosphere of his mother's hut.

He thought of Kraloch. They had been friends for eons, would even complete their ordeals within a ten-day of each other, yet his comrade had the one thing Urgon did not—the respect of Shular. He tried to convince himself he was not being objective, but the truth was staring him in the face. In Kraloch, his mother saw someone who had the potential to master the Magic of Life. Urgon, on the other hand, had no such talent and must be content with becoming a hunter. There was no shame in that, but somehow he didn't believe his mother saw things that way.

He let his eyes roam the village, taking in all he surveyed. What was his strength? Was being a hunter truly where his future lay, or was there something else? He resolved to speak to Kraloch of his thoughts at the next opportunity.

# FOUR

## The Mystery Deepens

SPRING 948 MC

U rgon dangled his legs over the cliff, Kraloch by his side. Below them stretched the Rugar Plains, a flat area heading west as far as the eye could see. The Human city of Eastwood was said to be two days' walk away, and beyond that lay the great forest known as the Deerwood. Orc hunters had trod that land before, but the round trip typically took at least a ten-day to complete. Kraloch turned to face his companion.

"Have your questions provided any answers yet?" he asked.

"No, only further questions." Urgon grimaced, keeping his eyes to the west. "No, that is not entirely true. Yesterday, I learned the hut was built fourteen winters ago, although I have yet to determine to what end. Something must have happened at that time, something that required a specialized hut. I gave it much thought, but the solution eludes me still."

"Then you must speculate," said Kraloch. "Give thoughts to your wildest imaginings, and maybe something will suggest an answer."

Urgon turned to his closest friend. "Mud is hard when dried. Could that be the answer?"

"How so?" asked Kraloch.

"Perhaps it is not so much a hut as it is a cage."

"A cage for what?"

"Something dangerous that was captured, do you think?" said Urgon. "Where better to keep such a creature?"

"What type of animal would still be in there after fourteen winters? Surely anything ferocious would have been heard? Such creatures are known to at least growl from time to time."

"Yes, and it would require feeding."

"I have seen food taken inside," Kraloch revealed.

"You have?"

"Yes. Why else would I say so?"

"And what form did this food take?"

"That I am unable to answer. It was in bowls, if it is any help, carried by your sister."

"I suppose that would make sense," said Urgon. "The door is sealed by magic. I suspect only a shaman could open it."

Kraloch frowned. "What type of animal eats from a bowl?"

"Rockjaw does. I saw him take a drink from the bowl of Latuhl."

"A wolf I can well imagine, but I hardly think such an animal would require walls of mud and sticks, not to mention a magical seal on the door. And I would suspect a wolf could easily dig its way out."

"What if the seal is not to keep something in but to keep others out?"

"Possibly, but then why take in food?" Urgon pondered the situation further. "It must be something else. What about a bear?"

Kraloch shook his head. "I see no reason to keep a bear locked up. They are very dangerous when confined."

"Agreed, and I would imagine that bringing a bear through the village would be noticed."

"There are other creatures that live amongst the mountains. How about a Troll?"

"Not likely," said Urgon. "Such creatures are said to be massive, far larger than would fit comfortably into that hut."

"Then what can it be?"

"That is what I intend to find out."

"And how will you do that?" asked Kraloch.

"I shall watch the hut, night and day."

"You might be discovered, or you could step on sacred ground. Your mother used it—do you think she conjured something from the spirit realm?"

"Doubtful. While she is quite capable of summoning spirits, the Ancestors are all deceased. Why, then, would they require food?"

"A valid point," agreed Kraloch. "But then that puts us back to it being an animal of some sort. It is the only explanation. If only we knew the nature of the food."

Urgon climbed to his feet. "You may be onto something there. Tell me, my friend, are you willing to help?"

"Of course. What would you like me to do?"

"I have in mind a course of action."

"Which is?" asked Kraloch.

"I propose we take turns watching the hut."

"And what will that accomplish?"

"By observing, we can determine how frequently food is taken in. Besides, if we identify the contents of those bowls, we might have a clearer picture of whatever creature that hut imprisons."

"IF it is a creature," clarified Kraloch.

"Why else take in food?"

"I honestly have no idea. Maybe it is part of a ritual?"

"I know of no ritual that requires food," said Urgon. "And I have lived in my mother's hut for my entire life."

"I might remind you that you have only seen thirteen winters, as have I. I wonder if it is simply a creature that neither of us is familiar with?"

"Aside from my sister, have you seen anyone else enter that hut?"

"Only your mother," said Kraloch, "and only late at night, after the sun has sunk below the horizon. Do you think that significant?"

"Possibly. Did Kurghal deliver food when it was dark? Perhaps the creature is nocturnal?"

"No. I saw her while the sun was up, shortly before noon."

"Then we shall watch closely. I must know the truth of the matter."


Over the next few ten-days, Urgon and Kraloch took turns watching and waiting. Each morning, Kurghal entered the hut bearing two bowls. Each evening, well after darkness had fallen, Shular did likewise.

Urgon took to shadowing his sister instead of watching the hut, determined to ascertain where the food was coming from. Much to his surprise, he discovered it was part of the tribute given to shamans. As a community, the Orcs relied on the generosity of their hunters to keep others fed. Food was considered communal property and thus shared out with the other inhabitants upon returning from the hunt. His mother, as a shaman, was in theory entitled to an equal share of such game, but he soon realized she was taking more than was required by her family. His next step was to find out exactly how much more she was collecting.

For five days, he carefully monitored his own meals, taking stock of how much actual food he was consuming. A quick check with Kraloch's cousin Urzath, a hunter herself, soon revealed the extra share was similar in size to his own.

He rushed off, eager to share his news with his comrade. Kraloch was beside Latuhl's wolf pen, from where he had an unobstructed view of their target.

"I made a discovery," said Urgon.

"As have I," replied his friend. "Tell me what you learned, and then I will share my own revelation."

"I watched my sister these past few days. She takes food into the hut, in a quantity not too different from my own meals."

"Are you suggesting an Orc is held within?" said Kraloch. "Orcs do not imprison other Orcs."

"True, but I would surmise whatever is in that hut is roughly the same size as us."

"What other creatures would fit that description? A Dwarf, or possibly even a Human?"

"That," said Urgon, "I have yet to determine. What of your own discovery?"

"Have you ever observed Master Latuhl at work?"

"Not for any real period of time, no. Why?"

"He has, on occasion, cleaned out the wolf pens. When he does, he takes the scat and dumps it over the cliff edge."

"How does that help us?"

Kraloch smiled. "I saw your sister doing the very same thing after visiting the hut."

"Do you think she was cleaning up after a wolf?"

"No, of course not, but she must be looking after something, and that tells us it is a living being inside. Whatever it is, its scat is now at the base of the cliff."

"Are you suggesting we climb down to investigate?"

"No," said Kraloch. "I doubt I could tell the difference between an Orc's and a wolf's. Can you?"

"Maybe one day, when my training as a hunter is complete, but not at present. How often does she carry out this task?"

"Every day, when she leaves the hut with the empty bowl."

"More frequently than Latuhl's wolves, then."

"From what I saw, yes," said Kraloch. "And that would suggest something with intelligence, something that does not like the smell of its own scat."

"It is beginning to sound more and more like an Orc," noted Urgon, "yet if it were so, would they not leave the hut of their own accord to relieve themselves?"

"What if they are unable to? A physical infirmity, perhaps?"

"What type of injury could not be healed by my mother's magic? She can heal flesh as well as cure diseases or even remove poisons. What does that leave us with?"

"A curse?"

Urgon thought for a moment. Curses were not unknown, but magic of that sort was forbidden. The only way a curse could be inflicted was through great power. Urgon suddenly felt his stomach turning. Was there an evil Hex Mage somewhere in the Artisan Hills, using the Orcs as subjects in their terrible experiments? He shuddered at the thought.

"Well?" pressed Kraloch. "What do you think?"

"It is possible, but what kind of curse would lead to imprisonment?"

"That," said Kraloch, "is something that eludes me, yet I feel it the most likely answer we discussed so far."

Urgon felt the pieces begin to fall into place. "Could it be some sort of changeling—a creature half-Orc, half-wolf?"

"I have heard of such things," admitted Kraloch. "My mother used to tell me stories at bedtime. I thought them flights of fancy, but maybe there is some truth to them?"

"Whatever it is, it must be relatively docile. It has, to my knowledge, never attacked my mother or sister."

"Could it be old?"

"Or young," suggested Urgon. "The hut was built fourteen winters ago. What if a youngling was born with a curse?"

"Would we not have heard of it?"

"We were not born yet!"

"Yes, but someone must remember."

"Who is to say they do not? When a youngling is lost at birth, it is never celebrated, only mourned. And they rarely speak of such things, especially to younglings like us."

Kraloch's eyes lit up with excitement. "Agreed, but I would prefer not to wait for my ordeal before I discover the details. I say we take some sort of action now to determine if this is the truth of the matter."

"As do I," said Urgon. "And I believe I have the perfect solution to our problem."

"Tell me more!"

"I propose that one of us enter the hut."

"How?" asked Kraloch. "You said it was sealed by magic runes?"

"Only the door. We could go in through the wall."

"That would take much work," said Kraloch, "and whoever, or whatever is in that hut, would likely hear you."

"I would be willing to take that chance."

"Who died and made you chieftain? I have as much right to enter as you do."

"True," said Urgon, "but you were chosen to become a shaman. I would not have you throw that away on a foolish errand."

"Foolish, is it? Now you are mocking yourself. Make up your mind, my friend. Is this a daring plan, carefully thought out and executed, or a reckless flight of fancy?"

Urgon grinned. "Can it not be both?"

"I will agree to this mad scheme of yours, provided we do our best to keep things quiet. How do we proceed?"

"The first difficulty will be in the approach. To that end, I propose we do so under cover of darkness."

"A wise choice," said Kraloch, "but will your mother not expect you to be at home?"

"I shall tell her I am visiting your hut."

"And I will tell mine that I am visiting yours. What is the next step?"

"We rendezvous by the wolf den," said Urgon. "You will remain there, watching for any sign of trouble while I make my way around the back of the hut. It is there that the greatest chance of discovery exists."

"How so?"

"I must get through the wall, and that requires me to dig out the mud, not to mention the sticks that lay beneath."

"And how do you intend to do that?" asked Kraloch.

"With my axe and knife. It will be a time-consuming process, but I see no other way."

"Could you not dig out the ground beneath it?"

Urgon looked back at his comrade with a gleam in his eyes. "An excellent idea. I wish I had thought of it myself."

"You will need to make sure you are not digging at a post hole."

"Easy enough to avoid, but I shall require a shovel or pick if I am to get inside before daybreak."

Kraloch frowned. "Yet another complication. Someone might notice the missing tools."

"No one is going to miss them at night, and they will allow me to dig much faster."

"It is not the speed that concerns me but the sound it will produce. The back of the mud hut is close to a hunters' longhouse."

"I shall dig quietly."

"How does one do that?" said Kraloch. "A pick striking the ground makes noise, noise that will attract unwanted attention."

"Then I will use a shovel instead. Have you any other concerns?"

"Yes, we do not know what actually lives within that hut. It could be hostile."

"I will be careful," said Urgon, "and in any case, I have my axe. Remember, I only seek to determine what is held there. Once I know, I can withdraw."

"There is so much that could go wrong."

"True, but with risk comes great rewards."

"Now you sound like Latuhl," said Kraloch. "Are those his nuggets of wisdom?"

"No, they are mine. Now, what did we overlook?"

"Nothing I can think of, although perhaps time will allow us to better determine if there is more to consider."

"Nonsense," said Urgon. "We must strike quickly. The better to put an end to this mystery."

"Only a fool rushes into the wolf's den."

"We should go in at night. Whatever it is will likely be sleeping."

"You do not know that," said Kraloch. "and there is still the risk of discovery. The consequences could be dire if you are found."

"The risk is all mine," said Urgon. "Come now, have faith in me, my friend. It takes confidence to do this. Something I have in abundance."

"There is a fine line between confidence and foolhardiness."

"You are well suited to be a shaman, for you stick to the rules like a fly to honey."

"And you are the exact opposite," said Kraloch, "breaking the rules at the drop of a spear."

"I think of myself not as breaking the rules so much as reshaping them to suit my needs."

"The results are the same."

"I would beg to differ," said Urgon, "but we will not argue the point. It is our very differences that allow us to be friends, would you not agree?"

"And I would not change that, for it gives us strength and tightens the bonds between us. I will always be there for you, Urgon, despite any disagreements we may have. I am your brother in all but birth."

"And I yours," said Urgon, grinning, "even when you are old and wise, and your head filled with the pride of being a shaman."

"Filled with pride? I will strive to do better than that and remain humble, I promise you."

"I shall hold you to that, my friend. Now, are you ready to help me enter the hut?"

"Now?" asked Kraloch.

"Of course, there is no better time than the present."

"I disagree. The endeavour will take most of the night. It would be better accomplished on a full stomach."

"Ah, Kraloch, ever the wise one. Fine with me, have it your way. Go and eat your fill, but try not to overindulge. I would prefer you stay awake as you watch over me."

"And you, my friend, should avoid your mother's soup. You know how it upsets your stomach. The last thing we need is for the growling of your belly to give you away."

Urgon chuckled. "I will follow your advice. Let us meet by the wolf pen when the sun sets."

"Agreed," said Kraloch. "In the meantime, I will visit the storage hut and gather a shovel." He turned, heading off towards his home.

Urgon watched him go, his heart racing at the thought of what he was about to do. He tried to calm himself, taking a deep breath and letting it out slowly, but it did little to suppress the energy that threatened to explode from within. Counting was another option, and so he closed his eyes, determined to get control of his pounding heart. He jumped into the air as a voice interrupted him.

"You there, Urgon. What are you up to?"

Opening his eyes, he saw Latuhl. The old master of wolves was in the pen, tossing chunks of meat to his charges as was his usual custom. He wandered over to the fence, resting his arms upon the timber.

"Well? Do you have an answer for me?"

"Sorry," said Urgon. "I was deep in thought."

"About what?"

"Nothing important. Why?"

"Merely curious. Did you ever find out more about the mud hut?"

"I did, although nothing that would confirm its contents. In any event, I decided to move on. There are far more interesting things to occupy my time."

"Good," said Latuhl. "Then you can move along and stop pestering my wolves."

"I assure you that was not my intention. Is my mere presence a problem?"

"It is," the old Orc replied. "They often form a bond with those who care for them, making them less effective on a hunt."

"You mean like Rockjaw?"

"Rockjaw is old and hunts no longer. These, on the other hand"—he waved his hand—"must still remain focused on prey."

"Worry not, master of wolves. My work here shall soon be done." He smiled as he walked off, leaving Latuhl with a confused expression.

# FIVE

## Infiltration

SPRING 948 MC

The clouds blocked out the moon, leading Urgon to stumble as he made his way through the village. He pressed himself against the side of a hunters' longhouse, peering around the edge to gaze in the direction of the wolf pen. He could see little through the inky blackness, leaving him with scant choice but to blindly close the distance, so he moved into the open, calling out softly, "Kraloch?"

"Over here," came the reply.

Closer he drew, until he recognized the dark shape before him. "Kraloch? Is that you?"

"Of course it is," came the hushed reply. "Who else would be out and about at this time of night."

"Fair point."

"Here. Take the shovel and be quick about it before someone overhears us."

Urgon grasped the wooden pole, feeling the weight of it. Now all that remained was to get into position and dig. He stumbled towards his target, cursing his luck. As an Orc, he could see quite clearly by moonlight, but his advantage was effectively neutralized with the clouds overhead.

When his boot struck a rut in the pathway, he almost lost his balance, and the shovel flew from his hands, clattering to the ground. Urgon froze, straining to hear any response. His heart felt as if it were in his throat, his pulse beating faster than ever, while the hair on the back of his neck stood upright.

He sighed in relief when not a sound came in reply. And then, at that moment, the clouds parted, allowing moonlight to filter through, restoring his night vision. Picking up the shovel, he ran to the mud hut and pushed up against its side while casting about, looking for any sign of others. He moved farther along the wall until he was between his target and the bigger hunters' longhouse behind it.

From his current position, Urgon could see the chieftain's hall, where two hunters stood watch. Lucky for him, they appeared uninterested in the hut of mud, preferring instead to gaze north, although to what purpose he couldn't surmise.

He knelt, feeling the ground at the base of the wall, only to let out a soft sigh of relief when he realized it was packed earth, for he had feared stone which would block his attempts at digging. He placed the shovel as quietly as possible, then dug in, putting all his weight into the effort. The dirt soon parted under his ministrations, and he heaved it up, ready to dump it off to the side. It was then he realized his predicament, for he must rid himself of it without raising suspicion. Standing there with a shovel full of dirt, he felt a bit foolish. In his rush to discover the truth, he had failed to look at all the repercussions, leaving him in a difficult position. He tried to reason things out but could see no solution that would keep his endeavours undetected.

Urgon took a step back, bumping into the longhouse. From inside drifted the sounds of snoring, leading him to finally relax. If he were to be discovered, then so be it. He would learn the secret of this hut if it was the last thing he ever did!

Soon, he could see the bottom of the wall, yet still he dug, for he needed enough clearance to crawl beneath it. He was covered in sweat by the time the hole was several hands deep. Once he hopped in, he dropped the shovel and took out his knife, plunging it up into the dirt. It took only a dozen stabs to reveal the underside of an animal skin.

Flush with his success, Urgon squeezed into the hole, feeling the tightly packed dirt hard up against his shoulders. Reaching up, he pushed the skin aside, then poked his head through the opening.

Light flickered off the walls from a small fire that illuminated the inside of the hut. Something, or more likely someone, sat before the fire, its back to him. He let his eyes adjust, trying to make out any details, but his position on the floor made it difficult. Aware that whoever was there could turn at any moment, Urgon placed the knife between his teeth, then pulled himself into the hut, moving closer, trying to be as quiet as possible.

Now that it was easier to see, he realized the figure was not dissimilar in size to himself and was covered in coarse robes of rough skins. Urgon held his breath, transferring the knife back to his hand. He inched along the wall, trying to view the face of whomever or whatever this thing was. He had only gone two paces when a clear voice sang out.

"Who are you?" it said.

The figure turned, revealing a female Orc unlike any he had ever seen before—it was as if all the colour had been washed from her face. A mantle of white hair framed her ghostly visage, giving the appearance of someone of advanced age, yet at the same time, he swore she was much the same age as him.

Urgon felt his throat constrict. "My name is Urgon," he finally squeaked out, "son of Urdar. Who are you?"

"My name is Zhura."

"What are you?"

"I am a ghostwalker, one who is doomed to exist between two worlds—the living and the dead." He gazed into her pale eyes, a look she returned with intense interest.

"You are not a shaman," she said.

"No. I hope one day to become a hunter, but I have yet to undergo the ordeal."

"And yet you sought me out? Why?"

"Curiosity. How old are you?" Urgon knew the answer immediately. "Never mind, I already know. You were born fourteen winters ago."

"I was. My mother was the hunter, Narduk. I am told she died soon after I escaped her womb. My… condition was obvious from the very beginning. They brought me here to keep me safe."

"Safe? From what?"

Zhura closed her eyes, and he saw turmoil crease her brow. "You must excuse me," she said. "It is difficult to concentrate when so much is going on around me."

"Around you? It is only me!"

"You are wrong, Urgon, for the spirits are plentiful here within the village."

"You see them?"

She nodded. "Indeed. They pass through these walls as if they did not exist."

"Then why the mud?"

"It dampens the sound and gives me rest from the voices."

"Voices?" said Urgon. "You mean you can hear them as well?"

"Yes, they speak to me. Their voices drone on endlessly, echoing through my mind." She opened her eyes, turning her intense gaze on Urgon. "You, however, are quite different."

"Different, how?"

"You are quiet."

"Well, I AM somewhat stealthy."

"No," said Zhura. "I mean, your spirit is at rest."

"What does that mean?"

"Normally when an Orc enters this hut, I can see the spirit within them, as if a ghost is fighting to get out. You, though, show no sign of that."

"And is that a good thing?"

She smiled. "It is peaceful and a welcome respite from my usual visitors."

"Ah," said Urgon. "That would be Shular, my mother, and Kurghal, my sister. Is it they who keep you prisoner here?"

"I am not a prisoner, but someone who is gifted… or cursed, depending on your point of view. They come seeking the wisdom of the Ancestors."

"I thought they used magic to do that?"

"Why use a spell when I can speak with them directly?"

"But surely you deserve a life?"

Zhura looked around the hut, her face falling. "This is my destiny."

"Nonsense. You have a right to be as free as any other Orc."

"Were I to step outside, I would be overwhelmed by the spirits of the dead. It would likely drive me mad."

"But are you not lonely?"

"I survive."

Urgon felt a burning in the pit of his stomach. "This is no way for you to live. What of companionship? Have you no wish to talk to others?"

"Of course, but what am I to do? I am trapped here, unable to walk amongst my own people."

"Then the village must come to you."

Zhura smiled. "That, I fear, would be too hard to bear. Even the presence of Shular and Kurghal can, at times, be too great a burden for me, and there are only two of them."

"I know what you mean. I sometimes feel the same."

She laughed, and the hint of a smile creased her lips. "You are refreshing, Urgon. It is a pleasure to talk with one whose spirit is calm."

He moved in front of her, letting the dim light wash over him. "May I sit?"

"Of course."

He lowered himself to the ground. "What do you know of the village?"

"Very little, for I have never set foot outside these walls."

"And yet you speak as one well versed in the language of our people. Has my mother given you instruction?"

"No, it is the spirits."

"You mean the Ancestors?"

Zhura nodded. "As I said, they are amongst us."

"Are they here now?" asked Urgon.

"No, at the moment, it is only you and I."

Urgon struggled to make sense of her situation. "Why do they not acknowledge your existence?"

"It is tradition. Those of my ilk are rare amongst our people. We are both cursed and blessed. On the one hand, we are a direct connection to the Ancestors, but on the other, we often go mad."

"Mad? You look normal to me."

She smiled again. "I am young, only a few months older than you, I would guess. People like me live brief lives, Urgon, or so the Ancestors tell me."

He felt a sorrow tugging at his heart. "Then prove them wrong, Zhura."

"How do you propose I do that?"

"You said you felt I was at peace. Let me return in the future."

"To what end?"

"I would offer you friendship."

"And how would that work?" Zhura asked. "I must remain in this hut, and you are forbidden to enter."

"Yet I am here. I would do so again if it helped you."

"Even at the risk of punishment?"

"Yes, even then."

They sat in silence, Urgon too afraid to speak, lest he interrupt her thoughts.

"Very well," she finally replied. "I will accept your offer of friendship, but you must promise you will reveal nothing of my existence."

"I promise."

"Good. Now you need to go before you are missed."

He stared at her, noting how the light played across her features. "You are quite unlike any other Orc I have ever seen, Zhura."

"As are you, Urgon. Now leave me and make sure you cover your tracks to avoid discovery."

He rose, unsure of himself. Zhura was alone, and he desperately wanted to reassure her. When his hand brushed up against his knife, an idea took root. He pulled forth the blade, handing it to her with open palms.

"Here," he said. "Take this as a token of my friendship."

"I have no need of a weapon."

"True, but perhaps you need a reminder that you are not alone."

"I shall keep it," she declared as she took the knife, "though I must hide it from the others, lest they know of your visit."

Urgon made his way back to the hole while Zhura watched. He lowered his legs into the shallow depression, keeping his eyes on her.

"I will return," he promised, "but I cannot say precisely when that will be."

She smiled. "I have waited a long time for a visitor. What are a few more days?"

He forced himself into the hole, squeezing through the opening to emerge outside where the cool evening air caressed his face. He stood for a moment, wondering if he had imagined the pale Orc with the hair of moonlight. Glancing down at his belt, he noted the absence of his knife and smiled. It appeared the Ancestors finally looked on him with favour.

# SIX

# Zhura

## SPRING 948 MC

U rgon tossed and turned as he slept. In his dreams, he hid in the darkness, fearing discovery, although what was after him was difficult to fathom. He awoke with a start, the furs soaked with sweat, and Shular bending over him, concern on her face.

"Are you unwell?" she asked.

"No," he replied. "Why?"

"The sun has been up for some time, and you have yet to rise. To sleep for so long is most unlike you. I fear you may be coming down with something."

"I found it difficult to get comfortable."

"In that case, I think it best to cast a spell or two if only to ward off any illness."

He was, in fact, tired due to his nighttime exertions, but to admit so would be to put an end to his endeavours. Arguing with his mother was useless, so he simply nodded, then stifled a yawn as he watched her invoke her magic.

The hut echoed with words of power, the air buzzing with energy as Shular's hands glowed. She placed them on her son's chest, and a warmth enveloped him.

"There," she said. "That should help."

Urgon threw off the covers and stood, trying desperately to hide his fatigue.

"How do you feel?" she asked.

"Fit as a mountain bear."

"Then come, have something to eat. I saved you some red berries from the morning meal."

He took the bowl, picking away at its contents.

"What are you up to today?" asked Shular.

"Not much. Kraloch and I thought we might set up some snares to see if we can catch anything."

"I wish you good hunting," said Shular, "but try not to stray too far from camp. There have been reports of a mountain cat in the area."

He looked up in surprise, his meal all but forgotten. "A mountain cat?"

"Yes, it looks like with the coming of warmer weather, the deer have returned, and with them their natural enemies."

"Then we shall be careful. I promise." He gulped down the rest of his food, then set the bowl aside. "Thank you for the meal."

Shular looked at him in shock. "Are you sure you are well?"

"Yes, why?"

"Your manner is strange. Never before have you thanked me for a meal."

"I have come to appreciate all you do for me. Now, I must be off, or else Kraloch will leave without me."

He stepped outside, eager to escape his mother's prying eyes. Kraloch stood by the great firepit, watching a group of Orcs Urgon didn't recognize. He soon crossed the distance, coming to stand beside his comrade.

"Who are they?" he asked.

"Tribe members from another village, here to trade."

"Where lies this village?"

"I have no idea. Why? Do you want to visit it?"

Urgon smiled. "One day, it would be interesting to see how others live."

"Truly? I imagine their village looks much like ours."

"I know our tribe is scattered amongst these hills, but how many villages do we have?"

"At least ten, possibly more. An elder would be able to give you a full count. Why? Is it important?"

Urgon shrugged. "Not really." He let out a yawn.

"Tired?"

"More like exhausted—digging is hard work. I could use a nap."

"You never told me what you found last night," said Kraloch.

Urgon looked around before answering. "I would prefer to talk of such things away from the ears of others."

Kraloch smiled. "I know the perfect place." He set off at a fast pace, forcing Urgon into a run in order to catch up.

They passed by the shaman's hut, heading farther into the hills where the terrain grew steeper. A brief pause allowed Urgon to look back from whence they had come, the village's leafy roofs clearly visible in the sunlight.

"How much farther?" Urgon asked.

"Only a few more paces. It will be worth the trip, trust me."

They scrambled up a steep slope to find a ledge that stood before a cave opening, an eerie green light flickering from within. Urgon halted, grabbing his comrade by the arm.

"What is this place?" he asked.

"An ancient cave said to be built by those who came before us."

"But it glows with an eerie light."

"It does," said Kraloch. "And wait until you see inside!"

He stepped into the cave, leaving Urgon to contemplate his next move. His heart began to pound, and he fought to hold back the fear building within him.

"Come along," urged Kraloch. "There is no danger here, despite what you might think."

Urgon took a deep breath and then stepped through the entrance. The cave was nothing special, but the source of light mesmerized him. Someone had stacked stones, forming a small step pyramid. However, instead of a peak, a green flame grew out from its flat top, hovering in the air a finger's width above the stone blocks, its light throwing shadows that danced across the walls. He moved closer, peering into the flame.

"There is no heat," he said, "and why is the flame green? I have never seen its like."

"It is magical in nature," explained Kraloch. "I am unsure how it works, but it has been this way for generations, or so my mother says."

"Why did no one ever tell me of this?"

His comrade shrugged. "I have no idea. It is a place of contemplation and peace."

"Peace?"

"Yes. Animals will not willingly enter the cave."

"Fascinating. I wonder why it was built."

"As do I," said Kraloch, "but such speculation will not provide an answer. Now come, you said you were tired. Here, you can sleep, far from the prying eyes of your mother."

"And what will you do while I sleep?"

"That I have yet to decide. Perhaps I shall spend some time contemplating the flame. I find it quite captivating."

"As do I," said Urgon, then let out another yawn.

Kraloch chuckled. "As I suspected you would, but the time for such study is later. Close your eyes, my friend. Your mind will be clearer after a good nap."


Urgon opened his eyes to an empty cave. He got to his feet, wondering what time it was, but a quick glance at the entrance revealed daylight streaming in. The strange light drew him, but then his gaze shifted to the stones beneath that formed the peculiar pyramid. Each one had a symbol upon it, reminding him of the runes that bedecked his father's monument. Was this, then, a product of Dwarven smiths?

He leaned in closer, noting the intricate work. Dwarven runes were made of straight lines, but these symbols were formed of curves and circles, something he had seen before. His mind drifted back to the recent past. The door to the mud hut had been adorned with markings that bore some similarity to these. Did that mean Orcs had made this place? And if so, why?

Footsteps approached, causing him to turn around and face the door. Kraloch had returned, bearing a small sack.

"I brought some food," he said. "Did you sleep well?"

"I did," said Urgon, "though not nearly long enough. Where did you go?"

"To get this"—Kraloch held up the sack—"and to check on your recent digging. Fear not, my friend. If anyone has noticed it, I have heard no word. It appears people care little for such things."

"Still, we must do better. If I am to return, I must find an easier way of hiding my tracks."

"You intend to return?"

"Of course," said Urgon. "Why would I not?"

"I had assumed now that you know what lies within, your appetite for this is satiated."

"Zhura will expect my return."

"Zhura?"

"Yes, she is who was within the hut. Did I not mention it?"

"You most certainly did not," said Kraloch. "Who is this Zhura?"

"She is a ghostwalker, or so she tells me. Have you heard of anything like that?"

"No, but I am no shaman, at least not yet."

"They are said to walk the thin line between the living world and that of the spirits."

"And you believe this to be true?"

"It would explain much," said Urgon. "When her mother died in childbirth, she was taken to the hut to keep her safe."

"From what?"

"The prying eyes of others, I would suspect, although she did mention something about keeping the spirits quiet."

"Tell me more," said Kraloch.

"She is pale of skin, with hair the colour of moonlight, and her eyes…"

"What about her eyes?"

"They are a strange colour, like a red berry. Her gaze can be quite unsettling, yet somehow she is… fascinating."

"Careful, Urgon, it sounds like you are attracted to her."

"Nonsense. I am only intrigued by her uniqueness. She speaks to the Ancestors, you know, and says they walk amongst us."

"That would explain why your mother visits her regularly. What else did she tell you?"

Urgon struggled to remember her words. "She was educated by the Ancestors and speaks much as an Orc many times her age."

"Exactly how old is she?"

"Fourteen, or close to it. The hut was built specifically for her, likely as soon as word got out of her birth."

"An incredible story," said Kraloch. "What do you intend to do about it?"

"I shall visit again," said Urgon, "and find out all I can about her."

"To what end?"

"She is lonely and would appreciate the company. That alone should be enough to justify my visit. What of you? Would you care to meet her?"

"While I am tempted, it would be better for me to remain aloof."

"Aloof?" said Urgon. "You sound like my mother."

"In this, I believe her to be correct. Better that I maintain a separation from this Zhura, at least for now. I can well imagine what will happen when Shular learns of this."

"IF she finds out," insisted Urgon.

"Well, I certainly intend to keep silent on the matter."

"As do I, but I suppose it is inevitable she will find out sooner or later. In the meantime, we must keep this secret for as long as possible."

"Agreed," said Kraloch. "Will you return tonight?"

"I will. Why?"

"I shall accompany you, but only to the back of the hut. I want to see if there is a better way to hide your method of entry. Simply throwing the dirt aside might prove troublesome in the long run."

So it was that as the moon climbed high, the two stalwart companions found themselves squeezed in between the mud hut and the hunters' longhouse. Urgon set to work at once, while Kraloch kept an eye out for trouble. The work was easier tonight, for the dirt had been loosened the night before.

Urgon made a shallower hole this time, more of a depression, his intention to go through feet first, using Kraloch to aid him. Sitting by the edge, he pushed his feet into the dirt, then scuttled forward to sit in the hole and push up with his knees. The dirt soon gave way, and then a pair of hands yanked him by the ankles, pulling him forward halfway through the gap.

Kraloch moved to grab him, but Urgon waved him away. Moments later, he was dragged beneath the hut's wall, disappearing from sight. Kraloch was beside himself with worry, but then Urgon's hand appeared with a brief wave, signalling all was well. Inside the hut, Zhura let go of his ankles.

"Thank you," said Urgon. "I wondered how I was going to get through." He stood, brushing the dirt from his arms and legs.

"Come," said Zhura. "Let us sit by the fire so I may see your face."

She took his hand, and he felt the warmth of her soul. He stared at her for a moment, unable to express the feeling.

"Is something the matter?" she asked.

"Your touch," he said, "it feels... unusual."

"As I said before, I tread the thin line between the worlds of the spirits and that of the living. When I touch your hand, I do so in both worlds. Do you find the feeling unpleasant?"

"N-no," he stammered. "Quite the opposite, in fact. It is soothing."

She led him to the fire, but instead of sitting across it, she sat next to him, turning her side to the heat. He sat in a similar state, watching her with great interest.

"You have questions," she said. "I can see it in your eyes."

"Kraloch took me to see a wondrous cave today."

"The cave of the Eternal Flame?"

"Yes," said Urgon. "You know of it?"

"It is an ancient structure, built long before our tribe settled in this area."

"By who?"

"The First Race."

"The Elves?"

She grimaced. "No. Did no one teach you the history of our people?"

He frowned. "My mother sees little point in such things."

"The First Race is the name we give to the Saurians, those who trod the world long before we appeared. After them came the Dwarves, Orcs, and Elves, those we call the Elder Races. Lastly came the Humans, who bent the land to their will."

"Humans, I have heard much of them. They are said to live in a great city that lies to the west of us."

"Yes," said Zhura. "In a place they call Eastwood."

"Eastwood? I have heard of it, but it is a curious name as it lies to the west. Have they no sense of direction?"

She laughed. "To our west they might be, but to their eyes it lies on the eastern border of their domain."

"Domain? You mean there are more of them?"

"Many more. The race of Humans spreads quickly, building great cities as they go, the same as we once did in the distant past."

"What nonsense is this? Orcs do not live in cities."

"Ah, but they did, many generations ago."

"What happened to them?"

"They were destroyed in a great war that encompassed the entire land."

"A war?" said Urgon. "With who?"

"The Elves."

"Why has no one ever told me of this?"

"It was a long time ago," said Zhura, "but the Ancestors speak of it still."

"How is it that we now live here?"

"After the loss of the great cities, the survivors wandered about in small groups, the better to avoid destruction. You see, the Elves hunted us down, killing all without mercy."

"Is that when the tribes were formed?"

"In a manner of speaking, yes, but the term tribes came about much later when we began to settle down again. For many generations, our people hunted and trapped, living off the land and then moving on before depleting the region of food. In those days, we called ourselves clans. Some of our people still live this way, but most settled down, as we have, building huts and gathering in large numbers."

"And the Elves," said Urgon, "will they come for us again?"

"No, for the war cost them dearly. So much so that when the Humans appeared, there were far too few to resist their expansion."

"And you learned all this from the Ancestors?"

"Yes," said Zhura. "I have little else to do but talk, and they are an endless source of information."

"This is all quite fascinating."

"And yet I fear I steered you away from your original question. You spoke of the Eternal Flame. What would you like to know about it?"

"It has a base of stone," said Urgon, "upon which are strange symbols, symbols that are very similar to those on the door to this very hut."

"Those are symbols of power. What others might call the letters of magic."

"Others?"

"Yes, such powers are not limited to Orcs alone. They are found within all the races, even Humans."

"Are you suggesting Humans had something to do with that cave?"

"No. As I said earlier, that place was built by the First Race. Words of power, or symbols in this case, are the same in any language. In a sense, they are a universal language, although only for the application of arcane forces."

Urgon struggled to keep up. "You are talking of things for which I have little understanding."

"My apologies if I babble. I am unused to having company that allows me such freedom. I hope I have not offended you."

"No, not at all. I find the discussion most enthralling."

"I talked far too much. It is your turn."

"My turn?" said Urgon. "What shall I talk of?"

"What are your goals in life?"

"I suppose I shall become a hunter."

"I suspect there is more to your future than that," said Zhura.

"Meaning?"

"You have an inquisitive mind."

He screwed up his face. "Is that a good thing?"

"It is," she replied. "It led you to me, and I suspect it is that very trait that will determine your future, perhaps even that of the entire tribe one day."

"Why would you say that?"

"I talk to the Ancestors, remember? Orcs are, by nature, inclined to follow the rules. Very few would ever consider taking the risk you did in coming here. You have a willingness to bend the rules, even break them if it suits your purpose. That can lead to great change."

"Change can be dangerous," he warned.

"It is merely the result of choices."

"And how do I know if my choices are good?"

"You must follow your heart," said Zhura. "Such choices will not be easy, but if you act from a sense of selflessness and choose what you think is best for others, that should suffice."

"I feel as though a great weight has been placed upon my shoulders, and I have not even passed my ordeal."

She reached out to him, placing her hand on his knee. "I do not mean to upset you, Urgon, but I sense you are quite unlike others of our race. I mean that only in the nicest way. You have the courage of a bear and the heart of a wolf. The village is your pack. I know you will do whatever it takes to protect us."

"A heavy burden considering I am still a youngling."

"The ordeal is merely a ritual. It does not determine your maturity. It is what lies here"—she placed her palm on his chest—"inside you, that is important."

She removed her hand, leaving Urgon with a sense of loss.

"I should get going," he said, "before someone notes my absence."

"But you will return?"

He smiled. "Most certainly. You have given me much to think on, Zhura."

"Is that not what friends do?"

Urgon stepped close, grasping her hands in his. "It is," he said. He wanted to stay. There were so many questions unanswered, yet he knew he couldn't.

"Go in friendship," said Zhura. "I look forward to our next meeting."

He forced himself to release her hands, then made his way back to the shallow entrance, looking once more in her direction before exiting.

# SEVEN

## Training

SUMMER 948 MC

Spring soon made way for summer, and Urgon's visits to Zhura continued. Rather than dig himself in each night, he laid out a large skin on which the dirt sat. He and Kraloch would pull it up, then return it when the visit was complete, filling in the edges with soil to erase any sign of their endeavours. This made the job much more manageable, not to mention relatively quick. On the inside, Urgon and Zhura dug a proper hole, covering it with furs to hide it.

The visits grew longer. And then, each night, he would relate to Kraloch what had transpired once he returned. Several times he tried to convince his comrade to join him, but Kraloch adamantly argued someone should keep watch.

Urgon learned more of his peoples' history and how the Orcs of the Black Arrow came to live here, in these hills. He absorbed every fascinating word like a sponge. He began to take pride in his heritage, something he had heretofore given little thought.

On Midsummer Day, the entire village celebrated by holding a feast around the great firepit. Food was eaten in abundance while the hunters talked of their skill and valour. That evening the fire burned late, and the presence of so many Orcs nearby made a visit to Zhura impractical. As a consequence, Urgon lay in his furs, unable to think of anything other than the Orc with the hair of moonlight's glow. He slept little and was rudely awoken by his mother.

"Come, my son," she called. "You have a visitor."

Urgon sat up, wiping his bleary eyes. As they swam into focus, he noted the presence of a large Orc.

"Urzath?" he said. "Is that you? What are you doing here?"

"Looking for you."

"Why? Is something wrong? Is Kraloch hurt?"

The hunter chuckled. "No, my cousin is well. I come at the bidding of Shular."

"Why would my mother send for you?"

"Why do you think? You are almost an adult, Urgon, and before you undergo your ordeal, you should be prepared."

"Prepared?"

"Yes, I come to teach you the skills of a hunter."

"I can already hunt."

"Oh?" said Urzath. "So you know how to track, do you? Or use an axe?"

"Well, maybe not as well as you, but tomorrow would be better for such things. I am far too tired for it today." He lowered himself back into his bed, pulling the furs over his head, only to have them rudely removed. Urzath held an axe over him.

"Here, take this. It is not the weapon of a youngling but that of a hunter."

He wanted to argue the point, but agreeing was easier. Resigned to his fate, he got to his feet, taking the weapon and examining it.

"It is a fine tool," he said.

"It is not a tool, but a weapon."

"Is there a difference?"

"Note the head," said Urzath, ignoring the remark. "It is made of steel, not stone. Such a weapon will last much longer than others, but it must be cared for."

"Cared for? What do I do, put it to bed each night and tell it stories?"

"No, but even Dwarven steel will rust when wet. To prevent that, you must learn to take care of it. Beeswax is the best coating, but any kind of animal fat will suffice. Be careful to only put it on the blade, though, or you may find your grip is no longer secure."

"Anything else I should know?"

"Much," said Urzath, "but you will retain little of it here, in this hut. To truly learn anything of the hunt, we must go beyond the confines of the village. Gather your knife and spear. I shall await you outside." She turned, leaving the hut.

Urgon tied on his belt, then went to tuck in his knife but remembered he had given it away. He looked around, worried his mother might have noticed, but she tended to something at the fire with her back to him. He dug through his things, pulling forth the knife of his youth. Far smaller than his gift to Zhura, with a shorter blade, but it would have to suffice. He grabbed his spear, then rose, coming to stand before his mother.

"Why did you arrange this?" he asked.

"Your ordeal approaches," replied Shular, "and you have done little on your own to prepare."

"And so you thought me unable to survive?"

"It is no laughing matter, my son," she said. "Many die out there in the wild. You need to take this seriously."

He looked at her a moment, noting her look of concern. He had not always gotten along with his mother, but she still took care of him.

"Yes, Mother," he said. "I will heed Urzath's word and make you proud."

"That is all I ask."

Urgon stepped outside to find Urzath waiting for him. "Where do we start?" he asked.

"We shall head south for a while. Once the village is out of sight, you can show me what you know about setting snares."

"Are we not to hunt deer?"

"Not yet," she said. "I must take a measure of your basic skills first."

"And what constitutes a basic skill?"

"Setting up a camp, building shelter, setting a fire, and, of course, cooking."

"That will take some time."

"Yes," agreed Urzath. "Likely the better part of the morning. I also have to show you how to find water—a very important part of survival."

"I know where the streams lie."

"Yes, the ones around here, but one day you may find yourself in unknown territory. You must learn to look for the signs."

"What kind of signs are those?" Urgon asked.

"Plenty, if you know where to look. Animals need water as much as we. Following their tracks can often lead to a pond or stream. How are you at reading the ground?"

"I can see the hills well enough."

Urzath halted. "Look south," she said, "and tell me what you see."

"Not much. The hills stretch as far as the eye can see."

"And how far is that?"

"A few hundred paces, I would say, but if I look eastward, I can see the mountains. They must be a day or more away."

"True," she said, "but it is the hills that are of more import. You say you can see a few hundred paces, but what lies beyond that?"

"How would I know?" said Urgon. "I have never been this way before."

"Precisely. Danger can lurk anywhere. It is best, when travelling, to keep to open areas. That way, you can see danger approaching. On the hunt, however, such distance can warn potential prey of your approach."

"But that would put you in more danger."

"So it would," said Urzath, "but from what?"

"A bear, or maybe a mountain cat?"

"Bears are seldom dangerous, so long as you maintain your distance. They are also exceedingly difficult to kill. My advice if you see one would be to move off in another direction."

"But a bear is a valuable source of meat, not to mention fur."

"It is, but such an animal is best taken down by a group of hunters, not an individual."

"And a mountain cat?"

"That," said Urzath, "is the most dangerous creature in these parts and is a deadly foe. Retreat from such an encounter can often be disastrous as they have a habit of closing the range quickly."

"What, then, do we do if we spot one?"

"If it is too close to avoid, then you retreat, keeping your weapons handy, but do not turn your back to it. If it is farther away, then conceal yourself. Be warned, however, they have a good sense of smell, so if the wind is behind your back, it may notice you regardless."

"How common are they?" he asked.

"They are seldom seen in these parts, although there have been rumours of one in the area of late. Now, turn your attention to the plants. What do you see?"

"Some trees, a few bushes, and some wildflowers."

Urzath knelt, indicating a purple flower. "Do you see this?"

Urgon nodded.

"This is Nargun's thumb," she said.

"Is it a healing plant?"

"No, but it has deep roots and a thirst for water. If you find yourself unable to locate a stream, you can dig down into the roots."

"To find water?" he asked.

"In a manner of speaking. The roots absorb much, so eating them will moisten the mouth. Be sure to get as much dirt off them as you can, or else you will find it hard to swallow."

"Why is it called Nargun's thumb?"

"Nargun was one of the first of our people to tread these hills. He was lost and injured when he stumbled across this plant. The colour reminded him of his bruised hand."

Urzath stood, then glanced to the north. "We have, I believe, put enough distance between us and the village. Show me what snares you are familiar with."

Late afternoon saw them sitting before a fire. Urgon's snares had managed to procure them a rock lizard. This he had promptly skinned and then thrown the meat on the fire. The skin was used for many things, so Urzath showed him the proper way to clean it.

With their stomachs full, they headed off once again, this time watching the ground for any sign of tracks. They soon spotted those of a deer, following it to find a small body of water fed by a tiny stream.

The deer was drinking thirstily, and the Orcs had no problem sneaking up on it. Two throws of the spear was all it took, and then there was another carcass to prepare.

Urzath had a wealth of knowledge, and Urgon took in all he could. He knew, at least in theory, all that was necessary to be a hunter, yet that was a far cry from actually doing it. By the end of the day, they returned to the village, carrying the deer they had brought down.

The meat was divided up in the traditional way. Then Urgon retired for the night, too exhausted to even consider visiting Zhura. Hunting was hard work, and he worried that once he was no longer a youngling, he would have little time for her.

He collapsed into his bed and was soon asleep, but his dreams worried him. Something was chasing him, and he fled to the village only to find it deserted. He woke to a darkened hut, and for only a moment, he thought his dream must have come true, but then he heard the rhythmic breathing of his mother.

Urgon rose, heading outside as quietly as he could. He gulped in the night air, desperate to put his fears behind him. Was there meaning to his nightmare? He had always thought of dreams as nothing but the imagination, but now he began to wonder. Could the Ancestors be trying to warn him of something?

He shook his head. It was a preposterous idea. The Ancestors cared little for such things, and in any event, they were dead—that did not give them the ability to see the future. Perhaps Zhura might have the answers he craved.

He gazed across at her hut. All was quiet within the village as it usually was this time of night, but the occasional trail of smoke told him fires burned still.

Moving as quietly as possible, he walked past the great firepit and came to rest by Zhura's hut. He placed his hand upon it, seeking reassurance, but felt nothing, and why would he? It was, after all, only a hut covered in mud. What he sought resided inside, not within the walls themselves.

He went around back to the secret entrance, pausing for only a moment before he dragged the cover aside—a difficult task when done alone. There was a very real danger his entry might be discovered, for without Kraloch to assist, he had no way to hide the hole while he was inside. His compulsion to see her, however, outweighed the risks, so he squeezed his bulk through the opening, emerging inside the hut.

The room was completely dark. Outside, this wouldn't be a problem, for his night vision would compensate, but here, inside, there was no moonlight to light his way.

"Zhura?" he whispered.

She stirred and then called out, "Urgon? Is that you?"

He crawled forward, feeling his way to her. His hand brushed against her leg, and then she caressed his face.

"I am glad you are here," she said.

"Urzath took me hunting," he said, his face warming. "I am soon to undertake my ordeal, and she wanted to make sure I was ready."

"I understand. Come, sit by my side and tell me of your day."

She removed her hand, and he fought back the impulse to grab it. His mind whirled as his emotions conflicted within him. Many times he had sat before Zhura, yet here, even without light, her voice brought a warmth to his heart as if a piece of him had been missing. He reached out, feeling the floor until he was before her.

"Shall I start a fire?" she asked.

"No," he said, not wanting to spoil the mood, "but I would take your hands if you would permit."

"Gladly," she whispered.

He felt the warmth of her palms pressed against his, and then their fingers entwined.

"I missed you." She breathed out the words, laying bare her heart.

"As I have you." He felt light-headed, his pulse quickening. "What is wrong with me?"

"Are you ill?" she asked, concern in her voice.

Her forehead pressed against his, and the smell of her overcame him. His lips touched hers, lingering. Time stood still, and at that moment he knew he and Zhura were destined to be more than mere friends. Like all Orcs his age, he was fully aware of the attraction between sexes, but the experience was far more overwhelming than he had ever imagined.

"I… " he mumbled.

"Shush," she said. "There is nothing that need be said."

They sat in silence, the heat between them palpable. Finally, Zhura slowly pulled back.

"You had better go," she said, her voice turning melancholy. "It is late, and the sun will soon rise."

"I want to stay."

"You cannot. What you seek can never be yours. I am a ghostwalker, Urgon. We can never be together in that way. Those of my ilk can never bond."

"Nonsense. You are an Orc, just like me."

"An Orc, yes, but I am nothing like you. My pale skin and white hair are merely the outward signs of my condition. Inside, I am completely different."

"I refuse to believe that," said Urgon.

"Your belief changes nothing. The fact still remains I am a ghost-walker, and such relations are forbidden to me."

"That may be true, but is our friendship not real?"

"It is," said Zhura, "and I prize it above all else, but you can have no future with me."

His chest tightened, and he knew she was right. Despair welled up inside him. "Then I shall bond with no other."

Her hand tightened its grip. "A noble sentiment, but in time you will change your mind. You have a bright future ahead of you, Urgon. I would not have you waste it on the likes of me."

Tears came to his eyes. Not since his father died had he felt such a loss, yet still, inside, he held hope.

"I shall always remember you, Zhura," he promised.

"And I will always be here for you, dear friend. Now go. Leave me while you still have the strength to do so."

He crawled to the back of the hut and rummaged around, searching for the exit. His hands finally found it, and he pulled himself through the hole, emerging to a low growl. He looked up to see the snarling face of a wolf.

"What have you found, Rockjaw?" came the voice of Latuhl.

A figure loomed over him. "Urgon? Is that you?"

He looked up, shame on his face. "Yes."

The old Orc knelt, offering a hand. "What are you doing?"

"I was digging under the wall of the hut to see what lies within."

"And what did you find?"

Urgon struggled to find an answer. "My heart," he finally let out.

"You look like you need to talk, youngling. I think you should accompany me back to my hut."

"I must fill in this hole first. Will you help me?"

"If I can," said Latuhl.

Urgon showed him how to drag the skin back into place, then they piled stones and dirt on top. Once complete, he let the master of wolves lead him back to his home. Latuhl said little until they were within.

"Take a seat," he said, "and I shall fetch us something to drink."

Urgon waited, feeling a heavy weight descend upon his shoulders. It was over. He just knew it. The old Orc would tell everyone of his discovery, and then he would never be permitted to visit Zhura again.

Latuhl passed him a skin, and he tipped it back, feeling the warmth slide down his throat.

"So, what did you find in the hut?"

"A ghostwalker," said Urgon.

"You said something earlier about your heart. Am I to understand this Orc is a female?"

Urgon nodded, unable to say more.

"And you have been seeing her for some time, unless I miss my guess?"

"I have." He sensed doom about to break over his shoulders.

"Good for you."

The words came as a shock. "Good? I thought you would berate me?"

"For what? Befriending someone? You may put your mind at ease."

"But it is forbidden," said Urgon.

"So it is, but it is not my responsibility to tell the chieftain, and I would have never found you had Rockjaw not been prowling the village."

"Prowling the village?"

"Of course. He keeps us safe while we sleep. How better to alert us to danger?" Latuhl smiled. "I was young once too, you know, and I know the look of an Orc in love."

"I never said I was in love."

"Maybe not in so many words, but the result is obvious. Tell me, do you think of her all the time?"

"Yes," the young Orc quietly admitted.

"And when you are apart, do you long to be in her company?"

"I do."

Latuhl sat back. "Then that is all that matters."

"But it is forbidden!"

"So you said, but the heart wants what it wants. You have little say in the matter."

Urgon cast his eyes down. "It matters not. She has refused me."

"Refused? Did she then tell you she had no wish to see you further?"

"No, she said she would always be there for me."

"I would hardly call that a refusal. She is likely only being realistic. After all, as you are so fond of saying, it is forbidden. She likely sees things the same as you."

"Thank you for your kind words, Master Latuhl. You helped me deal with a difficult situation."

"I am pleased I could be of assistance."

Urgon put down the skin. "I should leave you now. My mother will soon start looking for me."

"Nonsense. You are in no shape to face Shular. Stay here and rest. I shall tell her you have been helping with the wolves."

# EIGHT

## Coming of Age

SUMMER 948 MC

The sun was high in the sky by the time Urgon returned to the hut of his mother. Shular was out and about, but his sister, Kurghal, tended to the fire. At his arrival, she looked up.

"I hear you have been helping Latuhl over at the pen. Is that what you want to be? The new master of wolves?"

He found the question irritating and spat out an answer with a little more venom than he had intended. "Why? Does that bother you?"

"Believe it or not, I want only what is best for you, Brother. We still share a bond, despite that we had different fathers."

"Sorry, I have slept little."

"Is something wrong?"

He realized with a shock he had said too much and struggled to recover. "The wolves were noisy last night. As a consequence, my rest was disturbed."

"Understandable." She sat down on a fur, indicating with a hand he should do likewise. "I think it time you and I had a chat."

"You are not my mother."

"No, but I am older. I would talk to you of your ordeal."

He moved closer, taking a seat. "I will listen."

"You are almost fourteen, Urgon," began Kurghal, "which means you are now the size of a full-grown Orc."

"I know that."

"Let me finish. You may have the body of an adult, but you still lack the skills of one. The ordeal is meant to prepare you for the brutal life in which we find ourselves. The Orcs have always lived on the edge of extinction, something you would be aware of if Mother had done her job of educating you."

"Our mother is the shamaness of this village," said Urgon. "One can hardly blame her for being busy. And as for the rest, you are wrong, Kurghal."

She looked as though he had slapped her. "What did you say?"

"I said you were wrong."

"About what?"

"We have not always lived on the edge of extinction. We were a proud race once, living in great cities."

"Who told you of such things?"

Urgon felt his chest tighten. He had let himself get carried away and now had revealed knowledge he should not possess. How, then, would he explain this without implicating Zhura?

"Answer my question," Kurghal demanded.

"The Dwarves," he lied. "I was told as much by Gambreck Ironpick, the one who brought back the body of my father."

The answer appeared to mollify her. "Sounds like they told you their version, but you should know the true story. It was many generations ago before the Humans trod this land."

He let her ramble on while his thoughts drifted to Zhura. What would his sister say if she knew the truth? Would she be pleased by his actions or furious he had broken the rules by visiting the ghostwalker? One day, perhaps, he would talk to Kurghal of such things, but today was not that day. He let her speak at length, nodding his head dutifully as if hearing the history of the Orcs for the first time.

Kurghal finally came to the point. "So you see, we are at significant risk of being forever removed from the land. It is each Orc's duty to learn well the lessons of survival and pass them on to their younglings. You, too, shall one day bond, and then that same knowledge will be taught to your own younglings."

"Yes, I understand."

"Good. You and I have had our differences, but that should not prevent us from working together for the betterment of our people. I bear you no ill will, Urgon. We are family and ever shall be. Whether you become master of wolves or simply another hunter is entirely up to you. Find your passion, my brother, and then happiness will surely follow."

Urgon was unsure of how to proceed. Never before had his half-sister talked this way, but then again, he had always avoided spending time with her.

"Tell me," he finally said, "are you happy?"

"This discussion concerns you, not me."

"Still, I would have you answer the question if you are willing. Are you happy?"

"Yes, I am."

"But you are not bonded."

"True," she replied, "but being a shamaness is not without its benefits. I made many friends amongst the tribes—others with similar gifts."

"Tribes? Have others visited the village without my knowledge?"

"No, we shamans are able to communicate with the other tribes through the use of magic. It is how we keep abreast of what is happening to our people."

"And what IS happening to our people?"

"I fear nothing good," said Kurghal. "Our numbers dwindle due to the encroachment of Humans into our lands. Tribes everywhere are being forced into the far reaches of the known lands, there to eke out an existence."

"There must be a solution!"

"What would you have us do? War with the Humans? They are far too numerous."

"We could find allies?"

"With who? The mountain folk? They hide behind their stone fortresses, seldom venturing forth."

"But we trade with them," said Urgon.

"We do, but trade is a far cry from being allies. The Dwarves are not a numerous people. True, they have large cities, but that is the extent of their civilization. They have little else."

"Could we not learn to live alongside the Humans?"

"A nice idea," said Kurghal, "but history tells us they have no desire for friendship. In fact, it is quite the opposite. The number of tribes has dwindled over the last few generations—the direct result of Human interaction."

"They fight us?"

She nodded. "They see us as savage brutes, good for little else other than killing."

"So we are doomed?"

"So it would seem, but that is yet some time in the future. Our duty is to delay the inevitable for as long as possible."

"I see now why the ordeal is so important. Thank you, Kurghal, for your words of wisdom."

"You are welcome. Now, as the eldest of Shular, I have taken it upon myself to have a word with Urzath on your behalf."

"Am I to go out hunting again?"

"You are," Kurghal said, "but this time, it will be for a few days."

"A few days? There are things to do here."

"Such as?"

Urgon paused a moment, gathering his thoughts. "Latuhl is not getting any younger, and I need to help him with the wolves."

"Latuhl has managed well enough for many winters. A few more days will make little difference. When you are on your ordeal, he will be on his own for a ten-day. I think he is more than up to the challenge of a few days without you."

Urgon wanted to scream but held his tongue. He needed to talk to Zhura and sort things out between them, but now his meddling sister had thrown a spear into the circle. There was no choice but to take up the challenge.

"Of course, Kurghal," he said. "When am I to leave?"

"Urzath will come for you today when the sun is at its peak."

"That soon?"

"Your ordeal is almost upon you, Brother. There is no time to waste. I would suggest you get some sleep, for hunting while tired is not a good way to start a trip."


By the time Urzath arrived, Urgon was ready, not that he had much to prepare. On his ordeal, he would be permitted a knife, a spear, and an axe, but nothing else, save his clothes.

Urzath, similarly equipped, led him eastward, taking him deeper into the hills. The terrain here grew quite rough, forcing them to climb several cliff faces, a task Urgon found difficult, not to mention tiring.

Urzath appeared to have no end of energy for this, and her enthusiasm soon had Urgon looking forward to the rest of the trip.

That night they camped by a mountain stream and speared fish, a skill that proved difficult to master. He was stubborn, however, and finally succeeded in stabbing his dinner. Urzath, of course, was much more capable, catching five. They cooked the meat over the fire, but when Urgon moved to help himself to some, he was stopped by his mentor.

"You may only eat what you yourself catch," she said.

"But you have far more than I."

"I do, but when you are on your ordeal, you will not have me to feed you. You must feast or starve by your own hands."

He went to bed hungry that night but was determined to do better on the morrow.

The second day saw them into the mountains themselves. Urgon had never gone this far east and was surprised by how cold the air became.

"This is nothing," said Urzath. "I have been to the peaks. There the ground is forever covered in snow and little lives."

"Then why go?"

She smiled. "To see what lies beyond."

"And what did you find?"

"More mountains, stretching as far as the eye could see. It would take half a season to cross them, and so I turned back."

"Maybe one day I shall cross them," said Urgon.

"You are more than welcome to try, but if you do attempt such a feat, make sure you take lots of food with you. Oh, and dress warmly. The air there is frigid, much colder than even the harshest of winters in Ord-Dugath."

"If it is so bleak, then why have we come here?"

"It is the peaks that are bare of food. Here, at the base of the mountains, you can find goats. They have thick fur and tasty meat, but you must be willing to navigate the rocks to catch them. A bow would be preferable for this type of game, but we must make do with what we have."

"Have they no enemies?"

"They do," said Urzath. "Primarily the mountain cat. Little else threatens them in these parts, save for our own wolves."

"Have you ever hunted with one?"

"A wolf? I have, as a matter of fact. It is a most enjoyable experience, although it takes some getting used to. Wolves, by nature, hunt in packs, and so you must mimic their hunting style."

She halted, grabbing Urgon's arm to still him, then raised her spear, using it to point at a distant outcropping of rock.

"There, you see?" she whispered.

In the distance, a strange-looking animal with thick fur covering its torso and two horns protruding from its head, stood watch. The goat stared right at them while it chewed away at some type of plant.

"Come," said Urzath. "We must work our way uphill and come at it from above."

"It is in a precarious position."

"Yes, but where there is one, there are likely to be others, and it is those we seek, not this one who keeps watch."

It took them a large part of the afternoon to get into position, for the guardian moved around, watching for any sign of danger. They finally found a spot from which to launch their attack—a slight over-hanging of rock, no more than an Orc's height above their prey.

They moved up slowly, crawling on hands and knees, trying to be as quiet as possible. Urgon peered over the lip to see those below and selected his target. The objective here was to drop from above, pinning the unfortunate animal in place with a spear. A knife would finish it off, should it prove necessary, but the most challenging part would be preventing the goat from running off before they could kill it.

He looked at Urzath, who had selected her own target. With a nod, they both inched forward until they were perched on the edge of the overhang. Urgon gripped his spear in both hands, then leaped. The spear struck true, punching through the creature's head, and it fell to the ground, stone dead.

Urzath, meanwhile, had also struck her target but had hit its shoulder, the tip glancing off and leaving only a red gash. As a result, the beast ran off, forcing the Orc to finish it with a thrown spear.

That evening they ate roast goat and boasted of their deeds, finally settling down for a good night's sleep.

. . .

Over the next two days, Urzath showed him how to make use of most of the carcass. Sinew was kept for sewing and the bladder for making a satchel that could hold water. Even the bones were extracted, for they could be used to enhance primitive weapons as their ancestors had done or even be carved into wondrous pieces of art.

They lived a life of comparative ease, with lots to eat and plenty of water to keep them hydrated. They even dried some meat, cutting it into strips to make it easier to carry. On the fifth day, they turned towards home, making their way down out of the mountains. They were half a day's travel away when Urzath suddenly stopped, stooping to the ground.

"Look here," she said. "Tracks."

Urgon knelt, examining the marks. "A mountain cat?"

"Yes, a most dangerous foe."

"Shall I return to the village and gather more hunters?"

"It would be long gone by the time they got here. No, we must track down this beast ourselves."

Urzath led the way, her spear at the ready. Urgon wished he had a bow, but that would defeat the purpose of this trip. One had to survive the ordeal with only those items they left the village with, and bows were definitely not allowed. One could be made in the wild, of course, but such skill was rare amongst those of his age.

The tracks led back towards the mountains, leading them into a narrow defile. Here they slowed their pace, for the prints were fresher. A low growl caused them to stop. The sound echoed around them, making it impossible to tell from which direction it originated.

Urzath crouched, ready to spring into action, but the attack, when it came, still took her by surprise. A blur streaked past Urgon, then slammed into Urzath, driving her to the ground in a flurry of teeth and claws.

Urgon struck out with the tip of his spear while his companion rolled around, trying to dislodge the creature's jaws which had sunk into her shoulder. She went still, and the great cat let go, turning its attention on Urgon.

His pulse quickened, his heart trying to break out of his chest. When it came for him, he was ready, planting the spear and letting the cat's own weight work against it. The force of the attack knocked him back. The creature let out a roar of anger as it rushed past him, trailing blood.

Urgon turned, ready to finish the job, but it had disappeared in amongst the rocks. He was torn with indecision, for the creature was now wounded, making it even more dangerous. However, his primary duty was clear, and so he made his way over to Urzath, who lay in a pool of her own blood, growing wider by the moment. Her face was pale, but her eyes were still alert.

"You must stop the bleeding," she said, "or I shall be dead by nightfall."

He threw their prizes to the ground, then pulled out what was left of the goatskin and cut it into strips to bind her injuries.

Urzath had some experience in treating wounds, so she talked him through the process, but it was soon clear she wouldn't be moving anytime soon.

"You must leave me," she said. "Get back to the village and return with hunters."

"No," said Urgon. "If I leave you, the creature might return, and it would be the end of you."

"I cannot walk, for I am far too weak, and I am too large for you to carry."

"There must be another way." He glanced over at their prizes, then looked down from whence they had come. "I have an idea," he said, "but I must get you out of this defile first."

He moved around behind her, lifting her by the armpits and started dragging her westward towards the village. A few hundred paces and they were out of the defile, but Urgon felt as if his arms were ready to fall off.

"I need to gather some wood," he said.

"To do what?"

"I will build a sled, or at least the frame of one. Then I can pull you as the Dwarves pulled their supplies."

"That was the winter, Urgon. Such a task is made all the more difficult without the presence of snow."

"But not impossible." He stared down at her. "I must try, Urzath. To lose a valued hunter is not acceptable."


Kraloch was working clay, making a new bowl when shouts drifted his way. Instantly alert, he stood, wiping his hands with an old skin. The hunter, Agrug, rushed past him, spear in hand, to be joined shortly thereafter by Tarluk. Taking up his spear, Kraloch ran to join them, eager to discover what was happening.

They gathered, along with a few others, at the eastern end of the village. Off in the distance, a strange shape had come into view, and Kraloch struggled to make out what it was. As it drew closer, it solidified into that of Urgon walking with a strange gait. Only when he paused a moment did the reason for such movement become evident. Behind him was a series of sticks, tied together into a rough sled. A strap led from this up to Urgon, who had looped it around his chest and pulled it along.

The hunters all ran forward, and then the call came back for the shamaness. Kraloch managed to squeeze through the crowd to see his closest friend collapsed upon the ground in an exhausted state, while behind him lay the body of Urzath.

Shular soon forced her way through and quickly used her magic on the injured hunter. Urgon lay there, watching her work, content to finally be able to rest.

"You saved Urzath," said Kraloch.

"I did what I had to, for the good of the tribe."

"You did much more than that," came a familiar voice. Latuhl looked down at Urgon. "You did your father proud this day. It will be remembered for long to come."

"You would have done the same."

"True, but you are the one who brought her safely back, and that is no small feat. Celebrate your victories when you can, Urgon, son of Urdar. You never know when the hands of fate may turn against you."

# NINE

# The Ordeal

Shuvog, chieftain of the Black Arrow Tribe, sat across from Shular. They were in the shaman's hut, a rare occurrence for such a meeting as they would usually meet in the chieftain's home.

"He is not yet old enough," argued Urgon's mother, ignoring his presence.

"Yet Urzath stated he is ready."

"The fact still remains he is a youngling. He still has some months before he must face his ordeal."

The chieftain stretched her back, then looked over at Urgon. "He showed remarkable fortitude and perseverance. Had he not done so, both he and Urzath might have perished. He has saved not only himself but a valued member of our tribe."

"Is it not for me to determine when he faces his ordeal? I am his mother. I should have the final word."

"Ordinarily, I would agree, but his actions demonstrate he is much more mature than would be normal for an Orc of his age. It is, therefore, our duty to foster his growth by allowing him to finish his ordeal and get on with his life."

"Have I no say in the matter?"

"Your words are heard, Shular, but I consulted with the other elders. In this, we are all in agreement. Urgon's ordeal shall commence at first light tomorrow."

Urgon's heart skipped a beat. He was proud his accomplishment had been recognized, but the thought of being out alone in the wilderness for a ten-day sent shivers down his spine. And so soon!

The chieftain looked directly into his eyes. "Are you ready, Urgon, son of Urdar?"

He took a gulp of air. "As ready as I will ever be," he replied.

"Good. Then it is settled." She returned her attention to Shular. "Have him waiting by the wolf den at first light."

Shuvog stood, looking briefly at the young Orc. "Do well on your ordeal, Urgon. I look forward to welcoming you back as a full-fledged hunter of the Black Arrows."

That night, Urgon visited Zhura. He was unsure of how she might welcome him, considering their last encounter, yet she smiled as he crawled into her hut. She beckoned him to sit across from her and offered him a drink. He took a sip, watching her face for any indication of her thoughts.

"It is good to see you again," she said.

"Yes," he agreed. "I, too, feel the same. We left each other with matters unresolved, and then I was taken on a hunt."

"There is nothing to resolve. You and I shall remain friends, nothing more."

Urgon felt the pinch in his heart. "May I ask why?"

"It is forbidden."

"So is my being here."

A look of sadness crossed her face. "It is not only that."

"Then tell me," he pleaded. "I would know the truth."

"Ghostwalkers have short lives, often ending in madness. I would not inflict that upon you. Also, there is the matter of younglings. I am unable to bear them."

"I do not blame you," said Urgon. "I can scarce stand them myself."

She smiled at the jest. "The sad truth is my kind are barren."

"That does not mean you must live a life unloved. There is more to bonding than birthing younglings."

"What Orc would choose me as a bondmate?"

"I would," Urgon blurted out. "I have never found someone so well suited to my temperament."

"You are young. Your attitude towards such things will change in due course."

"Never."

"Easy words to say at this point in your life. In any event, the tribe would never consent to such an arrangement, and even asking might deprive me of that which I cherish above all else—your companionship."

It was a hard truth, but Urgon saw the wisdom of it. He choked down his arguments and took a cleansing breath. "Then I shall be content to remain so," he said at last.

"I sense there is more that troubles you. Let us have no secrets between us."

"It is my ordeal. It begins tomorrow."

"So soon?"

He nodded to avoid giving voice to his doubts.

"And this troubles you?"

"It does."

"Tell me," said Zhura, "can you hunt?"

"I can."

"And are you able to build a shelter to protect yourself from the elements?"

"Yes, of course," he said. "Urzath saw to that."

"It is normal to have doubts, but you are as prepared for this as anyone else. Admittedly, it is a ten-day, presumably the longest you will have been gone from Ord-Dugath. Am I correct?"

"You are."

"You may rest assured I will still be here when you return, although I will, of course, miss you."

"As I will miss you."

"Could it be the ordeal is not what you fear?"

Urgon was intrigued. "Meaning?"

"If all goes well, you will return as a full-fledged hunter of this tribe, which means a hunters' longhouse will become your home. No longer will you dwell in the hut of Shular."

"That does weigh on my mind, but there is something of greater concern."

"Go on," she urged.

"Shular is a heavy sleeper, as is my sister, Kurghal. Sneaking away in the middle of the night to be with you is a simple matter. Once I am within the hunters' longhouse, however, how will I steal away without being noticed?"

"You will find a way. I have complete confidence in you."

"I wish I thought like you."

"Wait a moment," Zhura said. "I have something for you, a gift." She dug through the furs withdrawing the knife he had given her. "Take this with you."

Urgon took it, noting the handle looked different. He held it to the fire, noticing she had carved small runes into the handle. "What is this?"

"A reminder of our friendship."

"Is it magic?"

"No," she said, "they are Dwarf runes. One of the Ancestors gave them to me."

"They are similar to the ones on my father's memorial. What does it say?"

"The Dwarf tongue is unknown to me, but I am assured the symbols mean 'wise hunter, devoted companion', although, of course, I have to take the words of the Ancestors for that."

"I shall treasure it," he replied.

Zhura stood, moving to stand beside him. "Am I permitted a hug?"

He threw his arms around her, holding her close.

"I shall return," he whispered. "I promise you."


The village gathered at dawn to witness the beginning of his ordeal. Shuvog led them out, stopping just beyond its perimeter, allowing everyone to spread out, then she moved to stand beside Urgon.

"We gather here this day to begin the ordeal of Urgon, son of Urdar. As in the days of our Ancestors, he shall leave us for a ten-day, armed only with knife, axe, and spear. Go now, youngling, and return to us a hunter."

Everyone cheered as Urgon turned and headed north. There was no set agenda other than survival. All he had to do was live on his own for ten days, then return. Yet deep down, he knew this ritual would change him.

He turned east and began searching for tracks. Water he could find, for the memory of the stream remained fresh in his mind. Food, on the other hand, was an entirely different matter.

By late afternoon he had found the water he sought. He set snares, built a fire, and even managed to build a small cage out of sticks and twigs, ready to hold any animals he might capture. Right as the sun waned in the sky, he caught a lizard which he cut up, keeping the skin for future use even as he ate the meat. With his stomach full, he crawled into his lean-to, content to sleep the night away.

Scratching noises woke him in the middle of the night. Some creature was out there, ransacking his camp. He peered from within his makeshift shelter, trying to see what was in the area, but with the moon hidden by clouds, his night vision was all but useless. By the sounds of it, something large was moving around. He thought at first it might be a bear, but its growl soon disabused him of that theory, for it was definitely that of a mountain cat, maybe even the very same creature he had wounded. He stayed hidden in place, knowing full well that to emerge now would give the beast the advantage.

By morning the camp had been destroyed. The mountain cat had broken his cages and wrecked snares, even dragged off what was left of the lizard. Clearly, it represented a significant threat. Should he track it down and risk injury so soon after starting his ordeal, or would it be more prudent to move his camp?

He tried to reason out what Zhura would propose. She had said he should follow his heart. Knowing the cat was a threat to his village, he chose what was best for them instead of shirking his duty by slinking off and hiding.

Urgon gathered his spear and began looking for tracks. The ground here was hard packed, yet he still found what he searched for. He followed his prey, all the while remembering his previous encounter and keeping a sharp lookout for danger.

The trail led him farther into rougher country, the land becoming broken, with more fissures and steep hills obstructing his way. The cat travelled quickly. Urgon was determined to find it and would have continued all day in this fashion, but the growling of his stomach reminded him he still had to eat.

Urgon turned around, convincing himself it was the wiser move. There was no point in facing a foe when weak; rather one should be strong, and so he made his way back to the stream.

He gave up on traps, preferring instead to spear fish. These he quickly ate raw, then returned to the trail, eager to pick up where he'd left off. Darkness put an end to his desires to follow, so he sought shelter, squeezing in between two large outcroppings of stone that created an excellent defensive position, allowing only one path of attack. Safe, he sat back, waiting for daylight.

Urgon, having nodded off sometime in the night, was awakened by the sun poking in between the rocks. He crawled out into the sunlight, his throat dry. The stream was some distance off, and not wanting to lose the trail, he cast his eyes around, searching for an alternative. He soon spotted some Nargun's thumb, poking out from between two stones. Remembering the words of Urzath, he dug it up, brushing off the dirt to chew on the roots, the moisture held within quickly wetting his mouth. He then tucked more into his belt, hoping they would retain at least some of their moisture.

For two days, he continued his search. He thought the creature had left the area right up until he came across the carcass of a small deer. He cut up what was left, taking the hide for later use. While he did this, he reasoned out a better course of action.

A mountain cat was far more mobile than he. Tracking was difficult in these parts, and without a wolf, very time-consuming. Better, then, to bring the creature to him. At least that way, he would have some control over the encounter.

Urgon had no doubt the beast was satiated for the moment, but it would need to eat again sooner or later. Likely it would return here, to the dead deer, so he built a fire, burning what was left of the body and using the flames for cooking some of the meat he had salvaged. The rest he kept raw, the better to attract his prey.

In order to mask his scent, he bathed his clothes in smoke. It wouldn't hide his smell completely, but at least he wouldn't smell like an Orc. The best protection, however, was to keep downwind from his prey. He started by placing the meat in an open area, then sought cover nearby. To facilitate this, he dug a shallow pit, then used leaves and twigs to cover himself. It wasn't a perfect solution, but he reasoned if the mountain cat was hungry enough, it should suffice.

Of course, there was always the possibility his target had eaten its fill, but he doubted it. A large predator like that required a lot of food, far more than a small deer would supply. Hoping it didn't favour Orc, Urgon settled in to watch.

Time passed, and it turned dark, yet still, he waited. Even as a chill seeped into his bones, he knew revealing himself now would spoil the trap, so he remained hidden, shivering as the cold took hold of him. Halfway through the night, he began to believe his plan had been in vain. The cat was, no doubt, far from here, likely feasting on fresh game. Then he heard a noise, an almost imperceptible footfall as if something large had just jumped down from somewhere.

Urgon cursed at his foolishness as he realized the beast had no interest in a dead carcass. Instead, it preferred fresher meat—he was now the hunted!

He grabbed his spear just as the creature struck, coming out of the dark to land on him with its full weight. Death would have come swiftly had it not been for his cover, for the twigs and leaves provided just enough protection that the great claws only scraped along his back.

Black blood welled to the surface as he flipped over, desperate to use his spear. His eyes saw only teeth reaching out for him, and he narrowly avoided having his face ripped off. With the spear useless this close in, he had to use his hands to try to force the animal from him.

Chaos ensued, for in the dark, he could see little but flying sticks and leaves being scattered by the attack. Even his night vision was of little use, so close was the predator. A blur of teeth and fur reached out, and then the beast clamped down on his forearm. Pain shot through him, and he knew he was as good as dead, yet the moment this realization hit him, his thoughts calmed. He found the presence of mind to grasp the hilt of his knife with his good hand and stab out, feeling resistance fail as flesh parted. Again and again, he struck, desperate to put an end to this fight. Blood poured down his arm even as he heard his foe's bones breaking under the onslaught, but still, it fought on.

As Urgon weakened, all he could think about was Zhura. Death did not frighten him, but it was the thought of leaving her behind, alone once more, that was too much to bear. All this drifted through his mind as his arm kept plunging the knife into the beast. A claw raked across his chest, cutting deep, right before a great weight fell against him, pressing him into the ground, then everything went still.

He lay there for some time, too exhausted to even move after so much of his blood had been spilled. He was almost ready to give up and admit defeat when his eyes wandered to the bloody knife still in his hand, the marks Zhura had carved in the handle staring back at him. Somehow he found the strength to push the creature off, and with the confusion of battle no longer upon him, he examined the carcass. He soon saw the old wound. This mountain cat was the same one he had wounded some days before! Thank the Ancestors, he thought. Had it not been weakened, he had no doubt it would have cost him his life.

His left arm was severely wounded—the elbow broken and bleeding heavily. He also had cuts on his back and chest that would need cleansing, but little could be done in his present state. He scrambled from the pit and got to work.

He had kept the skins of his first few kills, and although not cured, they would suffice to bind his arm, along with some sticks to hold it in place. His only hope to regain the use of his arm was to return to the village. Once there, his mother's magic could restore him.

With his wounds taken care of to the best of his abilities, he began building a fire to ward off the chill. Doing so with only one hand was awkward, but he managed well enough, and soon he sat before it, the heat restoring a bit of his energy.

Only as he warmed up did he realize how much the cold had saved him, for the pain of his wounds soon became quite intense. There was no magic here, no needles and gut to sew up cuts, nor anyone to help him other than himself.

With no other options, he dragged himself over to the dead mountain cat and cut off a piece of flesh. He knew his first priority had to be food. He would feel at least a little better after filling his belly.

As the first rays of the sun appeared to the east, he skinned his foe. A series of jagged cuts did the job. It would be nothing to brag about, but at least he would have something to cover him, even if it wasn't cured.

He tried to remember how long he'd been out in the wild. Had it been four days or five? If he were to return now, he would fail his ordeal, yet to remain here might prove fatal in his current condition. Every movement hurt, and as he worked, the wounds on his chest and back reopened, but what else could he do?

He sliced more meat from the carcass, cooking it over a fire, to preserve it. Food he had in abundance, but now he must somehow find shelter. He intended to start moving immediately, but as the morning wore on, his exertions got the better of him, and, lacking the energy to move any farther, sleep overcame him.

Urgon woke to a starless night. The air was cool, refreshingly so, and he took it as a good omen. Forcing himself to his feet, he started the trek homeward. In his weakened state, it was slow going, but he did at least manage to find a small, wooded area. Here he built a lean-to, protection from the clouds threatening to release the rain they held. He finished just in time, for the sky let loose with a torrential downpour.

As he watched, the storm unleashed its fury on the land before him. He dared the weather only once, gathering sticks and using some of the mountain-cat hide to make a water catcher, then settled back to wait out the storm.

Water was now plentiful, food as well, and although he had no use of his left arm, he was safe. All day he waited, yet the rain continued, the tiny rivulets running beside his lean-to soon became small streams.

Night came once again, but Urgon finally felt a little better. His wounds had scabbed over, and although he only had one usable arm, his back and chest were recovering. It was said Orcs were an incredibly resilient people, and Urgon wondered if it had something to do with their black blood. No other creature in all the known lands was so similarly blessed. Why were they so different, he wondered?

His pondering soon had his thoughts returning to Zhura. Would she know? And if not, would the Ancestors have such knowledge? For some reason, he doubted it.

# TEN

## Return

SUMMER 948 MC

K raloch gazed eastward, staring off at the distant hills. He sensed someone approaching and turned to see Latuhl.

"Any sight of him?" asked the old Orc.

"Not yet. I hope nothing went wrong."

"You worry too much. Today is the day of his return. I doubt anything could keep him away."

Kraloch noted the half-smile. "You know about Zhura."

"I do," said Latuhl.

"But you have not spoken to the elders."

"No. What happens between two Orcs is not the concern of others."

"But she is a ghostwalker."

"She is, but is she not also an Orc?"

"Of course," said Kraloch.

"Which, then, takes priority?"

"You ask me questions for which I have no answer."

The master of wolves smiled. "It is the advantage of age. A lesson I hope you and your comrade will learn long before you reach my advanced age. Always question why things are the way they are, Kraloch. Only in this way can true change happen."

"Change? I always thought elders like you wanted things to stay the same?"

"Wherever did you get that idea? We might be set in our ways, but that is a far cry from disliking change. Without change, we would be a stagnant race."

"How so?" asked the younger Orc.

"We use metal weapons, do we not? Those are not found in nature."

"Yet the other races still see us as primitives."

"Ah, yes, the words of Shular. Has she begun your training already?"

"Not formally, for I must complete my own ordeal first. I wish Urgon would hurry, I cannot wait here all day for him."

"Why?" asked Latuhl. "Have you somewhere else to be?"

Kraloch turned to him, ready to argue the point, but the old Orc's eyes were locked to the east.

"It appears your friend has deigned to reward us with his presence," he said.

The younger Orc followed his gaze to where Urgon appeared from over a hill. After watching for a moment, he noted something strange in the way his friend carried himself. Kraloch struggled to make sense of it, and only as Urgon drew closer did he realize the cause.

"Something has happened," he called out. "He is injured."

"Fetch Shular while I go and investigate."

Urgon saw the village as he topped the rise, giving him a needed boost to his waning energy. He noted the familiar sight of Kraloch and saw him run off, no doubt seeking help. Latuhl drew closer, and then Urgon smiled.

"You have made it," said the master of wolves.

"Not yet," replied Urgon. "I must set foot within the village once more to complete my ordeal." He held up his hand as help was offered. "Do not interfere. While I appreciate the offer, this is something I must do under my own power."

Latuhl noted the pelt. "Is that a mountain cat?"

"It is, the same one that wounded Urzath. It shall trouble us no more."

"A remarkable achievement. I sense it was a tough fight?"

Urgon grinned. "My arm is evidence of that."

"How long ago were you wounded?"

"Half a ten-day."

"But despite that, you did not return for help?"

"And be forced to repeat my ordeal? No, Latuhl, I would prefer to suffer the pain and become a full-fledged hunter."

"It appears you are much more than that. What hunter would take on a mountain cat single-handedly? Surely an act of bravery to rival our greatest heroes."

"No," insisted Urgon, "not an act of bravery, but foolishness. I never should have attempted such a thing. It almost killed me."

"Even so, you are here to tell the tale. I sense you have gained much from your ordeal."

"I have indeed."

They passed the outer huts, making their way to the great firepit. By tradition, the chieftain would be waiting there, and Urgon knew Shuvog to be a great believer in such things.

As Urgon drew closer, other Orcs followed, not only to welcome him but also to gape at his wounds. By the time the firepit came into view, almost the entire village had gathered.

He halted before the chieftain. "I have returned," he declared.

"So you have," said Shuvog. "I proclaim you a full-fledged member of the Black Arrows." She turned to Tarluk, who held out a bow. This was passed to Urgon, along with a quiver of arrows.

"I give these to you," she said, "as a symbol that you are a true hunter." She glanced briefly at her shamaness. "Take him and heal him, Shular. Once that is done, I shall come to visit him. He can then take his place in one of the hunters' longhouses."

Urgon's mother stepped forward, the magic already building within her. Her hands glowed as she placed them on his arm. He felt a strange sensation as his bones knit back together, and then his flesh crawled into place.

"I have healed you," she announced, "but you will be weak for some time yet. I suggest you rest."

"Where? I am no longer a youngling, Shular, and am yet to be assigned a hut."

"You shall rest here," said Shuvog, eliciting a gasp from the crowd. "You have shown great bravery, Urgon. Such actions are to be celebrated."

"I thank you."

"It is us who must thank you for ridding us of a great menace. Take him inside, Tarluk, and see he is taken care of."

"Of course," replied the hunter.

"As to the rest of you, go home. We shall celebrate Urgon's return once he has fully recovered."

Urgon followed Tarluk into the great hut, where one end had been closed off for the chieftain's personal living space. He was led through the inner door into a sizable room full of furs and skins. Here Tarluk showed him a bed.

"Rest," said the hunter, "and I shall get you some food. Have you had water?"

"Not since this morning. I was in a hurry to return home."

"Then I shall fetch some. Have you any requests?"

"Requests?"

"Yes, anyone you want to talk to?"

He immediately thought of Zhura but knew that was out of the question. "Kraloch, perhaps?"

"Then I shall summon him."

Urgon lay on the furs for a moment before sleep claimed him.


He woke to see the face of Kraloch bending over him.

"How are you feeling?" his friend asked.

"I have felt better."

"You should be thankful we have a shamaness. Without the efforts of Shular, you would be crippled for the rest of your life."

"Shular is not the only shaman."

"True, but would your sister aid you if your mother refused?"

"A good question."

"Of course, you could always travel to one of the other villages of our tribe. They have shamans of their own."

"Yes," said Urgon, "but none so skilled as Shular."

"I would agree, but I fear my opinion of her would be coloured by the fact she has promised to instruct me in the magical arts."

"A promise well earned. You will do well, my friend, even if you master only a portion of what she has learned."

"Tell me of your ordeal. My own is only a ten-day away."

"In the beginning, it was easy. Only the appearance of the mountain cat brought trouble. Now the beast is slain, you have nothing to fear."

"I do not have fear," said Kraloch.

"A poor choice of words on my part, and for that, I apologize. Still, it must give you some relief to know it no longer stalks the land."

"It does, although my own ordeal still weighs heavily upon me."

"Talk to Urzath. She prepared me. I am sure she can do the same for you."

"I shall, but I still believe the entire idea silly. I am destined to be a shaman. What need have I for the skills of a hunter?"

"An Orc must always be prepared," said Urgon. "You never know when such skills might be put to the test."

"I suppose."

"Come now, why so glum?"

"You are a full-fledged hunter now. There will be little time to visit with the likes of me."

"You and I are friends. Nothing can change that. You will stand beside me when I am bonded, just as I will stand by you when the roles are reversed."

"I am to become a shaman," said Kraloch. "I may never bond."

"Nonsense. My mother has bonded twice. If she can find two bondmates in her lifetime, then undoubtedly you can find at least one."

His companion smiled. "And what of Zhura?"

Urgon's face darkened. "That is another matter entirely. Hunting parties often travel days in search of game. I shall do my best to keep up my visits, but I fear they will be severely curtailed."

"Then permit me to visit her in your stead."

"You?"

"Yes. Once I am a shaman, I shall have free access to the mud hut."

"That is a long way off yet," said Urgon, "but I am glad she will have the company."


Urgon rested for two days in the chieftain's hut, each day receiving the healing powers of Shular. Urzath finally came to collect him and take him to his new home. He had little to call his own, save for his weapons and the pelt from the slain mountain cat, but such was the lot of new hunters.

Urzath first brought him to the hut that lay to the north of the great firepit, but Urgon claimed it was too close to his mother's. The village had seven such structures, but to Urgon's mind, there could be only one that was suitable, the one that sat closest to Zhura's home.

As luck would have it, there was an empty space at the northern end of that one. This way, he could be as close to Zhura as possible without actually seeing her. Urzath thought his choice strange, for it was the structure with the fewest hunters in residence, but Urgon insisted. When he was introduced to the other residents of the longhouse, they were friendly enough but obviously valued their privacy, for they were spaced out along the length of the hall, such that none could overhear any of the others.

Being summer, they all cooked on one fire, gathering at mealtime to share their food. Once complete, however, they each went their separate ways, something that worked in his favour.

He developed the habit of walking after dark, the better to hide his visits to Zhura. Some nights he would go and sit at the cliff's edge, while other times in the cave of the Eternal Flame. Each time he would make sure he was seen, establishing patterns that others would soon come to expect.

By the time he visited Zhura again, Kraloch was out on his own ordeal. Urgon fretted that he had waited too long, that she would forget him, but Latuhl reassured him such a thing would not come to pass.

With his usual ally absent, he asked Latuhl to stand watch, and so it was that on a cloudy night as the summer air grew cooler, he again entered the mud hut.

Zhura was quick to welcome him, inviting him to sit. Urgon expected her to bombard him with no end of questions, yet the only thing she asked surprised him.

"How do you feel?"

"Fully recovered," he replied. "Do you wish to know what befell me?"

"I already know."

"How?"

"Your mother could speak of little else."

Urgon frowned. "I suppose I should have expected that."

"She is proud of you, and why not? You are a full-fledged hunter now. What else could she wish for?"

"That I was a shaman?"

"You think her disappointed you lack the capacity for such training?"

"It has always been her dream. Look how proud she is of my half-sister."

"I believe you fail to see how much she cares for you," said Zhura.

"She has seldom shown much concern for my well-being."

"Nevertheless, here she was, talking endlessly of your accomplishments."

He chuckled. "I wonder how she might react if she knew I was here?"

"Badly, I would think. She dislikes those who break the rules. In any case, you are free of her now. How do you like the life of a hunter?"

He shrugged. "I have done little so far. Our first hunt will not be for another ten-day. Skulnug suggests we go west, down onto the plains. He says the hunting is good down there."

"Then why not go?"

"It would take me away from you, likely for some time."

She smiled. "I have survived without you for many winters, Urgon. I am quite capable of making do in your absence."

Now it was his turn to smile, something he found himself doing a lot lately. "I thought of you," he said at last. "Your words brought me comfort when I thought I might die."

He noticed tears brimming in her eyes.

"I worried about you too." Her voice trembled. "I asked the Ancestors to keep watch over you."

Urgon took her hand. "Then I have you to thank for my survival."

"It did little good. They are spirits, unable to affect things in the physical world, nor were they willing to even try. Your fate was yours to decide, or so they told me."

"Well, I survived without their help apparently." He looked into her eyes. "I would like to give you a gift?"

"A gift?"

"Yes, I have the pelt of the mountain cat. I should like you to have it."

"That would be inadvisable. You have made a name for yourself, Urgon. Were you to give it to me, how would you explain its absence?"

"That, I hadn't considered. I shall keep it with me, but only until such time as I can give it to you openly."

"You know that day will never come."

He leaned forward until he felt her breath on his face. "I know no such thing. I swear to you, Zhura, I WILL find a way for you to escape this life of isolation."

"Even if you could," she continued, "I shall never be considered a true member of this tribe."

"What utter nonsense!"

"Is it? I am isolated here. How, then, would I complete my own ordeal? And if I am unable to do so, how could I be considered a full member of this tribe? You know as well as I that I am ill-equipped to survive out there."

"And it should not be required of you. You serve the tribe in your own way, Zhura, and that should be enough. Were I the chieftain, I would allow you the freedoms all Orcs receive."

She laughed. "You have just become a hunter. Are you now to challenge Shuvog for the leadership of the tribe?"

"No, of course not, but I shall not be young forever. One day I will keep my promise, although I cannot say when."

"I hope you can, but I fear I shall not be around to see it."

"Why?" said Urgon. "Are you sick?"

"No, but ghostwalkers live brief lives. The Ancestors tell me we seldom see our twentieth winter. That leaves me with little time."

"Then we shall have to make the best of the time we have."

"What are you suggesting?"

"Come with me, outside this hut. Let me show you the stars in the night sky."

"No," said Zhura, squeezing his hand. "Much as I appreciate the offer, I would be overwhelmed by the spirits that inhabit this place. I am content to stay here, providing you promise to visit when you can."

Urgon nodded. "Agreed. I will, however, bring you back something from the hunt. How about a new fur for your collection?" He looked around the hut. "It would scarcely be noticed amongst those you have now."

"I like that. And when I wrap myself in it, I shall remember it comes from you."

He felt the blood surge to his face as he blushed. "I have missed you this last ten-day," he said. "The true ordeal was staying away from you."

"This from the Orc who was almost killed by a mountain cat?"

He grinned at the remark, then quickly sobered as a lump formed in his throat. "I… want to say something to you."

"You need not say it," said Zhura. "It is clear how you feel." She paused a moment, then added, "I feel the same."

Urgon's heart soared. "I understand we can never be together," he said, "but know there will never be another to take your place."

"I should hope not. Ghostwalkers are rare. For two such individuals to be born amongst our tribe would be unthinkable. There is only one of me, Urgon, just as there is only one of you. Make sure you take care of yourself, for without you, I am incomplete."

"I promise. And you"—he pointed a finger at her—"must promise me you will do all you can not to go mad!"

"I will heed your words, although I know not how it is to be accomplished."

"Then ask the Ancestors. Let us hope they can be helpful for a change, instead of standing around and watching what goes on around them."

"They hardly just stand around."

"What else is there for them to do?"

He saw her smile and knew she would be all right.

# ELEVEN

## Pressures

---

SUMMER 950 MC

The days turned into months, and in short order, the seasons passed. Urgon visited Zhura as often as possible, though he was lucky to manage two visits every ten-day. In the evenings when he couldn't visit her, he would talk about her with either Kraloch or Latuhl, sometimes even both of them when they were all gathered around the old Orc's fire while Rockjaw snoozed at their side.

Urgon proved himself an accomplished hunter while Kraloch, having completed his own ordeal with little fanfare, settled into the life of a shaman's apprentice. After half a year's instruction, Kraloch was permitted to meet Zhura in person, though always under the guidance of Shular. It wasn't until the autumn of 949 that he was finally allowed to visit her unaccompanied.

Both Urgon and Kraloch were kept quite busy, their lives carrying on with little to interfere with their interests, but all that changed in the summer of 950. Urgon was soon to be sixteen, a birthday he considered of no real significance, yet it was the beginning of what was to be the biggest disturbance to his way of life.

It all started innocently enough. Having just thrown some meat onto the fire, he was looking forward to an enjoyable meal when he looked up to see his sister.

"Kurghal?" he said. "What brings you here?"

"I bring word from our mother," she replied. "Though in this, she acts in her official role as shamaness."

"Then I shall come at once. Have you any idea what it concerns?"

"No, but I suggest we hurry. You know how much she hates to wait."

"I do." He used his knife to remove the meat from the fire, then tossed it aside. "Lead on."

They exited the longhouse, making their way past the great firepit. Just beyond lay the home of his youngling days, looking exactly the same as it always did. His sister pushed aside the hide and waved him in.

"I shall remain outside," she said.

Urgon stepped in. Little had changed, but that was to be expected.

"You wanted to see me, Mother?"

"Yes, come," said Shular. "Sit by the fire."

Urgon sat, and immediately the hairs on the back of his neck stood on end. Had she discovered his relationship with Zhura? He shivered at the thought. His mother misinterpreted his actions.

"Move closer," she urged, "and warm yourself. Can I offer you some refreshment?"

"No, thank you." He watched her sit. She was fidgeting, obviously trying to build courage for what was to come. He decided to tackle it head-on.

"What is it you wanted to see me about?" he asked.

"It occurs to me you have seen almost sixteen winters."

"And?"

"It is time you consider taking a bondmate."

Urgon laughed. "A bondmate? I have plenty of time for that."

"Do you? Look around you, Urgon. Most of the females your age have already bonded. If you wait too long, there will be none left."

"Would that be so bad?"

She looked as though he had slapped her. "It is your duty to bond in order to produce younglings. The future of the tribe demands it."

Urgon sat back. "Does it? What of Kurghal? She has not bonded."

"She is a shamaness. Bonding is not required of her. You, on the other hand, are a hunter. The risk to you is greater."

"The risk?"

"Yes, of injury or even death."

"You are a shamaness, Mother. I hardly think a fatal injury is likely when you are able to heal me with your magic."

He spotted the look of discomfort on her face. "Still, you could die. Better that you father younglings while you can."

"While I can? Am I to be prematurely aged?"

"Do not argue with me, Urgon!"

He bowed his head. "I respect you, both as my mother and as shamaness of this village, but whether or not I bond is not up for discussion. I must choose my own way in this."

"I see," said Shular. "And when might we expect such a decision?"

"That is for me to decide." He rose, bowing once more. "Now, unless there is something else, I will take my leave of you."

"You will leave when I give you permission to do so." She softened her features. "My only concern is for you, Urgon. I want you to have companionship. I promise not to press you on this, but please at least keep an open mind to the possibility?"

"I shall."

"And… inform me, should you change your mind?"

"You shall be amongst the first to know. I promise you."

"That is all I ask," said Shular.

"May I go now?"

"By all means."

He stormed out of the hut, only to run into Kraloch.

"What are you doing here?" Urgon grumbled.

"Where else would I go to learn the ways of a shaman? Is something wrong?"

"My mother is pressuring me to bond."

"That is to be expected."

"I am only fifteen."

"Yes," said Kraloch, "but if you were to have a youngling now, you would be thirty by the time they became an adult. That would make you almost as old as Latuhl. Can you see now why Orcs bond so young?"

"Easy for you to say. Your position gives you immunity from such pressure."

"Your mother is a harsh taskmaster," said Kraloch. "You may have it easier than you know. That reminds me, I have something to show you, something I think you'll appreciate."

"What is it?"

"Follow me."

He led Urgon through the village and right up to the door to the mud hut. "See this?" he asked.

"Of course. It is the door to Zhura's hut, locked by magical runes."

Kraloch grinned. "No longer." He parted the hangings.

"How did you do that?"

"I mastered my first spell, and with it, the secret of these runes."

"You mean I no longer need to crawl under the wall?"

"Unfortunately, the door will not open for you, so I must be present to allow you entry, but yes, that is essentially true."

Urgon grasped his friend by the biceps. "This is good news indeed!"

"Of course," continued Kraloch, "you must still wait until dark. It would not be wise to be noticed."

"And do I need you to exit?"

"No. The magic only works in one direction."

"How is it the magic of life has such powers?"

Kraloch grinned. "It is not the magic of life, merely the application of magical runes."

"You speak of things beyond my understanding."

"Let me try to explain it to you. Magic is sometimes referred to as the universal language. As such, it has its own symbols, shapes that contain power, whether they be uttered, as in a spell, or written, like the stones in the cave of the Eternal Flame. These magical runes"—he pointed at the door—"are a written manifestation of the power of magic. Only those who can interpret these symbols can invoke their power."

"Are you saying only a shaman can open that door?"

"From the outside, yes."

"And what of the cave?" asked Urgon. "If what you say is true, a shaman must have created that flame."

"That had not occurred to me, but yes, I suppose that must be true, although maybe shaman is not the correct term."

"Who else would use magic?"

"Ah," said Kraloch. "I see the confusion. Our tribe is limited in magic, having only those who can wield the magic of life. Other tribes have gifted individuals who can wield the power of the elements, such as a master of flame or earth. The Dwarves have another name for such magic."

"Which is?"

"Earth Magic, or Fire Magic, depending on which element is referenced."

"And they have no shamans?"

"Their healers are called Life Mages. I believe the Humans use similar terms."

"Mages," mused Urgon. "A strange name for a wielder of such power."

"It is from the term 'magic'."

"And only mages can read those symbols?"

"Anyone can recognize them, but it takes someone with the innate ability to use magic to actually harness their power."

"You have done well in your studies, Kraloch. I am proud to call you my friend."

"As am I, but I must be off. Shular will not be pleased that I am late."

Urgon watched him go, then looked at the door once again. He moved closer, scanning the area to make sure no one was within earshot.

"Zhura?" he called out. "Can you hear me?"

"Urgon?" came the muffled reply. "Is that you?"

He couldn't help but smile even though she was unable to see him. "It is. When I visit you this evening, I will tunnel no more. Instead, I will enter by the door."

"I look forward to it. Now be off with you before someone spots you talking to a door."

He chuckled. "Fair enough, but I am anticipating talking at length with you later."

"As am I."

He wandered off towards the wolf pen, his mood considerably lightened. That changed dramatically when he entered the hut of the master of wolves. Rockjaw lay on the floor beside the unmoving body of Latuhl. Urgon ran to his side, feeling his forehead. It was warm, thank the Ancestors, although the old Orc was very pale.

Latuhl muttered something, and Urgon lifted his head. "I am here," he soothed. "Let me call for Shular."

"No, it will do no good."

"But she is a healer, one of the greatest our tribe has ever known."

"She can do little for one of my advanced age."

"There must be something I can do?"

"Help me sit up," said Latuhl, "and perhaps get me something to drink?"

Urgon propped him up, stuffing furs and skins behind the old fellow to make him comfortable.

"Are you ill?"

Latuhl looked him in the eyes. "Have you any idea of my age?"

"You are the oldest Orc I know."

"Yes, but how many winters have I lived through?"

"I had always assumed forty or so," said Urgon. "Is that not accurate?"

"Forty? I should be so lucky! No, my young friend, only thirty-eight, a rare number for an Orc."

"Nonsense. They say we live much longer now than when we lived in cities."

"Perhaps," said Latuhl, "but that was ages past. My time amongst the living is drawing to its conclusion."

"But who will take care of the wolves?"

The old Orc clutched his arm. "I hoped you would want to take on that responsibility."

"Me? I hunt. What do I know of wolves?"

"More than you might think. You help me from time to time, Urgon. You know what is required to look after my pack."

"It is not my decision. Only the chieftain can name the new master of wolves."

"True," said Latuhl, "but as the present master, my recommendation would carry significant influence."

"And if I were to bond?"

"Then you and your bondmate would live here, in this hut. Would that be so difficult?"

Urgon frowned, an expression not lost on the old Orc. "Ah, I see the problem. You wish to bond with Zhura."

"It is forbidden."

"So are your visits, but that has yet to hold you back. Look at it this way, Urgon. If you bond with Zhura, you shall be unable to have younglings of your own. These wolves can fill that emptiness, maybe even provide comfort to Zhura when you are gone."

"Gone? Where would I go?"

"Why, to visit the other villages, of course. As master of wolves, you need to check in on the other packs."

Urgon sat back in surprise. "There are other packs?"

"Of course. The tribe is scattered throughout these hills. Did you assume we were the only Orcs in the region?"

"No, of course not."

"Yet you failed to consider that they, too, might have wolves?"

"It never crossed my mind."

"Well, now you know."

"I have never led the pack on a hunt," said Urgon.

"It is easy enough to do. Simply open the gate to the pen, and they shall return when the hunting is complete. The only one you need to watch is Grimtooth. He is the pack leader."

"Not Rockjaw?"

Latuhl chuckled. "No, Rockjaw is far too friendly to lead the others. He is my companion. Oh, he had his fair share of adventures in his youth, but like me, he has withered with age."

"And how do I control Grimtooth?"

"You do not control him, merely keep an eye on him. Where he goes, the others will follow."

Urgon passed him a waterskin, and the elder Orc drank deeply.

"I am much better, thank you. Now help me to my feet. We must go and talk to Shuvog if we are to see you named the new master of wolves."


The custom of Orcs was to select their chieftain by a count of stones, a process in which every adult member of the tribe could take part. There had been a large gathering ten winters ago, during which Shuvog had been selected to take that role.

In the time since, she had generally been seen as a great leader, overseeing the most significant population growth anyone could remember. That result had been achieved by encouraging Orcs to bond quickly after becoming adults, something Urgon knew would come up as they entered the chieftain's hut.

Shuvog, sitting by the fire sharpening her knife, looked up as they entered. If she was surprised by their arrival, she gave no indication of it.

"What brings you two to my hut?" she asked.

"May we sit?" asked Latuhl. "There are things we need to discuss."

"By all means."

Urgon noted the gaze of the chieftain and felt distinctly uncomfortable as they sat by the fire.

"For many winters have I been master of wolves," said Latuhl.

"And you have excelled in that role," said Shuvog.

"I am, however, growing old. Soon I shall be unable to continue my duties."

She glanced at Urgon once more. "Am I to presume you would name Urgon as your successor?"

The old Orc smiled. "I would. He still has much to learn but has shown great promise."

"I will consider it. What of you, Urgon?"

"Me?"

"Yes," said Shuvog. "Is this something you desire?"

"It is."

"Then I shall consider it."

"Is that all?" asked Urgon. "Have you another who desires the position?"

"No, but there is much to think on. You are young, Urgon, and have yet to... settle down."

"Settle down?"

"Positions like this are typically reserved for those who are already bonded."

Urgon screwed up his face. "But Latuhl is not bonded."

"He was, once."

He turned in surprise to the old Orc. "Is this true?"

"It is," said Latuhl, "but she died many winters ago."

"I had no idea."

"The death of a bondmate is not something generally discussed with others," said Shuvog. "In any event, I would be pleased to award you this position should you pick someone with whom to bond. I am aware of several females who are of a similar age."

"I know them all," said Urgon. "I could scarcely grow up here and not."

"Do you find none of them appealing?"

"There is nothing wrong with them. They are simply not right for me."

"You are being too particular."

"I need someone who can challenge me."

Shuvog smiled, and Urgon found the sight slightly unsettling. "Then maybe a visit to the other villages might allow you to discover one more suitable?"

A lump formed in Urgon's throat. He wanted to blurt out Zhura was the only one he desired, yet he knew it would do him no good. He tried to think up an excuse, but it proved unnecessary, for Shuvog herself gave him a temporary reprieve.

"I shall approve you as the new master of wolves, subject to training from Master Latuhl, of course. However, I only do so with the understanding you shall be bonded within the next two winters. Is that understood?"

"It is," said Urgon. "Thank you, Shuvog."

"You should be thanking Latuhl, not I. He seems to feel you have a lot of potential, Urgon. Were it up to me, you would remain a hunter for the rest of your days."

"You think so little of me?"

"No, quite the reverse. I have heard of your hunting skills, and you will be sorely missed."

Urgon was experiencing a whirlwind of emotions. He was to become master of wolves, a most prestigious position. Yet, at the same time, his chance of bonding with Zhura grew slimmer with the passing of the seasons. He must find some way to make it possible! His inner turmoil was noted by Shuvog.

"Have you a question?" she asked.

"No. My pardon, Chieftain. I was merely overwhelmed by your generosity."

"You must gather your things, few as they may be."

"To what end?"

"As of now, you are in training to be the new master of wolves, a position that requires you to live within the wolf hut."

"You mean Latuhl's hut?"

"I do."

"I have very few belongings."

"Then retrieving them will take but a moment. Now, off with you both. There are important things I need to attend to this day."

They left the chieftain's hut, Latuhl with a spring in his step, Urgon decidedly less so.

"Come now," urged the older Orc. "You should be celebrating."

"Celebrating? I feel as though my doom is approaching."

"Has this something to do with Shuvog's ultimatum?"

"Yes. It weighs heavily on my mind."

"And yet she gave you two winters before you must make a choice." He turned to Urgon with a grin. "Two winters in which you can come up with a plan to bond with Zhura."

"Two winters or ten, I fear it makes little difference. I can see no way to win over the village, let alone the entire tribe."

"You are a clever individual," said Latuhl. "I have every confidence you will find a way."

# TWELVE

## Master of Wolves

### SPRING 952 MC

U rgon emerged from Zhura's hut to a brisk evening wind, and Kraloch, ever the true friend, was waiting there for him. It had become their custom to return to the wolf hut to talk of Urgon's visits to his beloved Zhura.

"I have an idea," said Urgon. "You must tell me what you think."

"I would love to," replied Kraloch, "but could we seek shelter first?"

"A good idea. Come, we shall warm ourselves by the fire as we talk."

They crossed the path, eager to be in out of the cold, Urgon taking the lead. He entered the hut and nearly tripped over Rockjaw. The old wolf had lain down against the door, perhaps feeling the need for some fresh air, but in the dark, Urgon had almost not seen him. He stopped short, then looked down at the poor beast, sensing something was wrong. He knelt, feeling the wolf's fur.

"Kraloch," he said. "You are the shaman now. Tell me, has he passed?"

His companion knelt, reaching out with his hand as he muttered words of power. They were short, and then Kraloch's eyes glowed briefly, but Urgon could tell it wasn't good news.

"Yes, he has passed into the land of the spirits," said Kraloch. "Latuhl will take it hard."

The mention of his mentor's name caught in Urgon's throat. "Wait," he said. "There is something else. The hut is too quiet."

They both rose, and Urgon made his way to where Latuhl lay,

covered in furs. The mere sight of the old Orc brought tears to Urgon's eyes, and his heart ached. Kraloch stepped past him, looking down on the master of wolves while his spell still lasted.

"He, too, has joined the Ancestors. It is somehow fitting they both passed to the land of spirits together."

"Together? Are you saying animals also live on as spirits?"

"They do, although they often fade much faster than Orcs."

"Fade?"

"Yes," said Kraloch, "but that is a discussion best saved for another day. There are preparations to be made."

"Of course."

"I shall need to summon Shular."

"You are a shaman, are you not?"

"I am, but she is the senior. Latuhl was no ordinary Orc, Urgon, he was the master of wolves. As such, the entire village will want to celebrate his life."

"He was a solitary Orc," said Urgon, "with few friends. I find it curious so many would want to celebrate his life."

"But he lived to an advanced age, rare in an Orc. That alone calls for celebration."

Urgon's voice was bitter. "A celebration that is simply an excuse for eating and drinking. They did not know him as I did. He was like a father to me."

"He was, and a good friend. I tell you what. After the feast, you and I shall go and visit Zhura. There, we can tell tales of Latuhl in private to one who can appreciate him."

"I should like that."


The next evening, the village gathered around the great outdoor firepit. Hunters had gone out during the day, bringing back meat aplenty. There was a general sense of excitement. Such celebrations didn't occur very often, but Urgon found the entire experience distasteful. Many talked of the old Orc as if he had been their closest of friends, even going so far as to mock him for his strange habits.

Urgon sat as others made speeches, but he himself was too overcome to address the crowd. Instead, he turned to Kraloch.

"You talked earlier of spirits fading," he said. "What did you mean by that?"

"When an Orc dies, their spirit lingers; this we know. In time, however, many of those spirits become weaker, eventually dissipating away to nothingness. We call this process fading, although even our most experienced shamans have no explanation as to why. Some have speculated they go on to an afterlife, as was taught by the ancient gods, but there is no evidence of it."

"And you said animals fade faster?"

"They do, although some remain, particularly those who form a powerful bond with an Orc. A shaman, if they are so blessed, can even summon them as a spiritual companion, though I am yet to master that skill."

"Skill? Or spell?"

"They are almost the same thing. Both require the application of magic. The difference is in the effect. A spell is the invocation of magic to a single purpose, such as healing wounded flesh. A skill, on the other hand, requires so much more. If I were so trained, I could summon an animal spirit, but summoning and befriending one are two different things. Think of yourself; you are now the master of wolves. Could you befriend any wolf?"

"No, of course not."

"The spirit world is no different."

"Do other races have spirits?"

"I would assume so, but our magic only calls the Ancestors of Orcs."

"Why is that?"

"Why would we not? And if we did call others, how would we speak with them? Very few would know our language."

"I suppose that makes sense." Urgon stared into the flames. "I wonder how the other races handle death? Do they burn the bodies as we do?"

"As you might remember, the Dwarves are said to bury their dead in stone," said Kraloch. "They believe the body is important."

"Yes, but I wonder why?" said Urgon. "Surely they realize the body is merely a container for the spirit?"

"It is the way of the mountain folk. Who are we to argue? The Elves likely have their own customs, as do the Humans."

"A valid point, I suppose."

"The important thing is we remember Latuhl as he was."

"Can you contact him now that he has joined the spirits?"

Kraloch frowned. "Perhaps."

"You make it sound unlikely."

"Contacting spirits is not something you can control."

"Meaning?"

"When we summon spirits, it calls whoever is nearby. There is no control over who might answer."

"And yet Zhura can talk to many."

Kraloch lowered his voice. "True, but she is a ghostwalker who can see them all. It is her gift."

"Or her curse," said Urgon. "Though I suppose it depends on how you look at it." He fell silent as the crowd cheered on Shuvog, who spoke about Latuhl's accomplishments, of how she and the old Orc had grown up together. It occurred to Urgon that their chieftain was getting old, and as that thought drifted through his mind, he scanned the other villagers. Who amongst them would step up to be the new chieftain when she was gone? The beginning of an idea came to him at that moment, a mere spark that would be fanned to flames over the next few winters. He would seek the leadership of the Black Arrows, and then he would have the power to help Zhura.

He was deep in thought when he became aware of a sudden silence. Looking around, he saw all eyes were on him.

"They want you to say something," whispered Kraloch.

Urgon stood, as was the custom, aware of the stares that bore into him. No doubt they considered him an upstart, for he was young, far younger than anyone else who had spoken thus far.

"Latuhl was a great Orc," he began, his voice gaining strength as he spoke. "He taught me a great many things about the wolves, especially how much they mean to our people." Urgon was suddenly at a loss for words. He had wanted to talk of Latuhl's many accomplishments but found himself unable to remember them in his grief. He paused as tears welled up, and then he finally continued his speech. "From my side of things, his greatest accomplishment was being my friend and mentor. I shall miss him dearly."

He had spoken from the heart, and his words rang true with many.

Some Orcs wept openly while others cast their eyes downward, unwilling to let their emotions be seen.

Urgon sat, and then someone began a lament. It was unusual for his people to sing, except on special occasions, but young Gorath, the foster son of Arshug, stood before the entire village, his young voice reaching up into the night sky, emotion pouring from him as he sang.

Others took up the lament, and soon the entire gathering united in song.

*"Take me up into the stars, this land I tread no more,*
*for my body is no use to me, and my spirit wants to soar.*

*Guide me from this living world to where the spirits roam,*
*and show me those who lived before and take me to my home.*

*And to all those I leave behind, shed not a tear for me,*
*for one day we will meet again, upon the spirit sea."*

The gathering grew quiet, and then, one by one, those gathered left. Many openly wept now, the song reminding them of those whom they had lost. Kraloch stood, lifting Urgon gently by the arm.

"Come. We should leave now," he said, leading his companion back to the hut, where he poured a drink into a wooden bowl as was their custom. Urgon stared at it, wishing it were the milk of life. At least, then, he might sleep through the night and forget this overwhelming sense of loss. He drank, feeling the liquid burn as it cascaded down his throat.

"You talked earlier of a plan," said Kraloch.

"A plan? Well, it was more of an idea, really."

"What was it?"

"I thought to extend the hut."

"To what end?"

"To make it larger."

"That much I could work out on my own," said Kraloch. "My curiosity, however, wonders why you would contemplate something like that?"

"For Zhura." Urgon found himself warming to the task. "I would build a second hut, right behind this one, but with the walls adjacent, then I could cut a doorway between them."

"Like in the chieftain's hut?"

"Yes, though not as large, of course."

"But the mud hut protects her."

"So it does, but why not use the same technique here? It would double her living space and surely is not difficult to do?"

"You still have yet to bring your relationship to the attention of Shuvog."

Urgon frowned. "I know. I would do it now, but I fear the answer would destroy me."

"If not now, then when?"

"I wish I had an answer. My heart yearns for her, my friend, but I know the time is not yet upon us."

Kraloch moved to the doorway, peering outside. "Everyone is turning in for the night. Soon, we will be able to visit Zhura. Do you think it would be worthwhile to get her opinion on the matter?"

"I have no wish to give her false hope."

"She is running out of time, Urgon. You yourself told me few ghost-walkers live more than twenty winters."

"There is still time yet, but I promise you, I will find a way to make it work."

"And if she dies before the hut is complete?"

"Then I shall simply have a larger hut. As to the mudding, that can only be done once she has agreed to move."

"You mean once the chieftain allows her to be moved."

Urgon shrugged. "Do I?"

Kraloch stared back in shock. "You must not cross Shuvog. The consequences could be dire."

"How much more dire could they be? The worst thing she can do is banish me."

"Yes, and then you would never see Zhura again."

Urgon felt his frustration mounting. "I must do something!"

Kraloch took another look outside. "Let us both visit her now. The way is clear."

They made their way across the short distance to where the runes guarded the mud hut. Kraloch touched them, eliciting a slight glowing from their marks.

"Zhura?" he called out softly. "Urgon is with me. May we enter?"

"Yes," came the muffled response.

Kraloch parted the hides allowing Urgon to enter first. He followed, sitting across the firepit from Zhura while his companion sat beside her, his right hand interlocked with her left.

"There is a great sadness here," she said.

"Yes," said Urgon. "Latuhl has joined the Ancestors."

She squeezed his hand. "A sad day indeed."

"I feel his loss keenly, yet it is not the only thing I have on my mind this day."

"Oh?"

"Yes," agreed Kraloch. "Urgon has an idea. Well, the beginnings of one, at least."

"Tell me of this plan," she said.

"I thought to enlarge the hut of the master of wolves."

"Go on."

"The inside would then be divided into two rooms, one for greeting visitors, the other for privacy."

"An interesting idea."

"Tell her the rest," said Kraloch.

"I thought I might coat the walls in mud."

She smiled. "You would make this for me?"

"I would. Then we could live together as bondmates."

A shadow flickered across her face. "It would never be permitted."

"Shuvog is not an Elf. Sooner or later, death will claim her, and then I shall become the chieftain."

"You put much faith in this idea," said Zhura, "but I imagine Shuvog has a few winters yet before she leaves this mortal land."

"All right, I admit the plan is not ideal, but at least it would give me something to work towards. It drives me mad, knowing you are so close and yet being unable to spend my days with you."

"You must have patience a while longer. One day, maybe, events may fall in our favour, but that time is not now, and I would not have you do anything rash. I value our friendship too much for that."

"What, then, shall we do?"

"As she said," said Kraloch, "you must wait."

"I have been doing precisely that for too many winters."

"So you are used to it."

Zhura squeezed his hand. "Would you risk losing me now? If Shuvog denies you, you will be banned from seeing me. You know this to be true."

Urgon hung his head in shame. "I do."

"Latuhl has only just died. Let your life return to a semblance of normalcy, then reconsider this idea of yours. If you are still inclined to enlarge your hut, then do so."

"The other villagers will think him crazy," said Kraloch.

"Then let them," she retorted, keeping her eyes on Urgon. "In the end, it is only yourself who you must satisfy."

"Have you a sense of great events in our future?"

"The Ancestors do not see the future," said Zhura. "They only know the past. It is the lives they led as mortals that gives them the wisdom to guide us."

"And what do they say?" asked Urgon.

"They say you are capable of great things. You walk where others fear to tread, but not everyone can follow in your footsteps. You must be cautious."

"Does someone work against me?"

"No," she said, "but you represent change, and the unknown can scare people. Pushing someone off a cliff does not make them a climber. You must guide them, not force things down their throats."

"Let me be clear," said Urgon. "Are you suggesting I only make minor changes?"

"That is one way of interpreting their words."

"And the other?"

She thought a moment before answering. "Imagine you wanted someone to walk to the next village, but they feared being outside the village. Forcing them against their will would only increase their fear, yet if you did it in steps, you might eventually succeed."

"In making them walk?"

"No, you miss the point. You might start by taking them to the edge of the village. The next day you would take them a little farther, maybe only a few extra paces. Repeat that enough times, and they would soon lose their fear."

"It would take a long time."

"Yes," she agreed, "but in the end, they would no longer be scared to make the journey. You are full of energy and hope, Urgon. I believe you carry within you endless possibilities, but push too hard or too fast, and backs will be turned on you. Then it will all be for nothing."

"You are wise beyond your age."

"The Ancestors are wise. I only repeat their advice."

"Then I owe them much. I shall heed their wise words."

"What of the other females?" asked Kraloch.

"Other females?" said Zhura.

Urgon blushed, his face turning a darker shade of green. "There are no other females."

"There are, according to Shuvog," said Kraloch.

"Merely wishful thinking on her part," said Urgon. "Pay no attention to his ramblings."

"Why?" she asked. "Is our chieftain pressuring you to bond?"

"She is," said Kraloch, "though he has managed to hold them at bay for now. Unfortunately, his time is running out."

"Running out, how?"

Urgon buried his face in his hands, but Kraloch kept talking. "Our chieftain gave him an ultimatum of sorts when she made him the master of wolves."

"And this ultimatum is?"

"That he must bond before two winters pass, and that time is soon approaching."

Tears came to her eyes. She reached out, touching Urgon's arm as she choked out her words in a harsh whisper. "Then you must do so for the good of the tribe."

Urgon was incensed. "I shall do no such thing!"

"But you must. Duty demands it."

"Duty? What about the tribe's duty? Am I not as important as the next Orc? Do I not have the right to determine my own fate? What gives Shuvog the right to force me into a bonding?"

"I can see this is upsetting," said Kraloch. "I feel it would be best to leave such discussion for another time."

"Another time?" said Urgon. "And when would that be, my friend? Time works against us. The longer it takes to resolve this, the less time Zhura and I will have together."

"Still, I urge caution. There is too much at stake."

Urgon forced himself to relax. "You make a good point. I promise to make no rash decisions, but eventually, I will be forced to say something."

"And when that time comes," said Kraloch, "I shall be by your side."

# THIRTEEN

## Ultimatum

AUTUMN 952 MC

Urgon tossed the meat on the ground. Grimtooth came forward, sniffed it, then grabbed the biggest piece and started chewing on it. The other wolves, who had been waiting, came forward, each taking a share of the food. Urgon watched absently, his mind on other things. Life had become routine after the death of his mentor but also much busier. Time flew by, and before he knew it, the leaves had turned colour once again.

As the weather grew cooler, the village began stocking up on food for the winter. This required the presence of the wolf pack, and that meant even more work for Urgon.

He stood there as the wolves tore into what was left of the meat. He was exhausted. They had just returned from a three-day outing, and he had slept little. And, had it not been for Kraloch's quick thinking, they would have lost a member of the pack, all because a Human hunter had wandered into their territory.

Urgon remembered the strange steel trap that had caught the young wolf's paw, mangling the leg so severely the creature almost died. But the village's newest shaman had been along to keep him company, and his mastery of magic had saved the day.

"Urgon!" The call shattered his thoughts. Standing by the wolf pen was Tarluk, and Urgon knew that could only mean one thing.

"I assume Shuvog wants to see me?"

"She does," the hunter replied. "Are you finished feeding your wolves?"

"Yes. Allow me to clean up, and I shall join you directly."

"Of course," said Tarluk. "Take your time."

Urgon returned to his home. At the moment, he had three doors. One led outside while the second led to the pens. The third, however, lead to the half-completed hut he hoped would eventually house Zhura.

He wiped his hands, then steeled himself to go and visit the chieftain. Was Shuvog going to ask him about his hut? Somehow he doubted it. Far more likely, she would again bring up his bonding, something he did not look forward to, yet he knew he could no longer avoid the encounter. He stepped outside, then fell in behind Tarluk as they made their way to the chieftain's hut.

They passed by several villagers who stopped to stare, and suddenly Urgon had the distinct feeling they knew something about what was about to happen.

The sense of foreboding only intensified as they entered the great hut of the chieftain. Inside waited Shuvog, just as he'd expected. What shocked him, however, was the presence of his mother, along with three females, each similar in age to himself.

"What is this?" he demanded.

"Sit," ordered Shuvog. She waited while he took a seat. The hunter, Tarluk, took up a position by the door, although whether to keep him inside or others from entering was anyone's guess.

"Some time ago, I made you the master of wolves," continued the chieftain, "with the understanding that before two winters passed, you would choose a bondmate. That time is now upon you."

"My apologies," said Urgon. "With the death of Latuhl, I have been overwhelmed by looking after the wolves."

"That was last spring. More than enough time to put things in order. Shular has taken it upon herself to find several suitable candidates." She nodded at her shamaness.

Shular took a step forward. "This," she said, indicating one of the females, "is Wergu. She has come from the north to get to know you."

The Orc bowed. "Pleased to meet you, Urgon. It is an honour to be in the presence of a master of wolves."

Urgon kept his eyes on Shular.

"Or perhaps Galur is more to your liking? She is an accomplished hunter, a valuable asset in a bondmate."

Galur bowed. "I have heard tell of your ordeal," she said. "A most inspiring tale."

"And this," continued his mother, "is Rular. She joins us from the south and is a shaman in training."

"In training?" said Urgon. "Surely she is old enough to have learned anything you might teach her?"

"But I am not her teacher," said Shular. "And I might remind you it takes time to learn the ways of magic."

"Kraloch has already mastered it."

"Kraloch is the exception."

Shuvog looked at the three females. "Choose one," she said.

"I will not," said Urgon.

"You must," begged his mother. "It is our way."

"No. It is your way, not mine!"

"Why do you not understand the logic in this? You must do your part for the tribe, Urgon. Bonding is a part of life, and these three have all expressed an interest in you. Can you not see fit to show them some interest in return?"

"I do not love them!"

"But, in time, you would come to, I am sure."

"No!" roared Urgon. "I love another."

For the first time in his life, he saw a look of surprise on his mother's face.

"Good," said Shuvog. "Then out with the name, and you shall be bonded."

"Yes," said Shular. "Let us all share in your happiness!"

Urgon felt his life shattering—it was now or never.

"My heart belongs to Zhura," he declared.

His mother was furious. "Zhura? What do you know of Zhura? Did Kraloch put you up to this, because if he did—"

"It was not Kraloch, Mother. I met Zhura long ago, before my ordeal."

"How?"

"I became curious about the mud hut, and so I broke in, determined to discover what lay within. Little did I realize I would find the Orc who completes me."

"Completes you? You should never have set eyes on her, Urgon. It is forbidden!"

"And yet I have! And glad I am of it!"

"But why?" said Shuvog. "Surely you realize the futility of it?"

"Is it futile to seek companionship? Not every bonding produces younglings."

"True, but at least there is that eventual possibility. A ghostwalker is barren, Urgon. They can never bear young."

"Do you think I care?"

"This is outrageous," said Shular. "I thought I raised you better than this."

"I am following my heart."

"It matters not," said Shuvog. "You have, by your own admission, broken the sacred rules of our tribe."

Shular paled, but Urgon remained defiant. "Then so be it," he said.

"By our ancient customs, I shall call together the entire tribe. They will determine your fate, Urgon. There is no other way. What have you to say for yourself?"

"I welcome it. For too long, I held in my feelings for Zhura. She is an Orc and deserves a life like any other."

"She is a ghostwalker," spat out Shular. "To see her in any other way is a grave mistake."

"Think carefully on this," said Shuvog, "for your very life may be forfeited."

"That is a risk I am willing to take."

"Tarluk," said the chieftain, "take Urgon to his hut and keep your eyes on him. We will summon him once the tribe has assembled."

"The tribe?" said Shular. "Do you not mean the village?"

"Your son has violated one of our most solemn laws, a law meant to protect us all."

"What nonsense is this?" demanded Urgon. "The shamans have a right to visit Zhura. Why not me?"

Shuvog turned on him with an icy stare. "You will have an opportunity to speak once the tribe gathers. Until then, you must remain within your hut. Do I make myself clear?"

Urgon wanted to lash out, but the pallor of his mother gave him pause. Shular was worried, and not just about his visit to Zhura. With a shock, he suddenly realized his days of visiting the mud hut were over. Sadness welled up inside him as he turned to Tarluk.

"Lead on," he said, "and I will follow."


Urgon sat in his hut, staring at the flames. He had let his temper get the better of him, and now he would pay the price. Death held no fear over him, but the thought of no longer seeing the pale Orc with the hair of snow wounded him deeply. Voices outside soon drew his attention.

"Stand aside," said Kraloch.

"I shall not," replied Tarluk. "Urgon is forbidden to leave his hut."

"I mean to go in, not bring him out."

"He is being held pending his trial."

"Orcs do not take prisoners," argued the shaman.

"Nor is Urgon seen as one, but he is sequestered for his own good."

"That sounds suspiciously like imprisonment. Come now, Tarluk. Surely Shuvog meant only that he should prepare for what is to come?"

"I suppose that would make sense."

Kraloch's voice grew more authoritarian. "I am a shaman of this tribe, as you well know. Now stand aside. I must use my magic to judge his ability to stand trial."

"His ability? What are you suggesting?"

"He has been in the presence of a ghostwalker. It may have affected him."

The concern in Tarluk's voice was quite evident. "Are you saying he may be cursed?"

"There is always that possibility, but to determine the truth of it, I must see him."

Urgon smiled, for it appeared his friend would be granted access, but then Tarluk found his courage.

"Wait a moment," said the hunter. "You were in the mud hut as well, were you not?"

"I was," replied Kraloch. "What of it? All shamans visit the ghost-walker at one time or another."

"In that case, would you not also be cursed?"

"Of course not! Do you believe a shaman could be so easily swayed? Now stand aside, or I shall fetch Shular to teach you a lesson in manners."

Urgon held his breath, worried a fight might break out, but evidently, his guard backed down, for Kraloch soon parted the skins that formed the door.

"Urgon," he said. "So glad to see you in such fine spirits."

"Fine spirits? I am to face trial by the entire tribe. Why would you think me happy?"

Kraloch took a seat opposite him, although his face was anything but cheerful.

"Here now," said Urgon. "Why the glum look? It is my trial that is forthcoming, not yours."

"The charge is very serious, Urgon. We have few laws within our tribe, and you broke one of our most sacred."

"If you felt that way, why did you let it go on for so long? You are as guilty as I am." He took a breath, letting it out slowly. "I apologize, Kraloch. I got myself into this by my actions. You should not be punished for that. I shall say nothing of your involvement. You have my word."

"I am not worried for myself. I am concerned the tribe may vote against you."

"I do not fear death."

"It is not death you should fear. It is banishment."

"I can survive on my own."

"Can you?" said Kraloch. "I might remind you death almost claimed you when you returned from your ordeal."

"Nonsense. I walked into the village on my own."

"Yet in another two days, you would have died. You are not alone, Urgon. We shall see this through together."

"Together? And how would that work? I must defend myself, Kraloch. It is the way of things."

"Then challenge our traditions."

"In what way?"

"You bent the rules long enough, my friend. Now comes the time to break them. Convince the tribe you have the right of it. Your power of persuasion is strong."

"I am no chieftain."

"And you never will be with an attitude like that. Where is the Urgon I know, the one willing to risk everything to be with Zhura?"

"He is lost."

Kraloch leaned forward, shaking Urgon by the shoulders. "Then find him. Too much is at stake! This trial will determine not only your fate but that of Zhura as well. Would you see her deprived of your friendship? I see the way she looks at you. Do not abandon her!"

Urgon felt a fire building within him. Only a flicker, yet he knew if he tended it, it could explode into a rage of fury. He locked eyes with Kraloch, the hint of a smile curling his lips.

"You are right, my friend. I must do all I can to fight this."

"That's the Urgon I know. Now, what can I do to help?"

"Go and see Zhura; tell her all that has transpired. See if the Ancestors can give you some advice that would prove useful."

"I shall do so this very day."

"How long before the trial begins?"

"A difficult thing to predict. Word has gone out to the other villages, but the gathering will take some time to arrange. I would say at least a ten-day, possibly even two."

Urgon shook his head. "Too much time."

"Too much?"

"Yes. I know myself, Kraloch. I must tend the fire that burns within me. If I let it go out, I shall lose all hope."

"Then keep yourself busy."

"How? I am confined to my hut."

Kraloch looked around. "Your hut is only half complete. You have an entire expansion to finish."

"And how am I to do that when I am confined?"

"You are restricted to your hut, not incapable of working."

"But I will need sticks, leaves, even skins to complete what I started."

"All things I can see to. Put your mind to the task at hand, even while your hands build this home." He smiled. "Zhura would wish it."

Urgon stood. "Thank you, my friend. I shall."


That evening the wolves howled incessantly. It soon came to the attention of Shuvog, who showed up to look into the problem herself. Urgon, who sat sewing hides together, let his eyes drift up to her as she entered.

"What brings the chieftain of the Black Arrows to my humble abode?"

"You know full well, Master of Wolves. Why does the pack act so?" Urgon was blunt, but inside he smiled. "I did not feed them."

"What?"

"I am confined to my hut. How, then, am I to give them their food?"

"You are the master of wolves. It is your duty."

"You are the one who ordered me here," said Urgon, his voice quite calm. "Are you now saying I am free to leave the confines of my home?"

"Only to feed the pack."

He bowed his head solemnly, an action that appeared only to infuriate Shuvog. "I shall do as you command."

"Do not play games with me, Urgon. It will only make things worse for you."

"You are the one who is playing games, my chieftain. Your confinement of me is contrary to the ways of our people."

"Do not lecture me on our ways. You broke the rules."

"And that gives you the right to do the same? Careful, Shuvog, it is a slippery slope."

He saw the look of confusion. She was furious with him but, at the same time, fearful. Did he hold that much power over her?

"I want only what is best for the tribe," he continued. "I welcome the trial, for it will allow me to air my grievances. Are you prepared for that?"

She visibly paled, and he worried he had gone too far.

"I bear you no malice," he quickly added, "but change is coming, and you must learn to accept it."

"See to your charges," she barked out, then turned and abruptly left.

Urgon felt his legs begin to shake, and so he sat. It had been a gamble facing down Shuvog, but she would be the one speaking against him. Unsettling her could only work to his advantage. Grimtooth let out another howl, and he smiled.

"Time to get back to work," he mused aloud. The next howl was much more insistent. "I hear you," he called out. "Give me a moment to prepare it!"

Once he stepped outside, he pulled the meat from the drying rack and dropped it into a bowl. Tarluk watched him closely but said nothing. The wolves swarmed around him as he entered into the pen, their eyes on the food. Urgon tossed the meat, his mind elsewhere.

"I have news," came Kraloch's voice.

Urgon dumped the rest of the bowl, then wandered over to the fence that penned in the wolves. "It is good to see you."

Kraloch smiled. "And you," he replied, lowering his voice. "I spoke with Zhura. She promises to speak with the Ancestors. I also had a few discreet words with several members of the village."

"Oh?" said Urgon. "To what end?"

"I spoke of how, with you isolated in this manner, the wolves would be unable to help in the hunt. It caused quite a lot of concern, I can tell you."

"You are devious, my friend. Are you sure you are suited to be a shaman?"

"Whatever do you mean by that?"

"Only that shamans are supposed to be neutral in disputes such as the one I find myself in."

"We are all Orcs," said Kraloch. "Are we then to have no feelings?"

Urgon's face lit up. "You hit the spear on its tip," he said.

"I have?"

"Yes. Now I know how I must defend myself. Thank you, Kraloch. You have given me clarity."

"Have I? I wish you would explain it to me."

"My mind is racing, and I need to think more on the matter while it is still fresh. But I assure you, you will be the first to know once I reason things out."

"What can I do to help?"

"If I thought it would do any good, I would say pray, but the Ancestors do not heed such requests."

"They are spirits," said Kraloch, "not gods. They have no control over the world of the living."

"You are wrong, my friend. They lead us by the example of their own lives."

# FOURTEEN

## Tribal Council

AUTUMN 952 MC

After seventeen days, the largest gathering of tribe members in recent history had overtaken Ord-Dugath. With so many from the other villages in attendance, the trial had to be held outdoors, for they could not fit into the chieftain's hut. Even the great firepit had to be enlarged, along with adding several smaller fires to keep those on the periphery warm as the autumn winds turned cold, threatening an early winter.

Urgon sat some distance from Shuvog, who had gathered the other village elders around her. Even now, she was chatting with them, no doubt convincing them of his guilt. On the other hand, he sat alone, for no Orc wanted to be openly associated with his crime. His eyes scanned the crowd, seeking Kraloch, but his oldest friend was nowhere to be seen.

Shuvog passed the milk of life around to the other elders while the rest of the tribe talked in low voices, glancing his way. Urgon kept his composure by focusing on the flames before him, going over what he would say in his defence. He turned when someone sat beside him, expecting Kraloch, but instead he looked into the face of Urzath.

"Are you sure you want to be seen with me?" he asked.

"Have faith in your friends, Urgon," she replied. "Not everyone wants you exiled."

"Where is Kraloch?"

"I wish I knew. He told me he would be late but said little of the details. In the meantime, I am here to offer you my support."

"I appreciate it, Urzath, but the offer may draw unwanted attention to yourself."

"I have nothing to hide. And in any case, I am one of our greatest hunters. They could scarcely get rid of me."

"Have you spoken to Shular of late?"

"I have. She is worried for you, Urgon. She fears for your life. Are you not worried yourself?"

"Death no longer scares me. If I am to die, then it would be best to get it over with quickly."

Urzath nodded. "A good way to look at things, but maybe a bit maudlin. Have you already given up?"

"No. I know in my heart what I did was right. The difficulty is in convincing others."

"I wish you luck."

"Thank you," said Urgon, "but it is not luck that will get me out of this mess. I must somehow make them see reason."

"Reason? From this crowd? I think you have your work cut out for you. Shuvog has been talking the ears off those elders all morning."

"My sentence is not determined by the elders but by the entire tribe."

"True," said Urzath, "but the elders have great influence."

Urgon nodded, a lump forming in his throat. "I hear your words, but I must see this through to the end."

Urzath placed her hand on his forearm. "I understand. Know that I am with you, Urgon, son of Urdar, even in banishment."

"What are you saying?"

She leaned in close, talking in a whisper. "There are some amongst us who feel Shuvog has overstayed her welcome as chieftain. Should she choose to banish you, others will follow."

"That would split the tribe."

"So it would, but it is not the first time something like that has happened. The entire history of our people is full of such stories. It is how the other tribes came about. Come to think of it, it is how OUR tribe came about."

"Do not be hasty," warned Urgon. "The trial has yet to begin." He lapsed into silence, his eyes lost in the flames before him.

Shular rose, raising her staff on high and bringing the entire tribe to silence.

"Members of the Black Arrows," she began, "we have come here this day on a matter of great import. One amongst us has broken one of our sacred laws, and we must sit in judgement." She paused, and Urgon noticed her struggling with her duty. "Urgon, son of Urdar, has violated the sanctity of the mud hut."

The villagers sat in stunned silence. They all knew what this was about, for there had been talk of little else, but to hear it brought out in the open was still a shock.

"Not only that," Shular continued, "but he is accused of speaking with a ghostwalker, despite not being a shaman." She waited for the outrage to die down. "Today, you will hear both sides of the story, as is our custom. Only then will you be asked to decide what is to be done. Shuvog, chieftain of our clan, will present the argument for punishment, while Urgon will defend his actions." Her eyes roamed the crowd. "Does anyone object to this?"

Only silence met her gaze.

"Then let us commence." She turned to her leader. "Shuvog, you may begin the argument."

Shular sat, allowing her chieftain to stand as was the custom.

"We have few sacred rituals amongst our people. Thus it pains me to bring this charge against one of our own. Our master of wolves, Urgon, has defied not only tradition but has knowingly put our tribe at risk."

Urgon felt his heart quicken. "At risk?" he called out. "Explain yourself!"

The eyes of the tribe turned on him in distaste, but none spoke. Moments later, their gaze shifted back to their chieftain.

"As many of you are aware, Urgon somehow gained entry to the mud hut and consorted with a ghostwalker. This reckless action risks angering the Ancestors, without whom we would have no guidance. Not only that, but his distractions severely limit the ghostwalker's connection with them."

Urgon stood, unable to hold his temper in check. "Zhura," he yelled. "Her name is Zhura. If you are to speak of her, then use her name."

"A name you should not even know," replied Shuvog. "Do you deny the charge?"

"That I spent time with Zhura? No, I admit it freely. I gave her friendship when all you did was imprison her."

A murmur went through the tribe members, and Urgon took advantage of the opportunity. "She is an Orc and a member of this tribe, yet you took away her freedom."

Shuvog smiled. "She is not a member of the tribe, a fact you should be well aware of. Even the label of Orc is misleading, for she is afflicted with the curse of all ghostwalkers."

Urgon was caught off guard, something Shuvog quickly seized on. "Urgon, did you pass your ordeal?"

"Of course, but you know that already."

"Then tell everyone here what happens when you return."

Urgon felt the snare tightening.

"It looks like he has lost his tongue," she said. "And so, for the sake of expediency, let me answer the question for him. When a youngling passes the ordeal, they become a full-fledged member of the tribe. The ghostwalker has never passed such a test, and that means she is NOT a member of this tribe."

"Then what of the younglings?" said Urgon, grasping at straws. "Are they not allowed the protection of the tribe?"

"Younglings are cared for by their guardians," replied Shuvog, "and are typically kept under close supervision, for their own protection, of course." She turned her attention once more to the assembled crowd. "Urgon would have you believing we enslaved the ghostwalker, but it is far from the truth. Such a person is kept isolated for their own protection. They live a life in two worlds, you see—the land of the living and of the dead. Such a thing is a heavy burden, requiring the utmost concentration to delay the onset of madness. The actions of this Orc"— she pointed at Urgon—"endanger both it and us."

"Her," he corrected. "She is not an 'it', and her name is Zhura."

"It is clear you gave little thought to the well-being of your tribe-mates. Would you place your own happiness above theirs?"

"It is not my happiness I seek, but that of Zhura's. If you see fit to exile me, then so be it, but you must not blame her for my actions."

Shuvog smiled. "I have no intention of doing so. Ghostwalkers are precious to us, Urgon, not playthings to be defiled."

"I did nothing other than befriend her!"

"But you want to," she accused. "Go ahead, deny it. I dare you."

Urgon's pleas grew more desperate. "She is an Orc. Can you not see that? True, she has been afflicted by this curse, but, inside, her blood is as black as any of us."

Shuvog's temper rose. "You want to bond with her. Admit it!"

His blood boiled. He felt trapped, unable to breathe, his heart ready to explode. All eyes were on him, and then Shular spoke, sadness in her words.

"Is this true, Urgon?"

He swallowed, then opened his mouth but struggled to find the right words. Instead, he simply nodded, surrendering to the inevitability of his defeat.

"Say it aloud," ordered Shuvog.

"I love her," he proclaimed. "And I would have her as my bondmate, should she desire."

"There! He is condemned by his own words." The chieftain gloated at his admission. "There can be only one punishment for such a crime. I call on the tribe to render the sentence of death."

"No!" called out a frail voice. Everyone turned at the sound and then moved aside as Kraloch led Zhura by the arm. She struggled to maintain her concentration, stumbling as she moved, but she would not be deterred.

"I am Zhura," she declared, "ghostwalker of the Black Arrows, and I would have Urgon as my bondmate."

The entire tribe sat in stunned silence.

"Impossible," declared Shuvog. "This is not allowed."

"Not true," said Kraloch. "There is no such decree. A ghostwalker is free to choose her own destiny. Ask the Ancestors if you like. They will confirm it." He led her to her beloved, placing her hand in his.

Urgon felt her trembling, saw the fight happening within her to shut out all the spirits she must surely be hearing. He tightened his grip.

"You are safe," he soothed. "I shall not leave you." She gained strength from his touch.

"Yes, I am a ghostwalker," she said. "I have pale skin and white hair, and my eyes dislike the sun, but like all Orcs, I have a heart, a heart that beats for Urgon's embrace."

"You have no say in the matter," said Shuvog.

"On the contrary," said Shular. "Her words carry the wisdom of the Ancestors. Would you so callously disregard them?"

"I am the chieftain!"

"And I, the eldest shaman. If you wish to remain in charge of this tribe, I advise you to heed my words."

"Are you threatening me?"

Shular appeared to relax, her voice taking on a soothing tone. "There are limits to what a chieftain may do, Shuvog. You, of all people, should know that. As a shaman, I can dismiss this gathering or change its purpose to reconsider your own position as chieftain." The shamaness turned her attention to Urgon and Zhura. "I am saddened by the events that led to this day, but it is unthinkable to speak against a ghostwalker."

"My name is Zhura."

Shular bowed. "My apologies... Zhura."

"And the bonding?" said Urgon.

"That presents a problem," said Shuvog. "It is only allowed by full members of the tribe."

Kraloch stepped forward, raising his hands to get attention. "Perhaps I might offer a solution?"

"Speak," commanded Shular.

"It is, I believe, within our customs to grant an Orc status as a member of the tribe by vote. Is this not so?"

Shular smiled. "You have learned your lessons well, Kraloch."

"That law," said Shuvog, "was designed to permit outsiders to join our tribe."

"Zhura is, by the very definition of the term, an outsider," said Kraloch. "So much so, that very few have ever laid eyes on her." He moved to stand before Zhura. "How many Orcs have you spoken with before today?"

"Four," she replied. "Only the shamans, Shular, Kurghal, and yourself until Urgon came along."

Kraloch turned his attention once more to address the tribe. "There, you have it from her own lips. She has been confined to her hut since birth. Her only interaction with those of her race is controlled by others. It is clearly an example of imprisonment, and that"—he pointed at Shuvog—"is a far more serious charge than the one that faces Urgon."

All eyes turned towards the chieftain. A gentle breeze drifted past while all remained silent.

Shular was the one who broke the silence. "Shuvog, you and I have much to discuss. Let us adjourn to your hut along with Zhura and Urgon. I believe we can come to an arrangement that might prove beneficial to all."

"And Kraloch," added Urgon.

"That is acceptable," said his mother. "Now come, we must talk of this in private."

The small group headed into the hut, leaving the tribe sitting outside, waiting. Urgon kept a tight hold of Zhura's arm, worry flooding through him.

"It will be over soon," he soothed.

In answer, she halted, looking up at him. "It is difficult to concentrate," she said quietly. "The noise is overwhelming."

"Sit," ordered Shular, "and we shall talk of this situation we find ourselves in. And just to be clear, when I say we shall talk, I mean I shall talk, and you will all listen. Is that understood?"

Cowed by the shaman, they all nodded their agreement and took up places around the indoor firepit. Shular remained standing, gazing down at Zhura. Urgon recognized the concern in her eyes.

"I know this is difficult for you, Zhura, so I shall be as brief as I can. We find ourselves in uncharted territory here. Ghostwalkers are rare, so rare, in fact, no other tribe has a living Orc who remembers one such as you." She looked at each person present, gauging their response. "I might also remind you we are in communication with many other tribes through the use of spirit magic."

"Yes," said Shuvog. "Something Urgon put at risk by his actions."

"His actions had no effect on the spirit world," announced Zhura, "but they gave me comfort."

Shular grabbed at the statement. "Yes," she said. "I think I understand now."

"Then please explain yourself," said the chieftain.

"By all accounts, ghostwalkers do not live long, rarely surpassing twenty winters, but Urgon may have inadvertently changed that."

"I did?" said Urgon.

"People like Zhura go mad," continued Shular. "I believe the constant presence of the spirits has a debilitating effect on them. Urgon, however, has provided a distraction of sorts, something for her to focus on, to keep her mind from losing its grip on the material world."

"Are you saying he was right to do so?" asked Shuvog.

"Though I hate to admit it, I suppose I do. I also blame myself for not seeing it sooner. We put you in a terrible position, Zhura. We never should have isolated you the way we did. In our defence, we thought it the right thing to do, but now I see our mistake."

"So you are not opposed to our bonding?" said Urgon.

"Allowing you to see her is not the same thing as approving of your bonding. She is barren, Urgon. There is no future in that union."

"How do you know?" asked Kraloch.

The shamaness turned to him in surprise. "I beg your pardon?"

"How do you know she is barren?"

"It is the curse of her condition."

"According to who?"

Shular was at a loss for words.

"It seems to me," Kraloch continued, "that she is, physically, the same as any other Orc, save for the strange colouring and, of course, her ability to see the spirits. Does it not make sense she might bear a youngling at some point?"

"That does not bear consideration," said the shamaness.

"That is not your decision," said Urgon. "That is for Zhura to decide. And even if she WAS barren, I would still have her as my bondmate."

"As I would have you," said Zhura.

"There, you see?" said Kraloch. "The matter is settled."

"It is far from settled," said Shular.

"I would disagree. Urgon and Zhura are both mature Orcs. The choice is theirs and theirs alone."

"Not while I am the shaman. I refuse to bond them."

"You may do as you like," said Kraloch, "but I am more than capable of carrying out the ceremony."

"Do that, and I will no longer be your mentor."

"I have learned all I can from you, Shular. It is an empty threat."

"There is still the matter of Zhura not having undergone her ordeal," said Shuvog.

"A matter easily solved," noted Urgon. "We shall ask the tribe to permit her admission. Who would refuse a ghostwalker?"

"He has you there," said Kraloch.

"I will not permit this," said the chieftain.

"Yes, you will," said Shular, "or I will recommend your dismissal as chief of our tribe."

"But why?" hissed Shuvog. "You desire this union no more than I?"

"It is clear to me that this is what Zhura wants. Who am I to refuse such a request?" She looked at Urgon. "Understand, I still do not agree with this, but neither will I stand in your way."

"Thank you, Mother."

"Do not thank me, my son. I believe you may yet live to regret your choice."

"Never. I am strong in my convictions. Zhura has my heart as I have hers."

"Then come," said Kraloch. "We must return to the tribe and vote to welcome Zhura as a full-fledged member of the Black Arrows."

Urgon turned to Zhura first. "Are you up to this?"

She nodded, then let out a gasp.

"What is it?"

She held up her hand, then took a deep breath. "The spirits," she said. "My head can barely contain them. It feels as though my skull will erupt like a ripe melon."

Urgon turned to Kraloch. "Is there anything you can do for her?"

"I have no magic that will help. What of you, Shular? Any suggestions?"

"Returning her to the mud hut might help, but there is nothing else I can suggest."

"Then I shall take her there right now," said Urgon.

"No," said Zhura through gritted teeth. "Let us bring this matter to the tribe while the opportunity exists."

"Are you sure?" asked Kraloch.

Again, she nodded.

"Then let us proceed."

# FIFTEEN

# The Arrangement

AUTUMN 952 MC

The tribe had waited in relative silence while the small group met. But as they exited the shaman's hut, those gathered grew more vocal in their demands to know what had transpired.

Shuvog, as chieftain, sat at the end of the outdoor firepit, while Shular remained standing. Urgon, Zhura, and Kraloch sat on the other side of the shaman, leading to even more gasps from the Orcs assembled before them.

Shular held up her staff, calling them all to silence. "We discussed the matter at great length," she said. "The question of Urgon's guilt or innocence is now irrelevant. Instead, we must discuss another matter. I shall yield to Kraloch, a shaman of this tribe." She sat, allowing her protégé to stand.

"As you all witnessed," began Kraloch, "Zhura and Urgon desire to be bonded. What is perhaps less well understood is that Zhura is not considered a member of this tribe, for she has not passed her own ordeal. Considering her condition, it would be dangerous and foolhardy to ask her to undergo the same rituals the rest of us did. So I now ask this tribe to accept her as a full-fledged Black Arrow. That is the decision resting before you. Does anyone have any questions?"

Urzath stood, then waited for Kraloch to acknowledge her presence.

"Yes, Urzath. You may speak freely."

"I am all for allowing Zhura membership in this tribe," she said, "but Urgon is the master of wolves. Where would they live once bonded?"

"A good question, and one I believe best answered by Urgon." He looked at his comrade. Urgon rose, but Zhura clung to him, standing unsteadily by his side.

"I have been enlarging my hut," he said. "With help, I will cover the walls in mud, the same as Zhura's current home."

"How, then, would the shamans visit without your interference?" asked Shular.

"I have already considered the problem. The inside of the hut will consist of two rooms, much like the chieftain's, although clearly smaller in scale. It would provide the privacy required for such visits."

"And the wolves?"

"They would not bother me," said Zhura. "Their spirits are calming."

Urgon looked at her in surprise. "They are?"

"Yes. They do not chatter away endlessly as our Ancestors do."

He almost laughed out loud, then remembered where he was.

"Are there any other questions?" he asked the tribe.

Another Orc rose, this time Arshug the bowyer. "Would others then be able to visit the ghostwalker?"

"That would be for Zhura to decide," said Urgon. He looked down at her, but such was her discomfort he didn't press the issue.

"Then I have no further questions. I say we tally the stones," said Arshug as she sat.

Shular rose, picked up a wicker basket, and then made her way through the crowd and, with the help of Kraloch and Kurghal, handed a painted stone to each member of the tribe. They then returned to their previous positions.

"It is now time to collect the stones," Shular announced. "Kurghal shall go amongst you. A stone deposited in the basket means you agree to make Zhura a full-fledged member of the tribe. Its absence is a rejection of this. Kurghal will tally the vote once collected, and if there are enough stones to account for a majority of the tribe, then we shall welcome a new sister to our number."

Kraloch looked at her in surprise. "You will not conduct the tally yourself?"

"I am not impartial in this matter."

Kurghal moved amongst the tribe. Many dropped their stones into the basket, but it was by no means a unanimous decision. She eventually returned, dumping the stones out to count them.

The tribe quickly grew restless, talking amongst themselves. Urgon hated the wait, fearing it would do little for Zhura's condition, but then his sister finally moved to stand by the chieftain's side.

"It is the decision of this tribe," she said, "that we welcome our sister Zhura to its number."

Kraloch shouted out in triumph, then looked across to his friend only to witness Zhura's collapse.

Urgon scooped her up into his arms. "Quickly," he called out. "We must get her back to the mud hut. She is overwhelmed."

The Orcs parted as Kraloch led the way. It was only a short distance to her home, but Urgon fretted. They finally passed through the entrance to the hut, and he laid her out on the furs.

"Zhura," he said. "Can you hear me?"

Her eyes fluttered open. "I am here," she said, "though I am weak. I must rest."

Urgon let out a sigh of relief. "You had me worried for a moment."

"As was I," said Kraloch. "I suggest we leave."

"I would have you stay," said Zhura, taking Urgon's hand. "Watch over me as I recover. It would do me good to know you are nearby."

"I shall," said Urgon. "I promise."


Urgon stepped from the mud hut to see Urzath and a few others waiting there.

"Something wrong?" he asked.

"Not at all," replied the hunter. "I gathered some friends, and we are here to help you finish the work on your new home."

Urgon peered around her. "Gorath? He is still a youngling. Of what use is he?"

Urzath smiled. "He can fetch and carry like anyone else, and it frees up Arshug to assist as well. She was, I understand, involved in the original construction of the mud hut."

"She was," said Urgon, "and would be a fountain of knowledge, yet I do not see her."

"She says the mud here is unsuitable to the task and has therefore taken a group down onto the plains, to the same place they originally found it."

Urgon noticed a very tall Orc towering over the rest. "And who is that?"

Urzath looked over her shoulder and smiled. "That is Vulgar. He comes to us from one of the northern villages. Surely the largest Orc to ever tread these hills."

"You have done well, Urzath. Thank you."

"We are here for you, Urgon, despite what others may think. Will Zhura be joining us?"

"No. She is much recovered, but the noise of the spirits is far too loud out here. She will remain inside for now, but hopefully, once some of the walls are mudded, she will come out and have a look. Is Kraloch about?"

"He is over at the wolf master's hut, examining your work."

"Then let us join him."

Urzath turned to Vulgar. "Remain here, if you will, to keep Zhura safe."

The huge Orc nodded, then took up a position before the door to the mud hut.

"Is that truly necessary?" asked Urgon.

"There is a lot of bad feeling amongst the tribe," she replied. "It is, I think, wise to take precautions."

"Wise, maybe, but unnecessary. The door is protected by magic."

"Even magic can be destroyed by an axe."

Urgon felt an icy hand grasp his heart. "You believe they would stoop to that?"

"It is merely a precaution, my friend. Worry not. We are but a short distance away should any trouble present itself."

Kraloch stood inside the pen with the wolves at his feet while staring at the hut's walls.

"I see you are deep in thought," said Urgon. "Tell me what is on your mind."

"It occurs to me," his friend replied, "that the key to keeping Zhura comfortable is the mud."

"We know that already."

"Let me be more specific. I believe the mud used on Zhura's hut has something in it that helps dampen the sound."

"A reasonable assumption. Shular insisted on a particular kind of mud when they built the place all that time ago. Thankfully, Arshug remembers where they gathered it."

"I should very much like to examine it when she returns. If I can determine what lies within it, we may have other options."

"And if not?"

Kraloch shrugged. "Then we simply plaster the walls as they did in the past. I would, however, suggest we thicken the walls a little. I also have another idea."

"Which is?"

"Come, let me show you." He led Urgon to a place where the new hut's wall ran along the edge of the wolf pen. "I was looking over your work when I noticed this spot here."

Urgon stared at the frame of a wall, built of sticks and tied off with leather strips, but there was little else to note. "The wall is merely unfinished," he said. "Clearly, there is still work to be done."

"Yes, but if you look here"—Kraloch pointed—"there is an opening facing onto the wolf pen."

"As I said, only because the work is unfinished."

"Use your imagination, my friend. What if we kept a hole here?"

"To what end?"

"It would allow you and Zhura to look out upon the wolves when desired."

"That would also let in the sounds of the spirits."

Kraloch grinned. "I have a solution to that as well. We build a small panel which can hang from above. To open it, you would push it out and use a stick to hold it in place. Of course, the panel itself would need to be coated in mud."

Urgon saw the potential and smiled. "It would let her look out while not being overcome by all the noise. Wherever did you get such an idea?"

"The truth of the matter is Urzath told me."

Urgon turned to the shaman's cousin. "This was your idea?"

"I saw that sort of thing on a Human hut. They call it a window."

"You have met Humans?"

"I have," said Urzath. "There are a number of their dwellings on the way to the Deerwood."

"You entered their city?"

"No, but the Humans scatter their buildings everywhere. And they till the land and raise animals."

"What kinds of animals? Do they have wolves?"

"No, although some have dogs. They are similar to wolves, but... well, you would need to see them to understand."

"And you talked to them?"

Urzath nodded. "Those who live outside their city can be quite reasonable. We do not speak their language, of course, nor do they speak our tongue, but we manage well enough."

"And you trade with them? What do they have that would be of use?"

"Worked metal, mostly, although not as good as that of the mountain folk."

"And what do you trade for this metal?"

"Mainly meat or pelts." She reached into a small pouch slung over her shoulder and pulled forth a few flat metal disks. "They also have these. They call them coins. It is how they barter amongst their own people."

Urgon took one, holding it close to his eyes. "I have seen this metal before," he said.

"Yes, it is silver. Much favoured by the Dwarves."

"There is an image on this coin."

"The mark of their king. It is what they call their chieftain of chieftains."

Urgon shook his head, passing back the coin. "Such a strange people."

"They are much like us if truth be told, appearances aside."

"I have never seen a Human. What do they look like?"

"They are a little shorter than us but still taller than a Dwarf. Their skin tone varies from a dark brown to a very light colour, like that of a skinned mouse."

"And they are friendly?"

"Some are, but the closer one gets to their city, the more likely they are to be hostile. Perhaps one day you will accompany us on the long hunt, then you can see for yourself."

"I would enjoy that very much."

"Enough of these Humans," said Kraloch. "Tell me what you think of this idea of a window?"

"I like it, and I think Zhura will as well."

"Then the time for talk is done. Let us get to work."

It took them two days to complete what Urgon had started, then came the laborious task of applying the mud. Arshug showed them how to first mix it with rushes, then apply the mixture to the stick frame. The work was messy and made all the more challenging by the cooler weather that had moved in, but there was a feeling of camaraderie that couldn't be denied. A ten-day later, they stood back, admiring their work.

"A fine sight," said Urgon.

"A strange one to be sure," said Kraloch. "There is no other hut quite like it."

"I shall fetch Zhura. She is eager to see it." He entered the old mud hut to find her waiting, the excitement in her eyes bubbling over.

"Is it ready?" she asked.

"It is," he said, taking her hand. "Come, let me show you our new home."

"It is not our home yet," she reminded him. "We are still to be bonded."

"That will be taken care of shortly. In the meantime, let me show you what we did."

Urgon led Zhura from the hut, pausing to allow her to acclimatize herself to the outside world. She once told him the assault on her senses was as if hundreds of people were all talking at the same time. He saw her flinch, then put a reassuring arm around her. The others stood by, watching in silence as she slowly made her way to their new home. It was only when Urgon led her through the doorway that he felt her finally relax.

"It is quite spacious," she said, a smile gracing her features.

"This is the main room, and that door there"—he pointed—"leads to the wolf den."

"And the third door?"

"Come, let me show you." He pushed aside the hangings, revealing the interior. Furs lined the floor while a firepit crackled at its centre. "This will be where we sleep," he announced.

She looked around in awe. "I would never have dreamed of having so much space." She moved to the wall that faced the pen. "What is this?"

"Urzath calls it a window. It is a Human idea." He pushed it open, then propped it up with a stick.

Zhura stood before it, enjoying a gentle breeze. "Beautiful," she said.

"Yes, and if the noise gets too loud, you can close it."

"I look forward to moving in."

"Then come outside. I have another surprise for you."

"So many? What now?"

"You need to wait and see."

He led her outside to where a small group of friends waited.

"If you are ready, Kraloch will conduct the ceremony of bonding."

She looked at him with tears in her eyes. "Nothing would make me happier."

Kraloch indicated the Orc to his left. "You already know Kurghal, Urgon's sister. She shall act as witness on his behalf." He then turned to his right. "This is my mother, Maloch. She is pleased to perform a similar function on your behalf."

"Will your own mother not join us?" asked Zhura.

"No," said Urgon. "She has made her views quite clear on the subject of our bonding. We shall proceed without her."

"Stand before me," said Kraloch, "and we shall begin." He waited until they were in place, then continued. "Zhura, Urgon, you are here today to bond yourselves to one another, as is our custom." He turned to Urgon. "Do you, Urgon, undertake this bonding of your own free will?"

"I do."

"And you, Zhura, do you agree to this bonding of your own free will?"

"I do, most assuredly."

"Who here witnesses these vows?"

Kurghal stepped forward. "I, Kurghal, shamaness of the Black Arrows, do hereby witness these vows and do affirm Urgon commits to this bonding with a free heart."

Kraloch nodded to his mother, who also stepped forth.

"And I, Maloch, do hereby witness these vows and affirm Zhura, ghostwalker of the Black Arrows, commits to this bonding with a free heart."

"It is now time to exchange vows," said Kraloch. "Urgon?"

The master of wolves turned to Zhura, and they stood facing each other, holding on to hands. "Since first we met, we were destined for each other. In those days, I was but a youngling, ready to take on the world, yet without guidance. I was content to simply become a hunter, like most Orcs. Little did I realize I would find the Orc who would make my heart sing when I crawled into that hut. You complete me, Zhura of the Black Arrows, and I am pleased to name you bondmate."

Maloch sniffled, then wiped tears from her eyes, an action not lost on her son.

"And I," said Zhura, "I was lost and alone, abandoned to face a lifetime of loneliness and solitude, and then you came into my life. You set my heart aflutter, Urgon, son of Urdar, and your smile warms me. I am overjoyed I shall call you bondmate."

"Give me your hands," said Kraloch.

They both extended their arms, he, his left, she, her right. Kraloch took a braided cord and wrapped it around their wrists. "As I symbolically bind your hands, so too shall your hearts be bound in this mortal realm."

"And beyond," said Zhura, "for I would not see our spirits parted."

"Nor I," said Urgon.

"That is not part of the ceremony," said Kraloch.

"I know," replied Zhura, "but it is somehow fitting."

"Urzath?" called out Kraloch.

Urzath stepped forward, a bowl in her hands.

"Drink now of the milk of life," continued Kraloch, "but sparingly, Urgon. You remember what happened last time."

Urgon took a sip, then handed the bowl to Zhura, who sniffed it before she copied his actions. The milk of life was passed around to the others until they had all tasted it.

"And now," said Kraloch, "let it be known to all, Urgon, master of wolves and Zhura, ghostwalker of Ord-Dugath are bondmates." He grinned broadly. "Congratulations, both of you."

The others stepped in, adding their own words of encouragement.

"Now," said Urgon, "it is time to invite you all to enter this hut, OUR home where we shall celebrate our bonding."

# SIXTEEN

## Life

---

### SUMMER 955 MC

Z hura gazed out the window, watching as Urgon fed the wolves. Almost three winters had passed since the bonding, yet still, she marvelled at how her heart leaped as he turned to her with a smile.

"Like what you see?" he asked, tossing some raw meat to the ground.

"Best be quick," she answered. "I yearn for your embrace."

"In that case, I shall be there directly." He dropped the last of the food, then made his way inside, where Zhura waited for him. She wrapped her arms around him and held him tight.

"I missed you," she said.

"I have been gone but a moment."

"And yet it feels like forever. Now come, I prepared some food for you."

"You prepared food for me? I was unaware you could cook."

She smiled. "I have been watching you, bondmate mine."

He let her lead him into their private quarters, where two wooden platters held a collection of meat, fruit, and crushed roots.

"What have we here?" he asked.

"The mountain goat you have had before, but this is something new, at least to me."

"Red berries," said Urgon. "One of my favourites."

"Try these," she said, holding up a root.

He took one, chewing it quickly. "This is good. What is it?"

"Blackroot," she replied. "Maloch told me of it."

"You appear to have no end of visitors these days."

"Yes, and I owe it all to you." She was about to say more, but they were interrupted.

"Urgon? Zhura? Are you in there?"

"Yes," replied Urgon. "Where else would we be? Come in, Urzath. We shall meet you in the living area."

He held out his hand. "Shall we?"

Zhura took it. "Of course."

They walked into the next room to see Urzath. The hunter was obviously excited, for her face was a dark shade of green, with sweat beading on her brow.

"I just came from the chieftain's hut," she said, the words rushing out. "Shuvog is dead."

"Dead?" said Urgon.

"Yes. She had been ailing for some time. She joined the Ancestors in the middle of the night."

"We never saw eye to eye, but she was an efficient leader of the tribe."

"Is that all you can say?" asked Urzath.

"What else is there that needs to be said?"

"This is your chance, Urgon."

He screwed up his face, trying to reason what she meant. Zhura was the one who grasped the significance first. "The tribe will gather to choose a new leader, Urgon. That leader could be you."

"Me?"

"Certainly," she continued. "Who better to lead us?"

"Are there not those more suited to such a task?"

"We live in a time of change, my dearest. The Humans are encroaching on our lands. It will take someone with imagination and foresight to deal with them."

"And you believe that should be me?"

"Without a doubt."

"She is right," said Urzath. "As the master of wolves, you have gained many allies. Who better to lead the tribe?"

The hides parted again, revealing Kraloch. He quickly scanned the room, then looked at Urzath. "Well? Has he heard?"

"He has," she confirmed.

"And?"

"He is hesitant."

Kraloch turned towards Urgon. "Is this true? Where is the brash, young Orc I knew so well? The one willing to bend... pardon me, break the rules to accomplish his goals?"

"I am bonded now," replied Urgon. "I have much more to consider. Zhura's happiness for one."

"Nonsense," said Zhura. "I shall only be happy if you are happy. You often talk of this, dearest. I know it to be close to your heart."

"I would not have it take my time away from you."

"And why should it?" said Kraloch. "Do you think Shuvog spent much time being chieftain?"

"I had always assumed so."

"Then let me put your mind at ease. Aside from the occasional gathering, there is precious little to occupy a chieftain's mind."

"In that case, I shall put myself before the tribe. Have we heard of anyone else interested in the position?"

"Not yet," said Urzath, "but there is still time. Tradition calls for a ten-day of mourning before the new chieftain is selected."

"A ten-day?" said Urgon. "I had expected less."

"This is not the simple selection of a village elder," noted Kraloch. "The entire tribe has to be gathered. That has not happened since we welcomed Zhura into the Black Arrows."

"Who rules in her absence?" asked Urgon.

"Your mother is the senior shaman. She will oversee things until a replacement is selected."

Urgon frowned. "I doubt she will be pleased with my decision. Even now, when she visits Zhura, I must make myself scarce."

Zhura squeezed his hand. "I tried to talk to her about that, but she refuses to be in your presence."

"She took your bonding badly," said Kraloch, "and the only reason she meets with Zhura is because of her ability to communicate with spirits."

Urgon looked at his bondmate. "Does she speak of nothing else?"

"She is proud," she replied, "and is unable to let go of the past. It grieves me to know of your estrangement, especially considering I am the cause of it."

"Do not blame yourself, Zhura. It is she who is the cause, not you."

Urzath interrupted. "The tribe will be interested in what you would do as chieftain. Have you given it much thought?"

Zhura laughed. "When has he not given it thought? He is forever telling me of his plans."

Urgon blushed. "I admit the truth of it. I believe there is much we could do to improve our lot in life."

"Such as?" asked Urzath.

"We could reach out to the mountain folk."

"To what end?"

"They have many goods we would find to our advantage, and I know they have few hunters. Meat and skins could buy us better quality weapons."

"Would you have us go to war?"

"No, but the same weapons would be put to good use on the hunt. You and I both know the quality of Dwarven steel. It is much better than that used by the Humans."

"Speaking of Humans," said Kraloch, "what do you think we should do about them?"

"In what way?"

"Their hunters encroach on our lands."

"Then I would suggest we seek common ground with them."

"We do not speak their language," said Kraloch.

"I suppose that is also something we must remedy. Should we send a delegation to meet with them, much as we do with the other villages?"

"I doubt that would work," said Urzath. "We share the same culture as the villages, while we know very little of the Humans."

"What else can we do?"

"We could fight them."

"No," said Zhura. "The Humans far outnumber us. Going to war against them would spell the end of all we know."

They all looked at her in shock. "Are you sure?" asked Urgon.

She nodded. "The Ancestors speak of Humans breeding like rabbits. They move into an area and then reproduce at an alarming rate. Possibly, in days of old, when we lived in cities, we might have been a match for them, but then again, they only came to this land long after."

"Then we must learn more before making a decision."

"A wise move," said Urzath. "You sound like a chieftain."

"Yes," agreed Kraloch, "but you should adopt a pose that makes it look like you are wise."

"He IS wise," defended Zhura.

"True, but he doesn't LOOK it. A chieftain is typically much older and therefore wiser. See the problem?"

"I am twenty," said Urgon. "That means I still have at least another ten or fifteen winters left in me."

"Yes, but that would still make you younger than any of the village elders. We need some way to demonstrate your desire to better the tribe."

"I doubt that would work," said Urzath. "Many of our people dislike the idea of change. You broke tradition when you bonded with Zhura; that is not easily forgotten."

"Then I suppose we shall have to wait and see who else covets the position," said Urgon. "Until that time, there is little we can do."


In the end, it didn't take long for Urgon's opponent to announce himself. Agrug, the sibling of Arshug, was an experienced hunter and several winters senior. He regularly led hunting parties to the far reaches of the Rugar Plains. Some even said he tempted the wrath of the Elves of the Darkwood.

The period of Shuvog's mourning concluded with a feast in her honour, followed the very next day by the gathering of the Black Arrows.

With no other Orcs presenting themselves as potential chieftains, it came down to a simple choice—Urgon or Agrug. Each was allowed their say, and then the tribe would vote, casting their stones to decide who would be awarded the honour of leading them.

Urgon was nervous. Zhura had chosen to remain in the hut, the presence of so many Orcs and their spirits being simply too much for her to handle. Thus it was he found himself sitting amongst the tribe, surrounded by his friends.

"Nervous?" asked Kraloch.

"I am," he replied, "although I am loathe to admit it."

"You must relax. You are popular here in the village."

"True," replied Urgon, "but Agrug is well known amongst the other villages, an advantage I do not share."

"Yes, but you display a wisdom far beyond your age."

Shular rose, holding her staff on high, and the tribe grew quiet. The shaman swept her gaze over the assembled Orcs. "We are gathered here this day to select a new chieftain. Two Orcs have stepped forward to take on this heavy burden, and so it falls to you to decide which is more worthy." She paused, letting the words sink in.

"Chieftains must, by their very nature, have the courage to make hard decisions," she continued, "and the wisdom to guide our destiny. Choose wisely, fellow tribemates, for your choice will determine our future. We shall start the process by allowing each applicant to say a few words, then the counting of stones will begin. Is there any here who questions this?"

Gorath, eager to participate in the process, stood.

"Sit down, Gorath," said Shular. "You are still a youngling, and are only here to observe."

The Orcs around him all chuckled.

She waited, then, with no other Orc desiring to speak, looked to her right. "Agrug, as the elder Orc, you may speak first."

Agrug was an imposing sight, easily a head taller than Urgon, and physically very powerful. He towered over the seated assemblage as he spoke in a low, rumbling tone.

"I am Agrug," he said. "Many of you know me as a hunter. I have ranged far and wide, into the mountains to the east, and as far as the Deerwood, which lays to the west. South I have also been, skirting the edge of the Darkwood, and to the north, a desolate land of rock and stone. In that time, I have led many hunting parties, enriching the tribe with our bounty. I know what is required to survive in this harsh environment and what is needed for our tribe to prosper. Let me show you how we can be strong, like our Ancestors before us."

Orcs thumped the ground with their fists, showing their appreciation. Agrug sat, letting Shular take centre stage once again. She looked at him with a smile. "Wise words, Agrug. You have done yourself proud."

Urgon felt the heat rise within him. Shamans were supposed to remain neutral in these gatherings, yet it felt like favour was bestowed upon his rival.

"We will now hear from Urgon," continued Shular.

Urgon stood, feeling all eyes turn to him. He stared back, sweeping his gaze as he had seen his mother do, but was shocked at the looks of disapproval.

"Many of you know me," he said, "for I am Urgon, master of wolves, son of Urdar, who gave his life to save this very village." He paused, trying to gather his thoughts, but it had just the opposite effect, for he was now unsure of what to say. His eyes wandered to Kraloch, who simply nodded.

"If you do not know me," he continued, "then you likely know of my reputation, as I am bonded with Zhura, ghostwalker of the Black Arrows." His voice faltered, and he began to sweat.

"Agrug is a worthy choice for leader," he said, "but he offers nothing new. Choose him, and life will continue as it always has, stagnant and dead. Our people are dwindling, despite the efforts of our predecessors. Choose me, and I will see us thrive!"

He sat. A few thumps could be heard, but not nearly so many as had been given to Agrug, and he felt the sting of defeat. Urgon had no doubt how things would turn out, yet he swore to himself he would accept his fate with grace and humility.

Shular rose once more. "We shall now tally the stones." She held up the wicker basket. "The presence of a stone is a vote for Agrug, its absence marks one for Urgon." She nodded to Kurghal. "You may begin collecting the stones."

Urgon watched as his sister moved amongst the tribe. Orcs reached up, casting their stones into the basket, and it soon became clear he would be outvoted. He looked at Kraloch and shook his head. "We will not win today," he said.

Eventually, Kurghal returned to Shular's side, dumping the stones on the ground.

"Kraloch," barked out the senior shamaness. "Come and help count the stones."

Urgon closed his eyes, trying not to get his hopes up. Time seemed to stretch out for an eternity before Kurghal and Kraloch finally conferred. His sister then whispered something to Shular, prompting her to raise her staff once more.

"We have a decision," she announced. "The new chieftain of the Black Arrows shall be Agrug."

Everyone thumped the ground, save for Urgon and his closest friends. The defeat left a bitter taste in his mouth, yet he rose, offering his congratulations to his opponent. The rest of the tribe swept forward to offer their best wishes, pushing him aside. He felt Kraloch guide him from the scene, and the next thing he knew, he was sitting at home as Zhura took his hand.

"It is not yet your time," she soothed. "You are still young, and Agrug will not live forever."

"He will live for a long while yet," said Urgon. "And what have I accomplished?"

"You have me," said Zhura, "along with many other friends."

He smiled, gripping her hand all the more firmly. "I do," he admitted, "and I would not change that for anything."

"What will you do now?" asked Kraloch.

"Do? The same thing I always do. Look after the wolves, of course."

"Might I suggest an alternative?" said Zhura.

They all looked at her in surprise.

"Go on," urged Urgon.

"The next time Agrug goes on a hunt, accompany him."

"But I am the master of wolves. Who would take care of the pack in my absence?"

"I can," said Gorath. "If you would but show me how."

"There, you see?" said Zhura. "The problem is easily solved."

"But why would I accompany Agrug?" asked Urgon.

Now it was Zhura's turn to smile. "Associating yourself with him will let your name carry far and wide."

"Yes," added Urzath, "and the more Orcs who know your name, the more likely you will become chieftain one day, should that be your desire."

Urgon nodded. "It is, and I see the wisdom in this. The next time he sets forth on a hunting expedition, I shall ask to accompany him."

"As will I," said Urzath. "It will provide me with the opportunity to show you these Humans of which I have spoken."

"I should like that. They sound like a fascinating race."

"They are, but I think them dangerous as well. I have seen their hunters from afar, and they wear armour of metal."

"Those are not hunters," said Zhura, "but warriors trained to kill others. The Ancestors say the Humans are not to be trusted."

"This cannot be true of all of them?" Urgon asked. "Urzath herself has traded with them from time to time."

"The Humans are complex. Our people follow their leaders once they are chosen, but Humans feel no such obligation. They fight amongst themselves, and that conflict often spills over into our lands."

"And this has happened here? In these hills?"

"Not within recent memory," said Zhura, "yet the Ancestors tell of a time when the Humans first came to this region. Our conflict was great, and the villages that sat upon the Rugar Plains were lost to us. Now, all that remains of our people are the villages we now call home."

"Did we not fight back?"

"We did, but the Humans came in overwhelming numbers, far too many for us to defeat."

"Yet we still survived," said Urgon.

"Only because the enemy turned inward. Had they continued much longer, they would have driven our tribe to extinction."

"Then it is best we leave them alone."

"I would not suggest that," said Zhura. "The Humans spread across the land like a plague, and sooner or later, they will find us again. When that happens, it would be best we were prepared."

"Prepared, how?"

"We must learn all we can about them," she replied. "Only then can we truly learn how to keep our people safe."

Urgon chuckled. "What need have I for a shaman? I have the wisest of all bondmates."

"Do not dismiss us all so readily," said Kraloch. "Zhura may be wiser, but we can still heal those who are injured."

"And I would not deny your place amongst our people, my friend."

# SEVENTEEN

# The Gift

AUTUMN 957 MC

A grug proved to be a popular chieftain, although typically absent for long periods as he hunted throughout the land. These expeditions were highly successful, and they often brought back game not found in the hills they called home.

Urgon and Urzath accompanied their chieftain on longer and longer trips, although they had yet to meet any Humans. They were returning from one such trip with skins aplenty when Kraloch met them at the edge of the village.

"It has been a successful hunt," said Urgon. "Look at what we brought back!"

He noted the sour look on his friend's face and came to a halt. "What is it? Is Zhura well?"

"Zhura is fine," replied Kraloch, "but your mother is ill."

"Have you healed her?"

"It is not our way to use magic when age begins to conquer us."

"Here," said Urzath. "Let me take the skins. You should be with her."

Urgon handed over his prizes, then followed Kraloch. The two of them soon entered his old home. There his sister, Kurghal, held his mother's hand. Shular lay amongst the furs, her face pale, her brow sweating profusely despite the relatively cool interior.

She saw her son and had a sudden burst of clarity. "Go, Urgon, I do not wish you here."

"I am your son," he replied.

"You gave up that title when you defied me and became bondmate to that ghostwalker."

He felt the familiar surge of anger but fought to control it. "Zhura and I are bonded; that much is true, but I am happy, far more so than you could ever imagine."

"I warned you she would go mad."

"You did, yet Zhura has now seen twenty-two winters and is doing well. A far cry from the madness you spoke of. It is friendship that saved her, Mother, companionship and love, not isolation and fear."

"Begone," Shular shouted.

Urgon rose, his heart heavy, not with sadness but with pity. "As you wish. I shall leave you to your fate."

He stepped outside, Kraloch following him.

"She knows not what she says," said Kraloch.

"Shular knows her mind. This is not the first time we have had harsh words."

"True, but it will be the last." Kraloch looked into his comrade's eyes. "What will you do?"

"I shall return to my hut and sit with Zhura."

"Then I shall bring word when she has joined the Ancestors." He paused a moment, considering his words.

"Something wrong?" asked Urgon.

"I was suddenly struck by the situation. If your mother joins the Ancestors, does that mean she might answer when I call on them?"

"I hope not, for both our sakes." Urgon placed his hand on the shaman's shoulder. "Thank you, Kraloch. You are a true friend."

He wandered back to his home, his mind in turmoil. The last thing he wanted was to part with his mother on such terms, but there was little choice. That much she had made plain. Ever since he revealed his relationship with Zhura, Shular had turned against him. In his mind, she represented the past, Zhura his future. Urgon halted by the wolf pens, where Gorath sat amongst the newest litter of wolf pups, petting them.

"Your efforts will make them soft," warned Urgon.

The younger Orc looked up in alarm, then saw the smile. "I do only what I have seen you do, Master of Wolves."

Urgon laughed. "So you do. Is Zhura well?"

"See for yourself. She awaits you inside."

Urgon entered the hut only to have his bondmate rush across and embrace him.

"I heard about Shular."

"Do not be sad for me," he replied. "Her time has come."

"She is your mother."

"True. She is the one who birthed me, and I have no doubt she loved me in her own way, but all that changed once I became an adult."

"She was still a shaman and a great Orc."

"Yes, and I will honour her for it, but do not ask me to weep for her."

"That I would never do," said Zhura, "for I know your heart. It will always yearn for what never was."

Urgon sat by the fire. "You know me so well."

She sat by his side. "And is that a bad thing?"

"No, of course not."

The voice of Kurghal called from outside. "Urgon?"

"Enter, Sister."

She stepped into the hut, her face betraying her news.

"I gather she has passed?"

Kurghal simply nodded but did not leave. He noted her hesitancy.

"Speak freely," he said. "You are amongst friends."

She cast her eyes around, unsure. "There is something you should know. Something Mother kept from you."

Urgon's interest was immediately piqued. "Go on."

"When the Dwarves came, they left a gift."

"I remember hearing of it," said Urgon, "though Shular knew it not. What was the nature of this gift?"

"I believe it best if you saw for yourself," said Kurghal. "Come with me, and I will show you."

He looked at Zhura, a question in his eyes.

"I shall await you here," she announced.

Kurghal led them straight to the shameness's hut, where Kraloch stood watch over the body.

"She passed shortly after you left," the shaman explained, "but her words to you were her last."

"It matters little," said Urgon. "She has gone to join the Ancestors. No doubt she will lecture you from the spirit world in future."

"Here," said Kurghal. "Mother ordered me to bury the gifts. I held on to them for some time, hoping she would change her mind, but it was not to be. Eventually, I hid them beneath the fire."

"Beneath the fire? They will be burned to bits by now."

"Not so. I buried them deep." She extinguished the fire, then pushed the ash aside using her axe. Next, she dug up the dirt beneath, using her hands to scoop it off to the side.

"The mountain folk wanted us to have something to remember Urdar by. It is only fitting that these gifts go to you." She dug around some more, then a smile broke out. "Ah, here it is."

She pulled on something and then removed a large blue sack. It clanked as she set it down. "Open it," she said, "and see what lies within."

Urgon reached in, and the first thing he encountered was a metal hilt. Grabbing it, he hauled it out to reveal a sword in an ornate scabbard.

"A Dwarven sword," said Kraloch. "A gift worthy of a great hunter."

"No," said Urgon. "It is a warrior's weapon, not that of a hunter." He took hold of the hilt with one hand, the scabbard with the other, and drew forth the blade which sang as he pulled it free, echoing throughout the hut. It took but a moment for the noise to subside, and then Kurghal noted a faint blue sheen to its blade.

"That is a masterwork weapon," she said. "Such a tool could be blessed by the Ancestors."

"And what difference would that make?"

"Imbuing it with magic would make it even more formidable," said Kraloch. "I have heard of such a thing but am uncertain how it would be accomplished."

"YOU may not know," said Kurghal, "but my training was complete. I would be honoured to empower it for you."

"What would that entail?" asked Urgon.

"How much do you know about magic?"

"Very little."

"Then let me explain it to you. Magic harnesses an inner power to accomplish its effects. That energy replenishes over time, allowing us to cast more spells after a brief period of rest. Empowering an item, however, requires the permanent expenditure of some of that internal power."

"Permanent? You mean to say you would not recover it?"

"That is correct, although in time, I may regain it through rigorous study."

"And you would sacrifice that energy for me?"

"I would. You have been given a rare gift, Urgon, and I can make it rarer still. Our Ancestors speak of great weapons of the past, but no Orc in recent history has been so blessed."

"Thank you, Sister. I accept your offer." He held up the sword.

"Not yet," said Kurghal. "I shall need to consult the Ancestors before I begin the ritual."

"I suggest you talk to Zhura. Her connection to them might prove less taxing."

"An excellent idea," his sister replied.

"Might I remind you," said Kraloch, "something yet remains inside the sack."

Urgon put the sword back in its scabbard. Reaching in once more, his hand encountered the icy touch of metal, and he withdrew the prize —a shirt of chain links. He held it aloft, letting the light from the doorway reveal its design.

"This was made for an Orc," he said in awe.

"The Dwarves thought Urdar brave," said Kurghal, "and the mountain folk are said to have many such things in their halls of stone. It is not your place to question where it came from, but it is yours to wear. I said as much to our mother, but she preferred to see these items destroyed."

"But why?" asked Kraloch. "They are of such great value."

Kurghal shrugged. "Who can say? Perhaps she feared the influence of the mountain folk. Shular never liked outsiders."

Urgon looked at his sister. "You should have this."

"What need would a shaman have for such things? No, they are yours, Brother. Do with them what you will. I only ask one thing."

"Name it, and it shall be yours."

"Use these items for the betterment of the tribe, not for your own enrichment."

Urgon smiled. "Agreed. Of course, now I have a problem."

"Which is?"

"How does one use a sword?"

"I have no idea," replied Kurghal. "Do you, Kraloch?"

"No, nor do I know of any Orc hereabouts who is familiar with the weapon."

Urgon screwed up his face. "Then let us hope the Ancestors have knowledge of such things, or it shall become a very expensive stick with which to poke the fire."

"At least the armour would protect you from the tusks of a boar."

"So it would, although it might attract some unwanted attention."

"What if it does?" asked Kraloch. "It is a gift from the Dwarves, Urgon. You should be proud of that."

"What of this hut?" asked Kurghal.

"You are now the senior shaman, Sister," said Urgon. "It is yours, as is the custom. Now come, let us all see what Zhura makes of these gifts."


Zhura closed her eyes. Her hands were palm up in front of her, the sword resting there as she tried to make sense of the voices that drifted to her from the spirit realm. Occasionally she opened one eye, searching for some detail on the weapon, and then she closed it again.

Urgon had seen this sort of thing before, but it never grew old. Zhura was communing with the Ancestors, a powerful link to the spirit realm that allowed her to talk freely to those who had lived before.

Her voice bubbled from her mouth with such speed, he struggled to make out words, yet still, she talked. On and on she chatted until she finally opened both eyes and fell silent.

"Well," said Urgon, "it appears Zhura has succeeded."

"I have," replied the ghostwalker. "This blade bears the mark of Kalidor Bloodrock, the legendary swordsmith of Stonecastle."

"And can it be enchanted?"

"Empowered," interrupted Kurghal.

"What?"

"When we place magic upon something, it is empowered. Enchantments are a particular type of magic that is not commonly found amongst those of our race."

"Whatever you call it, can it be done?"

"Yes," said Zhura. "It is as your sister says."

"And what would be the actual effect?" asked Kraloch.

"That is difficult to say," said Kurghal. "It all depends on which Ancestors arrive to bless it when the spell is cast."

"She is correct," said Zhura. "Only then will the magic reveal itself."

Urgon turned to his sister. "Are you sure you want to go through with this?"

"Quite sure."

"What can we do to help?"

"I will require some rest. The ritual will be quite taxing."

"Where will you conduct this ritual?" asked Urgon.

"Here will do as well as anywhere else, although I must warn you not to interfere once my casting begins. In the meantime, I should like to lie down to recover my strength."

"Use our sleeping room," said Zhura. "You will find it dark and quiet."

"Thank you," said Kurghal. "I shall take you up on that offer."

Urgon waited until she had left, then turned to his bondmate. "Do any of the Ancestors know how to use a sword?"

"They do," said Zhura, "but it will be difficult to impart such knowledge to you, for I must act as a go-between."

"Learning weapons can be difficult," noted Kraloch. "You must take great care not to hurt Zhura."

"Then you and I will learn, Kraloch."

"Of what use is a sword to a shaman?"

"Come now, you never know when such a skill might come in handy, and in any case, it will be fun."

"Fun? What can be fun about killing?"

"You must make some wooden swords," said Zhura. "Do you think that is something you can manage?"

"I shall ask Arshug," said Urgon. "If I show her this Dwarven sword, she might be able to make a copy out of wood."

"Definitely worth a try," said Kraloch, "but she will need to make two if we are to fight each other. I have no wish to see either of us in need of healing."

Urgon chuckled. "You worry too much, my friend."

"And you, too little."


They gathered around the fire that evening, all eyes on Kurghal. She sat cross-legged, the sword resting on the ground before her. With her eyes closed, she uttered the words of power. Kraloch was familiar with the sounds, yet even he had not heard them combined in this way before.

Urgon watched with intense interest, eager to understand what was happening.

Kurghal's chanting continued for quite some time until the sound became a droning that threatened to lure them all to sleep. Urgon shook his head, then his sister spoke three distinct words in rapid succession, and he felt a slap as if the air itself had suddenly crackled.

"It is beginning," said Zhura. "I feel the spirits being drawn to her."

Urgon stared at his bondmate with a look of worry. Her face was starting to contort in pain, and he knew in his heart she could hear the sound of the spirits as they were closing in on his sister. He moved closer, throwing his arms around her even as she tried to cover her ears.

The air came alive as if thousands of insects swarmed them, and Urgon felt the hair on his arms stand up on end. His head ached, and for a brief moment, he thought his head might explode. He wanted to carry Zhura to safety, but his legs were pinned in place by an inexplicable force.

Kurghal's voice rose higher, her hair splaying out as a great wind rushed around them. Urgon closed his eyes, pressing his forehead to Zhura's, willing her pain away. The flames of the fire leaped into the air, singeing the ceiling of the hut while outside, the wolves howled.

Kurghal let out a blood-curdling scream and then fell backwards, landing with a thump. The wind suddenly died, and the fire returned to normal.

Zhura shook her head. "It is done."

Kraloch moved closer to Kurghal, ready to invoke his powers of healing, but the shaman blinked, then held up her hand.

"I am well," she said, "merely tired."

She sat back up and lifted the sword, admiring the blade which now glowed with an inner light. "It worked," she declared as she passed the weapon to Urgon. "Take it, Brother, and use it for the good of the tribe."

"I will," he promised. The sword felt light, much more so than he remembered. He stood, then swung it experimentally, finding it easy to use. "A marvellous weapon."

"It will give you strength and cut through the toughest of armour. Note the blade. It now holds runes."

"I see none," said Urgon.

"Then hold it over the fire, and they will appear."

Urgon did as he was bid. Glowing runes appeared—magical symbols that imbued the weapon with the power of the Ancestors. He passed it to Zhura.

"There is powerful magic here," she said. "Much more than I would expect."

"I think it was you," said Kurghal. "I called the spirits, but far more responded than I thought possible." She leaned forward and wiped some blood from Zhura's nose.

"By the Ancestors," said Kraloch. "Let me heal you." He began casting a spell of his own, that of healing flesh. His hands glowed, and as he touched them to her face, the colour briefly transferred to her skin, then dissipated.

"How do you feel?" asked Urgon.

"Fine," Zhura replied, "but let us refrain from such actions in the future." She got to her feet but then staggered. Urgon was there in the blink of an eye, steadying her.

"Come," he said. "You should rest."

She nodded. "Perhaps I was premature in my reply. I feel a great fatigue, as if I had lain awake all night."

"The effects of the magic," said Kurghal. "I, too, am weary, although not as much as you, it would seem."

"I shall take your sister home," said Kraloch. "You, meanwhile, must watch over Zhura. Whatever has happened appears to have taken a lot out of her."

Urgon led his bondmate into the sleeping chamber and laid her down amongst the furs. When her eyes closed, he turned to leave.

"Stay," she begged. "I would have you by my side, even if only in sleep."

"Then sleep, my beloved, and I shall stay here beside you until you awaken."

## EIGHTEEN

## Trade

SPRING 958 MC

It took only a good night's sleep for Kurghal to recover from the ordeal. True, her magic power had been diminished, but her physical condition improved immediately. Zhura, however, was another issue.

Whatever had taken place during the ceremony had produced a marked effect on her. She lay immobile for more than a ten-day, her mind seemingly lost and rambling. At Urgon's urging, Kraloch threw spell after spell at her, healing flesh and even removing toxins, but there was little improvement. It wasn't until halfway through the next ten-day that she finally found the strength to begin moving around the hut a little.

Urgon stayed at her side the entire time, determined to help in whatever way he could. Once they started getting regular food into her, her progress improved, and by spring, she was back to her former self.

Urgon swore off the sword, for in its empowerment, it had drawn too much energy from her, or so he told himself. In truth, he had no idea what had happened at all, but the glowing blade reminded him of the pain her infirmity had caused him.

Zhura, for her part, urged him to pick it up. "There is a part of me in it," she said. "And when you carry it, I am with you. All that remains now is for you to learn how to use it. Take it to Arshug, and have her make the wooden swords you spoke of months ago. Then you and Kraloch can begin."

"I shall," he promised, "although I have my reservations about using such a weapon. I am a hunter, not a warrior."

"Still, this sword has come into your possession. Use it to forge your destiny, Urgon. Lead the tribe into greatness like those of our past."

He shrugged it off, tried to see it as a flight of fancy, yet somehow it sank into the recesses of his mind, her words always there, a constant reminder of how things might be.

Urgon was thinking on this very matter when word came that Agrug had called for volunteers. It appeared he had a special expedition in mind, one, he had said, that would greatly enhance life for the Orcs. Urgon had his doubts, but word spread quickly, and many speculated on what their chieftain might have planned.

So it was that the master of wolves found himself in the chieftain's hut, along with a dozen others, waiting to be addressed by Agrug.

Urgon turned to Urzath. "What do you suppose this is?"

"A hunting expedition?"

"Then why all the secrecy? Why not come out and say that? We have gone on many such hunts in the past. What makes this one any different?"

"I have no answer for you. We shall just have to wait and see."

Agrug finally appeared, looking quite pleased with himself.

"Greetings," he said. "I can well imagine how curious you are, so I will get right to the point. For a long while, we have traded with the mountain folk which has brought us much to appreciate, whether it be their fine weapons or the soft cloth they weave. I am now proposing we expand our horizons and increase trade, not with the Dwarves, but with the Humans."

"Humans?" said Vulgar. "They seek to drive us farther into the hills."

"Not all of them," replied Agrug. "I have come to learn that they, like us, are divided into different groups, much as we have tribes. However, unlike us, their tribes do not get along."

"And so we antagonize one by trading with another?"

"I am not proposing an alliance, merely trade. We shall take that which we have in plenty."

"Which is?"

"Pelts, meat, possibly even some of our Dwarven goods."

"What could the Humans possibly have that we could use?"

"A good question," said Agrug. "I have been watching them for some time, and it has become quite evident they have much to offer."

"Such as?" asked Urzath.

"Knives, axes, even bows."

"We have a bowyer."

"Yes, but it takes Arshug days to craft a bow. The Humans have them in abundance."

"How do you know this?"

The chieftain stood tall. "I have been to their city."

They all looked at him in stunned silence.

"When?" said Urgon.

"Three nights ago."

"And they allowed this?"

Agrug smiled. "They were unaware of my presence. I walked through their village as they slept."

"What did you see?" asked Urgon.

"Their city huts are similar to those we saw in the countryside, but closer together." He wrinkled his nose. "It also stank."

"Do they not bathe?" asked Vulgar.

"There is no cliff from which to eliminate their waste. Instead they leave it outside their homes."

"That," said Urzath, "is disgusting."

"They also have armour to protect their warriors."

"You fought them?"

"No," said the chieftain, "but I saw them, although THEY did not see ME."

Urgon thought of his chainmail shirt. "What kind of armour?"

"The ones I saw wore a type of padded covering, along with a metal helmet and rings of metal that hung from their shoulders."

"Chainmail," said Urgon.

"What?"

"The metal rings are called chainmail."

"How do you know that?" asked Agrug.

"My bondmate talks to spirits, remember? She knows much of such things."

"These are things that would benefit us," continued the chieftain. "What say you?"

"I feel it worth pursuing," said Urzath, "although how to actually approach them is beyond me."

"I shall take care of that," said Agrug. "What of the rest of you?"

Skulnug nodded. "Armour would protect us on the hunt, especially when going after boar."

"When did you start worrying about such things?" said Urzath. "You are the stealthiest of us all. Would not wearing metal make your job more difficult?"

"Possibly, but I would gladly give that up to be protected from tusks."

Agrug looked around the room. "Mull it over for a day and let me know your answer."

"If we did agree," said Urzath, "when would we leave?"

"In three days. That will allow us time to celebrate the high spring before we go."

"Why us?" asked Urgon. "Why not consult the entire tribe?"

"You know as well as I that the tribe is too set in its ways. I need Orcs who are not afraid to try something new. The risk is great, but so are the potential rewards. Let us alter the course of our future, my friends. The Ancestors would wish it."

Urgon doubted Agrug had consulted the Ancestors but held his tongue. "We shall consider it." He rose, as did the rest, and made their way from the hut.

Urzath walked beside him but waited until they were outside to speak. "What did you make of that?"

"You mean Agrug's plan to contact the Humans? I must admit to some trepidation. The relationship between our two races is said to be a tumultuous one."

"Is that what Zhura told you?"

Urgon nodded. "The Ancestors have opinions on everything, but they are not always in agreement with each other. This is one such case."

"Meaning?"

"They say that once, in the distant past, Humans and Orcs worked together."

"I have not heard of this?"

"That is because it happened in a land far removed from here, in a place called Therengia."

"And what happened? Did we flourish?"

"For a while, and then the other Humans turned on them. Now they are scattered once more, and Orcs have become hunted where once they dwelled."

"Why such an interest in this?"

"Do you remember when Shular died?"

"Of course I do. It was scarcely more than two seasons ago. Why?"

"She hid something from me, a gift from the Dwarves."

"What type of gift?"

"A sword," said Urgon, "and some armour."

"You have armour?"

"I do, but it is the sword that interests me more. They are said to be common amongst the Humans."

"Ah," said Urzath. "So you had Zhura speak to the Ancestors about them."

"I did. It was most informative."

"You are starting to sound like a shaman."

Urgon grinned. "I shall take that as a compliment."

They halted before his hut. "Come inside, and we shall discuss it further."

"While this discussion is most intriguing, I must decline the offer. I promised Arshug that she and I would go hunting today, and our chieftain's meeting has already delayed me."

"Maybe another time," said Urgon. "I wish you good hunting."

He stepped inside to be greeted by Zhura.

"You have news?" she asked.

"Yes. It seems Agrug wants us to trade with the Humans."

"I gather you are not in agreement on this?"

"I have my doubts," he admitted.

"Then tell me of his plans, and we can reason out the best course of action."

"I have nothing against these Humans, but they often fight amongst themselves. How do we know these are the right ones to deal with?"

"Why would you think not?"

"You told me Orcs were once on friendly terms with Humans."

"Yes, I did," she said. "And that is precisely what the Ancestors told me."

"Yet our people have also been hunted by others. How, then, am I to tell the difference?"

"It is a difficult question."

"And what would be your counsel?"

"To judge for yourself," said Zhura. "Meet these Humans; form your own opinion of them, and, most importantly, follow your heart. It has served you well so far."

"Good advice."

"Of course. Nothing but the best for you, bondmate."

"Then I shall agree to accompany Agrug on this mission of his."

"Might I suggest something that might prove a benefit in the long term?"

"By all means," said Urgon.

"Take every opportunity to learn their language."

"Why?"

"The Humans you meet might reveal things in their own tongue that they have no desire for you to know. It would give you an advantage."

Urgon smiled. "So it would. I shall learn to speak their language. Anything else?"

"Yes," she said, moving closer. "You shall be gone for some time. Come to the sleeping chamber, and let me give you a proper send-off."

"It is three days until we leave."

Zhura smiled. "Then we shall have two days to practice for the parting."


Three days later found them heading west, descending into the Rugar plains. The terrain here was much flatter than that of their home, allowing swift progress. Had it not been for the goods they carried, they would have been even faster, but there was no point in going if they had nothing to trade in return, so they slowed to conserve their strength.

The land was abundant with game, and Urgon looked on wistfully as distant deer grazed the long grass. He briefly wondered why the Orcs didn't settle this region, and then he remembered—the Humans lived here, and they did not tolerate the presence of his people so close to their city.

They camped in the open, for the air was warmer out of the hills, and trees were plentiful, providing fuel for the fire. They spotted farmland as they drew closer, and then the great Human city of Eastwood came into view.

Urgon had never seen anything like it. The Human buildings were immense, with many made of stone, but it was not only their size that astounded him, it was the construction. Used as he was to the huts of his own people, they paled in comparison to the thatched and tiled roofs of this place.

These dwellings were made of stout timbers, with walls of mud mixed with straw. Even the smallest of buildings were three times the size of his own hut, leading him to wonder what the Humans did with all the extra space.

Agrug picked a field on the outskirts of the city, just off the strange pathway that led south. Here they set up a camp, building a fire and watching the road for any signs of movement. They didn't need to wait long, for right as they lit a fire, a small group of horsemen rode out from the city.

"Here they come," said Agrug. "Let me do the talking."

Urgon watched as their leader stepped forward, his hands held up on either side well away from his weapons. There was a brief discussion, but they were too far away to overhear.

"He speaks Human?" said Urzath.

"Apparently," Urgon replied. "It looks like he has met them before."

"Then why not tell us this beforehand? Something is amiss here. I do not like it."

"Nor I, but we must be patient."

One of the men climbed down from his horse, then walked towards the camp with Agrug at his side. There was more talk in the Human tongue, and Urgon heard his name and those of the other Orcs. Their chieftain looked quite pleased with himself.

"Come," Agrug said as he turned towards his hunting party. "We have been invited to enter the city. These men will accompany us."

"What of the camp?" asked Urzath.

"Leave it. We shall return before dusk."

"Someone should watch our goods," said Vulgar. "Else animals will get into them."

"A good point," replied Agrug. "I shall take Urzath, Urgon, and Tarluk with me. The rest of you can stay here."

"And if you should fail to return?"

"Do not fear, for we shall be safe. Relax and enjoy yourselves. When we return, there will be much to celebrate."

Urgon felt an unease settle over him. Agrug had arranged something; he was sure of it. The real question was what that something was. He grabbed a stack of skins, then made his way to the road, where the mounted men waited. Urzath soon joined him, loaded up with her own goods. Tarluk, easily the oldest of them all, carried a bag full of Dwarven hatchets, rumoured to be quite valuable amongst Humans. Urgon now had to wonder if he might not have been tipped off on this by Agrug himself.

They headed north, the horsemen riding on either side while their leader, atop his own mount, trotted beside Agrug.

The outskirts of the city gave way to the edge of town, and they were soon surrounded by buildings that felt too closed in on either side. City folk watched them go by, many with looks of horror or fear. Urgon thought it strange seeing all the Human faces, but the emotions on display were little different from those of his own people.

The maze of streets had them turning at odd angles as they walked, leading to the feeling that, should they wish to leave, they would be forced to wander the streets for days in order to find the countryside.

Eventually, they arrived at an enormous building with an open green space before it. Agrug turned to address the rest of the party.

"This," he announced, "is the home of the Human in charge. He is something called an earl, a chieftain in our own tongue. We shall go inside and be his guests."

Other soldiers, these on foot, soon arrived, allowing the horsemen to ride off. They then led the Orcs through a metal gate and past the open green area. Urgon had to look twice to realize it was grass, neatly cut to a short length. He shook his head, trying to reason out why something like that was done. It certainly looked pleasant to the eye, but there must be another reason why they trimmed it so short?

Into the massive building they went, to be swallowed up by walls taller than even the chieftain's hut. Towering stone columns supported a roof that appeared incredibly high. Urgon had to admit it was a comfortable feeling, with fresh air aplenty, but how did they warm it in the winter? It would require a bonfire the likes of which he had never seen.

They were escorted into a slightly smaller room in which a long, wooden construction stretched the length. Around it were strange structures made of sticks and planks. He struggled to understand the significance, then Agrug sat, explaining that these were chairs. Urgon copied the motion, resting his arms on the longer wooden construct.

"This," said the chieftain, "is a table. We meet thus because it is the Human way. The man we are about to talk with represents their earl and speaks with some authority.

"Like a shaman?" suggested Urzath.

"Yes, but without the magic."

"Their shamans have no magic?"

Agrug grew impatient. "I was making a comparison only. This man speaks for his master. That was the point."

"Master?" said Urgon. "Are they master and slave? We do not believe in such things, Agrug. Why did you bring us here?"

"This man is not a slave. They use the term master as a sign of respect only, not as an indication of ownership."

"There is so much to learn," said Urzath.

They waited in silence, the Humans taking up positions by the doors. Urgon used the time to survey his surroundings. The men guarding the exit wore chainmail that covered almost their entire body. He also noticed something else—the scabbards on their belts were similar to what held his own magic sword. What would it be like to fight such a person? Hopefully, the metal would prevent any actual damage. Did that mean they would need to whale on each other until the metal gave way? Urgon was keenly aware he had left his own mail at home. He promised himself not to do so again.

The door opened, revealing a beardless Human who said something only Agrug could understand. He was followed by a trio of other Humans, and then they all sat at the head of the table.

More doors opened, startling Urgon, and for a moment, he thought they might have sprung a trap, but it was only another group of Humans carrying platters of food. These they laid down in front of their guests before scurrying from the room.

All the while, Agrug chatted with their host. It was now crystal clear their chieftain had been in communication with the Humans for some time. The real question was, why? Why would Agrug hide this information from the rest of the tribe?

"Look at this," said Urzath, breaking open a loaf of bread. Steam rose from its soft interior while a pleasant smell drifted out. "I assume this to be bread, but it is unlike anything I have ever seen before? Certainly much different from our own."

Agrug chuckled. "The Humans grow their wheat in fields, not harvest it from the wild as we do." He returned his attention to their Human host.

"I do not trust this Human," whispered Urgon. "He lies, or Agrug does."

"How do you know?" replied Urzath.

"He called their leader an earl and described him as a chieftain."

"And what of it?"

"The Ancestors tell us the Humans are ruled by kings."

"Maybe he is only the equivalent of a village elder?"

"If you were welcoming outsiders," said Urgon, "would you not tell of your own chieftain?"

"I would. What should we do?"

"Keep your eyes and ears open, and a close eye on Agrug."

# NINETEEN

## The Price

SPRING 959 MC

They left their trade goods behind as they departed the city. Urgon found the entire situation confusing, for they had received nothing in return. Agrug, however, looked quite pleased, an attitude that earned him Urgon's attention once they returned to their campsite.

"Agrug," he said. "Why have we left them everything, while we received nothing in return?"

"Wait and see," replied the chieftain. "We are to receive riches beyond imagining."

Urgon scowled but said no more. They remained in their camp that night but talked little. Come morning, he expected to be up and moving, for home was a full three days of travel, yet still, Agrug waited. It wasn't until mid-morning that the answer presented itself in the form of a wagon pulled by two horses and driven by a man wearing a weather-beaten cloak.

Agrug had words with him, then turned to his tribemates. "Come," he said. "Pick what you will from the wagon. These are the goods that are offered in exchange."

"How many do we take?"

"As much as you can carry."

Urgon climbed up, rooting through the sacks and baskets.

"What do you see?" asked Urzath.

"Mostly knives and spears. There are also some arrows, but they appear to be of inferior quality." He picked up an iron pot. "What is this?"

Urzath came up beside him. "It looks like a metal bowl."

Urgon smiled. "A bowl such as this could be heated over a fire."

"I have seen something like this before. The Dwarves brought one with them when they visited. Of course, you were still a youngling in those days. I doubt you remember it."

"I remember the Dwarves, but not the bowls." He rooted around some more. "Blankets," he said, passing one to Urzath, "and plenty of them."

"They are soft. I think they would ward off the chill of winter quite well. I will take one."

"Only one? I would suggest we each take two. We can hand them out once we return home."

"And the metal bowls?"

"A little awkward to carry. Perhaps only one of those will suffice. There are knives aplenty, but they look ill-suited to the hunt."

"They are for eating," said Agrug, "not skinning prey. Did you not notice them when we sat at the earl's table?"

"You speak their language well," said Urgon. "Could you teach us their tongue?"

"Eventually, but I have more important things to look after for the moment. Now come, select your prizes. We must be on our way."

Urgon took several blankets, then dropped from the back of the wagon, allowing his tribemates to select their own rewards. He watched them pick through the goods, all the while wondering why the earl was so generous.

They set off soon after, crossing the flat land that led, eventually, back to the hills they called home. Urgon waited until the city had fallen from sight before engaging Agrug in conversation.

"Tell me, my chief, why is the earl so charitable?"

"It is his nature."

"To give so much with so little in return? I find that hard to believe."

"We can learn a lot from the Humans, Urgon. You would do well to remember that."

"I am not opposed to these gifts. I merely wish to know the price we pay in return. There must be more to this than pelts and meat?"

Agrug smiled. "There is indeed, but I shall speak no more of it at present. Suffice it to say our place in the world will be safe once more."

"And once we are home, will you tell us the rest?"

"Soon," the chieftain replied, "but I must gather the tribe first. When we are closer, we will split up: your group returning home to Ord-Dugath while I visit the other villages."

"And how long before we assemble as a tribe?"

"At least a ten-day, possibly more. In the meantime, pass your goods around, and tell everyone of the riches you saw. Mark my words; this is only the beginning, my friend. The Orcs of the Black Arrow will lead the way to a new future for our people."

Agrug jogged ahead, leading Urgon to ponder his words. Whatever he had planned, it was something big.


Try as he may, Urgon proved unable to get any more information out of their chieftain. Urzath proved no more successful than he, and so they found themselves once more sitting by the fire in the company of Zhura and Kraloch.

"Come," said his bondmate, "tell me of your suspicions, and I will tell you of mine."

"Agrug is up to something," replied Urgon, "although I am unable to ascertain what."

"Something big," added Urzath. "He mentioned it would shape the very future of our people."

"Yes," said Urgon, "but not our tribe. A distinction that might be important."

Kraloch leaned forward. "And you say he spoke the Human tongue?"

"He did, and quite well."

"Then he has been in contact with them for some time," said Zhura.

"Time enough to hatch some strange plan," said Urzath, "but once again, the question returns to what?"

Urgon shook his head. "Urzath and I spent the better part of three days trying to make head or tail of this, to no avail. Can either of you think of something that might explain all this?" He swept his arm to encompass the goods brought back from the city of Eastwood.

"Maybe he is currying favour?" said Kraloch. "We received far more than what our own goods warranted."

"But that would be Agrug's doing," said Urgon, "yet these goods came from the earl."

"Then it is the earl who seeks favour."

"We saw his city," said Urzath. "He has many soldiers with which he could conquer us. Why, then, does he offer these gifts?"

"He will ask for something else," said Zhura. "Something he has not yet named."

"Like what?"

"I do not know," she continued, "but I imagine the truth will eventually come out. No one can hold a secret forever, and if it is as big as Agrug says, he will need to address it at some point."

"He is gathering the tribe," noted Urzath. "I imagine that is when he will make the announcement."

"I have my doubts," said Zhura. "Orcs do not do well with sudden change. You experienced that yourself, my love, when you announced our intention to bond. I think this meeting of the tribe is only the beginning."

"What would you suggest we do?"

"Listen carefully to his words. He may yet give some clue as to what he has planned. In the meantime, I have another idea, but it is not to be shared."

"An idea or a plan?" said Urgon.

"Call it what you will, but it will take Kraloch to make it work."

"Me?" said the shaman. "What could I possibly do to help decipher Agrug's plan?"

"You can speak to tribes in distant lands through the use of your magic."

"And? What of it?"

"Some of them trade with Humans and would know their language."

"Are we sure they all speak the same language?"

Zhura smiled. "The Ancestors tell me Humans developed something they call the common tongue. It is used across most of the Continent, as well as those who settled in these lands. Seek out those who can speak it, learn it yourself, and then teach it to Urgon and Urzath."

"And what of you?"

"I shall learn it from Urgon, of course, although it is less important to me."

"Why would you say that?" asked Kraloch.

"I am not in a position to overhear anything. You, on the other hand, may be allowed to make another trip to Eastwood, in which case you must not reveal you know their language."

Urgon smiled. "We would be able to understand what was being said between Agrug and the earl's man."

"Yes, and that may prove their undoing in the long run."

As a shaman, one of the spells Kraloch was able to call upon was spirit talk. Using it, he could communicate with Orcs in places far removed from their own, for the spirit realm held no concept of distance. It took some time, but he reached out to all he could, finally contacting a tribe known as the Crimson Spears. They lived in a far-flung place they referred to as The Wilderness and traded with the Humans who had settled close by. Thus it was that Kraloch, shaman of the Black Arrows, began learning the Human tongue.

Agrug finally returned to Ord-Dugath, having sent word a day in advance that he was bringing the tribe elders with him. This sent hunters scurrying to track down food and fill their larders, for the population of their village was about to increase substantially.

They gathered, as was the custom, by the chieftain's hut, but with the weather being unseasonably warm, they chose to meet by the great outside firepit.

Urgon sat by Kraloch while Urzath made her way closer to the chieftain, the better to possibly overhear what was being said. Agrug chatted for a while before standing, an action that demanded everyone's attention.

"Greetings," he said. "I know many of you are wondering why I called this meeting, but fear not, I shall soon reveal that very thing. Let me first, however, talk of how life might be if things were different. Our people wandered for generations, finally settling down here, amongst these ancient hills, not by choice, but by necessity. The land we inhabit is sparse, and our hunters must range far and wide to feed us." Many of the elders thumped the ground with their fists, showing their agreement.

"Had we but lived on the plains," he continued, "we would have thrived!" He held up his hands as many argued his statement. "It is true that we would have perished living there, not through lack of game but because our enemies would have driven us out." He waited, letting his eyes scan the crowd. "Now, imagine a future where we could do so without fear of attack."

Urgon's ears pricked up.

"The ruler of the Humans, the Earl of Eastwood himself, has offered us this very thing—land to call our own in the fertile Rugar Plains."

"And what would he ask in return?" asked Urzath.

"Our friendship," replied Agrug. "The Humans have much to occupy their time. They wish only for peace and freedom from tyranny."

Urgon turned to Kraloch. "Tyranny? What is he talking about?"

His companion shushed him, too interested in what was being said.

"For too long, our people have scraped out a meagre living from these hills. It is time we took our rightful place beside the Humans."

"Are you suggesting we submit to their rule?"

"No," said Agrug, "of course not, but can we not benefit from their presence? You have all seen the riches the earl has sent us. I can assure you much more is coming."

This looked to garner an appreciative response, but Urgon felt the hairs on his neck stand on end. "What are you up to?" he whispered to himself.

"I called you together that I might explain how this can benefit us." The chieftain continued on, but Urgon's mind was racing. Agrug was leading them somewhere, but by the Ancestors, he knew not where this would all stop. He berated himself for missing the chieftain's words and turned his attention, once more, to Agrug.

"They have much to offer," he was saying.

"And what is the price?" came a voice.

Agrug searched the crowd until he found the source. "Stand, Arshug. You are my sister, and I would have you heard."

The bowyer stood. "What is the price we must pay," she demanded.

"The earl will be content with trade for the present."

"The present?"

"Yes, but the trading of goods can lead to so much more."

"Such as?"

Agrug waved his hands, dismissing the thought. "Future friendship. Now, is there anyone else who has questions?" He looked around, too quickly for Urgon's liking, then dismissed the assembly, making his way inside the chieftain's hut.

"That was short," said Kraloch.

"Agreed," said Urgon. "And still, we have no inkling of what he plans."

"We need help."

"What kind of help?"

"Someone who can get close enough to Agrug to hear what he plans."

"And do you know anyone capable of that?"

Kraloch smiled. "As a matter of fact, I believe I do."


The moon, high in the sky, cast its eerie glow over Ord-Dugath. Zhura sat, stirring the pot, letting its aroma fill the hut.

"You soon mastered that," said Urgon.

"How much longer must it cook?" asked Kraloch. "My stomach is already growling."

"It will be but a moment," said Zhura. "You must be patient."

"Are you in?" came a whispered voice.

"Skulnug?" called out Kraloch.

"Yes. Who else would be calling at this time of night?"

"Come in quickly before you wake the entire village."

The flaps parted, revealing the short-statured Orc known for his stealth skills.

"What did you learn?" asked Urgon.

"Too much and yet not enough."

"You speak in riddles," said Kraloch. "Explain yourself."

Skulnug moved to stand before the fire, taking a deep sniff of the pot. "That smells delicious."

"Would you like some?" asked Zhura.

"The news, Skulnug!" exclaimed Urgon. "Get to it before we die of hunger!"

Skulnug sat. "You were right to be wary of Agrug. I overheard him talking to Tarluk. It appears he does, indeed, have an ulterior motive."

"Which is?"

"He means to take us to war."

"War?" said Urgon. "Are you sure?"

Skulnug nodded. "Absolutely. The Earl of Eastwood desires the throne of Merceria, the Human name for their land."

"Throne?" said Kraloch.

"The symbol of their power," said Zhura. "It is the place on which the ruler sits, but I suspect when he says he desires the throne, he means he wants to rule the land as king."

"Precisely," said Skulnug. "And Agrug aims to help put him there. In return, the earl had promised us land to call our own."

"We already call this land our own," noted Urgon.

"Yes, but the plains are much more hospitable."

"And can we trust this Human, the earl?"

"I cannot say. I only repeat what I heard. The minds of Humans are a mystery to me."

"And have you any idea when this is to happen?"

"Not for some time, apparently," said Skulnug. "There was talk of the earl sending men here to Ord-Dugath before the plan can proceed."

"To what end?"

"To teach us how to fight."

"We already know how to fight!" insisted Urgon.

"Not with the weapons of Humans. They will come in wagons, he said, bringing armour, amongst other things."

"Are you sure of this?"

"Absolutely," said Skulnug.

"And who would we be fighting?" asked Kraloch.

"That remains to be seen. As I said, he spoke of taking the throne, but what that entails is meaningless to me. I know so little of the Human lands."

"A lack we all share. What think you, Urgon?"

"Summer is almost upon us," replied Urgon, "yet he says men are coming to train us. If he needs an army, as you say, he will need many Orcs to fill his ranks, and that would require time to train."

"So in the autumn, then?"

Urgon nodded. "Possibly even later. At a guess, I would say we would march next spring."

"That long?" said Skulnug.

"Remember what we learned at Eastwood? The Humans grow their own wheat. To support a population like we saw would require much food. Autumn is when such plants are at their highest, meaning many Humans would be needed to gather what has grown. Wouldn't you agree, Zhura?"

She nodded. "I believe your assessment accurate."

"Can we trust these Humans?" asked Skulnug. "Or will they turn on us once they have what they want?"

"I wish I knew," said Urgon. "The truth is, we lack the experience with Humans to say for sure."

"However," said Zhura, "it buys us time. If the Humans come here to train us, then we have the opportunity to learn more. You can put your training in their language to use."

"I have only learned a handful of words," said Kraloch.

"You have time yet," she replied. "Be patient. The opportunity will present itself."

"And when they come?" asked Urgon.

"Then we welcome them. Maybe you can convince them to train you in the use of the sword. The Ancestors know you have learned little in that regard so far."

"I have been fairly busy of late."

"I am merely stating facts, not assigning blame."

"This war," said Skulnug, "why does it bother you so? Do you not wish to fight?"

"War means battle," said Urgon, "and battle ultimately results in death. I would not see our numbers reduced only to satisfy the greed of others."

"But we would be given land," Skulnug replied. "Land in which we could live in peace."

"If that were true, it would be cause enough for war, but I still have my doubts. A person who is willing to fight against their chieftain, as this earl does, is not to be trusted."

"A wise observation," said Zhura. "Who is to say that one who turns on his chieftain might not also turn on his ally once no longer needed."

"An Orc would never betray their chieftain!" said Kraloch.

"True," said Urgon, "but the earl is no Orc, and their king no chieftain."

"Then what are we to do?"

"The path has already been laid before us. There is little we can do to change it. With the support of the tribe, Agrug will do what he feels is right."

"And if he is wrong?" asked Kraloch.

"Then we may all end up joining the Ancestors."

# TWENTY

## Strangers

SUMMER 959 MC

With the warmer weather came the first of the wagons. Loaded with blankets, pots, and spears, they were accompanied by half a dozen Human warriors who met with Agrug out of sight of the rest of the tribe.

Urgon began to worry. The change was subtle at first—Orcs becoming enamoured with the gifts, but then more wagons followed, each one carrying an increasing number of weapons. By mid-summer, the wagons were packed with bows, axes, and knives, the earl's men no longer caring to hide their plans.

With the weapons came more Human warriors, and then the training began. It started with only a few Orcs learning fighting techniques. Then, as others watched, interest grew until almost the entire village was participating.

Throughout the summer, Kraloch's knowledge of the Human tongue grew by leaps and bounds. He passed this on to his cousin Urzath and, of course, Urgon, but they all decided it would be best to keep such knowledge to themselves, at least for the present.

At Zhura's urging, Urgon took advantage of the training to learn the use of a sword, along with a dozen others. This he did with a weapon the Humans brought, for he wanted to keep the presence of his own sword a secret.

So it was that on the hottest day of the year, Urgon found himself sparring with a Human warrior named Haldrath. The man was quick but nowhere near as strong as an Orc, a fact which became all too apparent after numerous ten-days of such training.

Urgon parried a blow, then struck out with the tip, feeling the wooden blade sink into the man's padded jacket. He had not used his full strength, but he had no doubt his Dwarven sword would have had no trouble penetrating the armour. Haldrath raised his hands, the signal that the fight was over, then walked over to where a cluster of his friends gathered.

"*These greenskins learn fast,*" he said, using the Human tongue.

"*Perhaps TOO fast,*" replied his comrade. "*I should hate to fight them when the time comes.*"

Urgon struggled to appear uninterested in their discussion, settling instead for rummaging through the barrel of weapons. His attention, however, was far from unfocused.

"*Don't worry,*" said Haldrath. "*They'll wear themselves out fighting the king's forces. By the time the battle's over, all we'll need to do is mop up.*"

The words were hard to understand, but their meaning was clear. The Humans meant to betray them! How, then, should he proceed?

His first thought was to inform Agrug, but he wondered if their chieftain might not be involved in this plot. Urgon found it unthinkable that an Orc might betray his own people, but something about Agrug's secrecy bothered him. He resolved to seek advice from the others.

How ironic that he was the one to oppose change. He, who had broken convention by daring to befriend a ghostwalker and then bond with her. He glanced around, noting the looks of determination on the faces of his fellow villagers as they practiced their newfound skills.

Since their cities were destroyed, Orcs had prided themselves on their hunting skills. Yet, now the earl's men were turning them into the very things Humans despised—savage warriors.

Savage. Urgon found even the term distasteful. His tribe had lived in relative peace for generations, allowing them to flourish, but now, at the behest of this Human earl, they would march to war, unleashing a fury that could only lead to disaster. Clearly, Agrug intended to lead the tribe into ruin. What could he do? Challenge Agrug for the leadership of the Black Arrows? While Urgon could now wield a sword, he was also intelligent enough to know he was no match for the chieftain.

. . .

That evening found him sitting by the fire surrounded by friends.

"What will you do?" asked Kraloch.

"I am caught between the bear and the spear. If I talk of this to Agrug and he is aware of their treachery, I shall only endanger myself. Yet if I do nothing, the end will come as assuredly as the sun sets."

"There is always the possibility Agrug is unaware of the Human's betrayal."

"Agreed," said Urzath. "He is an Orc, and our people do not willingly bring destruction upon our own. I consider it far more likely he is as much a victim here as we."

"I would tend to agree," said Kraloch. "What do you think, Zhura?"

"It is a difficult choice, but one thing is for certain, if we do nothing, things can only get worse."

"Then I must talk to Agrug," said Urgon, "and make him see reason. I am sure he wishes only the best for the tribe."

"One would certainly hope so," said Kraloch. "Else he is unworthy to wear the torc."

"Torc?" said Zhura.

"Yes, the symbol of leadership. The Orc who wears it is recognized by all as the chieftain of the tribe. I thought you were aware of such things?"

"I have only seen a chieftain once, at Urgon's trial, and I was much too distracted by the Ancestors at the time. Tell me of this torc."

"It is made of metal and hangs around the neck as all torcs do. It bears the symbol of an arrow, representing our tribe, although how that came to symbolize our people is beyond me."

"That is easily explained," said Zhura. "Our founder, Dugath, wandered in these hills until near death. Unable to choose where to settle, he finally let loose with an arrow, founding this very village where it fell. Thus, we call this place Ord-Dugath, the village of Dugath."

"I have heard the story," said Urzath, "but I always assumed it a tale to entertain younglings."

"It is no tall tale," said Zhura, "for I have spoken to Dugath's spirit."

"And he told you naught of the torc?"

"That is a much more recent tradition," said Kraloch. "It dates back only a hundred years. The Dwarves of Stonecastle gave it to us as a gift."

"Is it valuable?" asked Zhura.

"Only as a symbol of leadership. We are scattered amongst many villages. Not every Orc would recognize our leader, thus we use this token to identify them."

"It is an interesting tale," said Urgon, "but we are no closer to making a decision on what to do."

"I say you talk to Agrug," offered Urzath.

"I would agree," said Kraloch, "although the decision would, of course, be yours to make."

Urgon turned to Zhura. "I would have your thoughts on the matter."

"We have little choice," she replied. "Thus, I agree with our friends."

"Then the choice is made. I shall seek an audience with Agrug come morning. There I will discuss our fears."

The next day Urgon rose early, but the closer he came to the chieftain's hut, the more uncertain he felt. Humans were now a common sight within the village, and the two standing on either side of the entrance were no exception.

Urgon gave them only a cursory glance, then entered the massive structure. He angled off to the right, heading towards the chieftain's room, only to see Agrug emerge.

"Urgon? Are you here to see me?"

"I am. I have an important matter to discuss with you."

He noted a flicker of annoyance, but the chieftain remained gracious, nonetheless.

"Then come inside"—Agrug beckoned—"and you can tell me what concerns you."

Urgon followed him through the doorway, then they both took a seat on the furs littering the ground.

"Let me guess," said Agrug. "You are uncomfortable with the Humans in our midst. I fear it is a common enough feeling amongst our people."

"Then why are they here?"

"To help make the tribe stronger."

"By arming us?" asked Urgon. "Such an act can only lead to war."

"And what if it does?" said Agrug. "We were once a strong race, Urgon. We can be so again."

"Preparing for battle will only lead us to it. Many lives will be lost."

The chieftain nodded. "There are always deaths in battle, my friend, but the rewards are well worth it. Imagine how our life will be living on the plains. We shall have all the game we want."

"At what price? How many lives must we sacrifice for that greater good? Would you be so eager to go to war if your own life were forfeit?"

"The strong survive," said Agrug. "It has always been the way with our people."

"No, we look after those who are unable to look after themselves. You brought Humans to Ord-Dugath, Agrug. Humans! This has never been done before."

"What else would you have me do? War is coming, Urgon, and to face it, we must take up arms, either that or be wiped out."

"You talk of a war amongst the Humans. It is none of our concern."

"Ah, but it is, and when the earl is successful, we will have a rich land to call our own."

"Do you seriously believe the Humans will allow us to live in peace after all is said and done? They armed us, but they will not permit us to remain so."

Agrug leaned forward, his eyes boring into Urgon. "Our tribe will prosper. What matters if a few must give their lives?"

"How can you be so callous? You, who have taken up the task of leading us? You speak of prosperity while just as easily dismissing the losses we must bear to do so. What gives you the right to make this choice on their behalf?"

Agrug tapped the torc that hung around his neck. "This gives me the right. I am the chieftain of the Black Arrows, and I make the decisions as to the fate of our people."

Urgon stood, his temper flaring. "I will NOT let you do this!"

"Oh? And how will you stop me? You had your chance to be chieftain, Urgon, and you squandered it. If you hadn't been wasting your time with your ghostwalker, you might have won the right to lead the tribe."

Urgon clenched his fist. He wanted to strike out and knock some sense into the chieftain, but it would only lead to a savage beating on his behalf. Agrug was a towering hulk and perfectly capable of taking him down.

"Then you will not change your mind?" Urgon asked.

"I will not."

"What if I told you the Humans are plotting treachery?"

"Is that how you hope to persuade me otherwise? By making up such things?"

"I am not making it up!" Urgon saw the smile crossing Agrug's face. There was no sign of shock or indignation to his news. No, clearly, the chieftain was fully aware of what was to transpire. His shoulders slumped as the full implications flooded over him. The tribe was doomed. Agrug and his followers would doubtless prosper, but at what cost?

"It is clear you have made up your mind on this," said Urgon. "We shall speak no more of it."

"Good, then our meeting is concluded." Agrug paused. "Oh, and Urgon?"

"Yes?"

"Keep your opinions to yourself. If I hear word you are spreading such thoughts to others, I shall be forced to take action."

Urgon felt his face flush. He wanted to argue the point, but something told him not to do so. "You may rest assured I shall spread nothing but the truth." He stormed from the room.


Urgon lay awake that evening, his mind churning. Sleep finally claimed him only for Zhura to wake him in the middle of the night. Through the open window, soft moonlight bathed the room, allowing him to notice the concern on her face.

"What is it?" he asked.

"A noise," she whispered. "Someone is in our hut."

He lifted his head, straining to listen, then heard a footfall coming from the living area. Urgon was instantly awake and reaching for his sword. He drew it, letting the blue glow of its blade fill the room.

"Stay here," he whispered.

The doorway between the rooms was separated by two hides, hanging side by side. These he parted with his left hand while his right tightly gripped his weapon.

The living area contained a firepit, and scattered around it were some of the pots and pans the Humans had brought here in trade. Even as he watched, the two intruders drifted around the room, stumbling in the dark, on the hunt for something.

It was when they lifted the furs that he realized what was happening. These Humans were searching for Zhura and him, but they struggled to accomplish their goal without the Orcs' night vision.

The room was illuminated with a blue light as Urgon stepped in, and the closest one gave a yell, swinging out with his sword. The blow was easily parried, and then Urgon struck, the tip of his blade scraping across the man's chest.

His opponent stepped back slightly, fearful of the magic blade, while the other advanced, mace in hand. Urgon jabbed at the nearest, letting the man think he had successfully blocked it, then raised his arm for an overhead swing. When his foe lifted his own sword for another block, Urgon's Dwarven blade came down, the Orc's strength more than enough to knock the weapon aside. His blade cut into the shoulder, driving the man to the ground with a scream. Urgon paused to watch the man fall, too engrossed to pay attention to his surroundings.

The sudden pain of a mace striking his arm soon reminded him of the second opponent. Urgon stumbled back, tripping on some furs and falling to the floor. The man with the mace loomed over the prone Orc, and then he screamed out in pain. Urgon struggled to comprehend what had happened until he saw teeth digging into flesh and then understood. While he had been busy fighting the intruders, Zhura had opened the door to the wolf pen. The sound of conflict had been all that was needed for the pack to respond.

Beside him, the first man struck out with his sword, a weak blow due to his wound, but it was to be his last. Urgon sat up and drove the point of his sword into the man's chest, feeling the steel penetrate flesh with ease. The screams behind him halted as the second one collapsed, the wolves tearing at the flesh.

Urgon's world swam before his eyes. He had suspected Agrug of conspiring with the earl's men but never imagined he would send someone to kill him. As his knees began to shake, he leaned back against the hut's wall, trying to overcome his fears. Zhura bent over him, concern written all over her face.

"You must leave Ord-Dugath," she said. "Agrug wants you dead!"

"And leave you alone and at his mercy? I would prefer to die!"

"Then I shall go with you."

He looked at her, recognizing the fear in her eyes. "The only place we could go would be farther into the hills, and there would be no mud to shut out the spirits."

"I would rather choose a short life out there than linger here, waiting for my death. When Agrug learns you left, he will take out his revenge on me. You know this to be true."

Urgon nodded. "Then we must go together." He forced a smile. "Who knows, it may be pleasant enough. Perhaps I can make another mud hut for us to live in?"

"Gather your things," said Zhura. "I will pack us some food."

"What of the wolves?"

"It will soon be evident we left. Gorath will know how to take care of them."

"I wish we could send word that we were leaving."

"You must not. Our safety lies in secrecy. Would you have Agrug's hunters follow?"

"What of our friends? They will assume we abandoned them."

"Fear not. I shall tell the Ancestors of our woes. The next time Kraloch talks to them, they will pass on the message. Now get your things, my love. We have little time before these two Humans are missed."

Urgon sought his chainmail shirt, pulling it over his head. Ordinarily, someone would have had to tie it up in the back, but there was no time for this now. He wrapped his belt around his waist, then tucked in his axe, looking around the room.

Zhura had gathered food, wrapping it up in a bundle she tied off with rope, another gift from the Humans. His heart reached out for her, knowing the sacrifice she was making. The Ancestors' voices would be so hard for her to shut out.

He grabbed his spear, then took her hand, leading her to the front of the hut and peering out. The village was quiet, so he stepped outside, keeping her close. Around the edge of the hut they went, staying in the shadows as much as possible. He sensed her hesitancy and turned to see her struggling to find her bearings.

"Is it the voices?" he asked.

She nodded. "Yes, but keep going. I shall survive."

Urgon looked back to the centre of the village. The great firepit was hidden from sight, but the light thrown off from it lit the area with a crimson glow, sending flickering shadows between the huts. Into these shadows he took Zhura, moving slowly while keeping a tight hold of her hand.

They were near the edge of the village now, with only the outer ring of huts to pass on their way to freedom. He stepped from the shadows to see a shape before him. At first, he took it to be a Human, but then a familiar voice spoke.

"Where are you going, Urgon?"

"We are leaving, Skulnug. Do not stand in our way."

"Why? What has happened?"

"I have no time to explain, but come daybreak, all will become plain. Must I fight you to pass?"

"No," replied Skulnug, "of course not. Have you any word for your allies?"

"Yes," said Urgon. "Tell Kraloch to seek answers from the spirits."

Skulnug stepped aside. "Good luck, Urgon. You too, Zhura. May the Ancestors watch over you both."

Zhura breathed a sigh of relief. "Come," she said. "We must go."

## TWENTY-ONE

## Exile

WINTER 959/960 MC

The wind howled across the mountains, driving sheets of white before it. Urgon crouched in the snow, ready to spring into action, watching his prey—a stout, woolly goat with a massive set of horns. It would have been an easy kill had he a bow, but in his rush to flee Ord-Dugath, he had left without one. So now he waited, shivering, with his spear in hand instead.

His prey moved closer, seemingly oblivious to his presence. His muscles tensed as he prepared to rise up and throw his weapon. The goat raised its head, suddenly on the alert. Urgon knew he would have only one chance at this. He staggered to his feet, weighed down as he was by the thick furs that fought to keep the chill at bay.

He chucked the spear, throwing with all his might, but the goat bounded away, disappearing into the blowing snow. Urgon cursed his luck. Now he must fight through the snow to recover his weapon, a job made all the more difficult by the flurries swirling around. As he trudged through the drifts, he cast his eyes about, but there was no sign of the spear. A low growl brought his advance to a halt, and he struggled to peer through the blizzard, desperate to find its source.

Again, a snarl. Now, he could have no doubt—a mountain cat had found him. He whirled around to see a large shape rushing towards him. It reached out, raking its claws across his chest, shredding the furs. The force of the blow knocked him off his feet back into the snow.

Only his presence of mind saved him, for even as he fell, his hand went for his sword.

Out the weapon came, its blade singing as it struck, easily slicing through flesh and bone. The cat's momentum carried it forward, and it fell on him with a great weight, its teeth a hand's breadth from his face.

The pressure on his chest suddenly increased as the massive head lolled lifelessly to the side. Urgon summoned what remained of his strength and heaved the carcass off of him. Now relieved of the burden, he sucked in the frigid winter air in huge gasps, his mind still trying to cope with what had just happened.

He struggled to his feet, gazing down at the body. The great mountain cat was dead when, by all rights, it should be him lying there in the blood-soaked snow. He had come here seeking a goat, but instead, this large predator had now provided him with the needed meat.

Urgon remembered the claw attack and glanced down at his chest. The furs there had been shredded, but his chainmail shirt, worn beneath, saved him, blunting the force of the creature's strike. His knife came out, and he began the process of gutting the carcass.

Zhura looked up as Urgon entered the cave.

"What have you there?" she asked.

He dumped the creature on the floor. "Fresh meat."

The corners of her mouth curled up in a smile. "I thought you were going to hunt down a goat, and here I see a mountain cat. Can you not tell the difference?"

"Do they not both have four legs?"

Her smile quickly disappeared as she saw the state of his furs. "Are you hurt?"

"Only my pride. The beast surprised me."

"You are lucky to still be alive."

"I was saved by my sword."

"I would say the armour was what saved you," said Zhura. "Fate was in your favour today. Had it not been Dwarven mail, the links would likely have parted."

"Fate did not bring me the chainmail, Gambreck Ironpick did. He was the one who returned my father's body to Ord-Dugath."

"So your father's death led to your life being spared today. Do you not perceive the fate in that?"

"When you put it that way, I suppose I must. Looking back, I can now see my entire life has been a string of chance occurrences. Had any of them changed, I would not be here today."

"True," said Zhura. "You would be tucked up in your bed with a normal bondmate instead of me."

He moved closer, wrapping his arms around her. "You are the one who captured my heart."

"And you mine, but do you ever stop to consider what drove you to look inside that mud hut all those winters ago?"

"No, and never have I regretted it."

"Good, because I intend to remain amongst the living for a good many winters yet."

"And here I thought you would have gone mad by twenty."

"But I did," she said, the smile creeping back. "I am mad for you!"

He looked around the cave, intending to pull her down into some soft, warm furs, but then he noticed she had cleared a spot on the cavern floor. She immediately noted the shift in his attention.

"What have you been up to?" he asked.

"Come, and I will show you."

She grabbed his hand, guiding him to where the furs had been cast aside. The exposed floor was covered in scratches, and he wondered why she would do that. He was about to say something when he recognized a familiar design.

"I have seen these shapes before," he said. "They were in the cave of the Eternal Light."

"They are magic runes, much like those that decorated the door on my old hut."

"Why did we not see them earlier?"

"They were covered in dirt that had accumulated over the winters. Had I not spilled some of the stew, I would likely never have discovered them."

"So this cave is magical?"

"Possibly, but it would take a shaman to know for sure."

Urgon crouched, reaching out to feel the markings. "I can feel... something, although I have no sense of what it is."

"Let me guess," she said. "It makes the hairs on your arm stand on end?"

He nodded.

"I felt the same thing. It might be some kind of protective ward."

"Protection from what?" asked Urgon.

"I have no idea, but you must admit it strange that an animal had not taken up residence in this cave."

"But why would someone create that here, in the middle of nowhere? It makes no sense."

"Do you recall the legend of Dugath?"

"The founder of our tribe?"

"Yes," said Zhura. "I suspect he and his followers might have lived here for a while."

"But his arrow founded our village. Ord-Dugath is far too distant for that to have worked."

"Most likely it was before the founding. I also believe he may have had a ghostwalker amongst his people."

"What makes you say that?"

"This cave," said Zhura. "It insulates me from the spirits. If I step outside, I can still hear the echoes of the Ancestors, yet inside all is quiet."

"And you believe these markings have something to do with that?"

"Possibly."

"You talked to the spirit of Dugath before," said Urgon. "Could you not do so again?"

"Were I a shaman, I might, but I am a ghostwalker, unable to choose when and where I communicate with spirits. Only happenstance allowed me to speak with Dugath, and that was while I still lived in the village."

"I suppose that makes sense," mused Urgon, "but why do you suggest he had a ghostwalker amongst his people?"

"Our people are all descended from those original Orcs."

"And?"

"Ghostwalking is said to be in the blood. In that sense, I am a product of my ancestors. I will never know for sure if one of Dugath's people was like me or whether they had it in their blood, but it had to come from somewhere."

"That would make sense," said Urgon. "That being the case, would we not have seen or heard more about it in our history?"

"Not necessarily. Orcs have a variety of eye colours, and not every blue-eyed Orc has younglings who match. Sometimes such traits skip an entire generation."

Urgon frowned. "But Shular told me ghostwalkers are barren. How, then, did they pass on their blood?"

"Through siblings. Think of yourself. You have certain physical traits you share with your sister—eye colour, for example. Even though you may not have younglings, who is to say she might not?"

Urgon laughed but stopped when he saw her serious expression.

"You find this funny?" she asked.

"Only the thought of my sister bonding."

"I only used her as an example," said Zhura, "though I understand your amusement. Kurghal can be quite obstinate at times, and now that she is the senior shaman of the tribe, I doubt she will consider bonding."

"It is her loss," he said, reaching out to her. "I find it very fulfilling."

"As do I, although I would welcome the chance to have a youngling."

He noticed her mood darkening. "Come, now. We are both getting a little old to worry about such things. You have me. Am I not enough of a handful?"

She brightened considerably. "Look at me, feeling sorry for myself. I should count my blessings. Without you, I would have wasted away to nothing, my mind completely gone. I have much to be thankful for."

Urgon glanced at the floor again. "So this stew you were making, did you spill all of it?"


Two days later, the storm abated. Blessed with clear skies, Urgon emerged from the cave with Zhura by his side.

"It is so bright," she said. "It hurts my eyes."

"Mine too," replied Urgon, "but they will soon adjust. Come, breathe in the fresh air."

Zhura took a step, her feet sinking knee-deep into the snow. A smile crept over her face, and Urgon was about to say something, but then Zhura's eyes darted left. Concerned she had heard something, he swivelled his own gaze, but there was nothing there except snowdrifts as far as the eye could see.

"What is it?" he called out.

"A spirit."

He wanted to know more but held his tongue. In all the time they had been here, there had been no sign of the Ancestors. Why, then, would one appear now? He felt affronted as if their privacy had somehow been invaded, then silently berated himself for his selfishness. Zhura had no control over the spirit world—she had not conjured this ghost.

Zhura took three steps to her left and called out, her voice echoing off the hills, carrying in the crisp, cold air. Whoever was there evidently answered her call, for she angled her head as if listening intently. Urgon waited, knowing she would reveal all to him once she was done.

Her voice grew soft and rapid, further evidence she was conversing with a spirit. He had seen it often over the years, yet still, it drew him in, fascinating him.

Finally, she turned to him. "It is the spirit of your father, Urdar," she said.

Urgon felt an icy grip over his heart. "What did he want?"

"The Ancestors have been searching for us. Only he was brave enough to come this far into the mountains."

"Why would they be looking for us? Are we in danger?"

"Kraloch told them of our plight," she replied. "It has taken them half a year to find us."

He moved closer. "So we can get word back to Ord-Dugath?"

"If you wish. What would you have me say?"

"That we are safe, but let our location remain a secret, at least for now. I would not have Agrug's Humans learn of our whereabouts."

"A wise precaution," said Zhura. "Anything else?"

"Have them ask Kraloch to notify us when the tribe starts moving."

"That will probably not be until spring, and we would be hard-pressed to catch up to them once they begin."

"You raise a valid point," said Urgon. "I shall have to rethink our strategy."

"Is there another option? What if we return to the vicinity of Ord-Dugath come spring. There, we can keep an eye on things from a distance."

"No, the risk of running afoul of a hunting party is too high. Unless…"

Zhura smiled. "You have an idea."

"I do, but it largely depends on your ability to get a message to Kraloch. Timing will be important."

"Tell me your thoughts."

"Hunting parties are common around Ord-Dugath's immediate area, but we have the advantage."

"We do?"

"Yes," said Urgon, warming to the challenge. "If we get word to Urzath, we could ensure only those friendly to us hunted in whatever area we choose to inhabit."

"I do not see how. Hunters go where the game is, do they not? How, then, do we stop them from hunting in a specific area?"

Urgon grinned. "Unless they are operating in a group, Orcs will seldom hunt near others, else they would be in competition for the same prey. As long as Urzath announces where she will hunt, there will be little chance of running into anyone else."

"And this is common behaviour for hunters?"

"It is, especially concerning Urzath. She is our greatest hunter. Who in their right mind would want to interfere with her craft?"

"You have, I believe, come up with a good idea, but it needs work. Where, for example, would we live? Any shelter we build would attract attention."

Urgon pursed his lips. "A valid point. It would have to be somewhere that it could be concealed, like amongst rocks or in a thick grove of trees."

"Or in a depression," added Zhura. "That way, it might not be seen until quite close."

"The real problem would be the smoke of our fire. It would be visible for some distance."

"Could we make do without a fire?"

"We could certainly exist on raw meat if we had to, but we would need heat to survive the cold, and that means fire."

Zhura re-entered the cave, leaving Urgon to scan the frozen landscape. His mind raced. He valued his time with Zhura, but the thought of returning to Ord-Dugath made his pulse quicken. His people needed him!

Eventually, he followed her inside.

· · ·

Urgon stared at the flames as the night air picked up, sending a chilly breeze into the cave. He had hung several skins over the door in an effort to block it, but the results had been only partially successful.

Zhura sat opposite him, her hands engaged in sewing together a bag. A gust hit the fire, wafting smoke into her face, and she coughed.

"It is as if this smoke is destined to burn my eyes regardless of where I sit."

"It is not your fault," said Urgon. "The hills here funnel the wind. It has little choice but to enter our cave."

Zhura looked at him, her eyes tearing from the smoke. "The wind always blows in the same direction here."

It took a moment for the idea to sink in. "So it does," he replied.

"Is it the same in Ord-Dugath?"

"It is. It always comes from the west, blowing up towards the mountains."

"Are you thinking what I am?"

Urgon grinned. "I believe so. As long as we remain downwind of the village, we can build a fire. It appears the Ancestors have provided the answer we needed after all."

"It was not the Ancestors," said Zhura, "but your bondmate."

He smiled. "So it was! You are quite remarkable, Zhura. Glad I am that we are bonded. You complete me." He stood, moving around the fire to gaze down at her with love in his eyes.

In return, she looked at him and held up her hand. "Not so fast, my love. There will be plenty of time for that later. Come and sit by my side so we may further discuss this plan of yours."

He sat, taking her hand in his. "All right, although I consider the plan not mine, but OURS." He stared into her eyes to see worry reflected back, then his gut tightened. "No," he said. "I think it best if we just stay here instead."

"Why would you say that?"

"I know the toll the spirits take on you. Returning to the village would only make your burden greater. Here you have peace and quiet. Is it not best if it remains so?"

Zhura forced a smile. "I am happy wherever you are," she said. "And in any case, the mud hut will protect me. I have enjoyed these last few months, but it places a heavy burden on you to provide for us. It might be different if I were a hunter, but look at me—I have barely enough muscle to walk for more than a few hundred paces, let alone sneak around looking for food. You belong amongst our people, Urgon, and I by your side. We shall return to Ord-Dugath, and then you must save our people from disaster."

He squeezed her hand. "You once told me to follow my heart," he said, "and that led me to you. I will not abandon you now."

"You will not be abandoning me but providing for our future. You need to claim the leadership of the tribe, Urgon, else this will become our life." She gazed around the cave.

Urgon sighed, seeing the practical side of things. "I see now that you speak the truth."

"Do I not always do so?"

He grinned. "Of course. What I meant to say is that I agree with you. The only way for life to return to some semblance of normalcy is to become chieftain. Only with Agrug removed from power can we stop this madness."

"Good. When do we start?"

"In the spring," said Urgon. "Once the snows have melted."

# TWENTY-TWO

## The Tribe Gathers

### SPRING 960 MC

Urgon peered out from behind the tree. Off in the distance, he could make out a campfire, a crude affair made from green wood and leaves, sending a plume of thick smoke skyward.

Clearly, whoever it was, lacked experience in such matters, so he watched, waiting for its owner to emerge from the lean-to that sat nearby.

He thought back to Zhura and their own primitive lodgings. They had come to the hills a couple of ten-days ago, determined to keep an eye on the village. They had encountered little, save for wildlife, but now he wondered if their luck had not just run out.

He spotted movement, and then a figure emerged from the lean-to. Urgon chuckled as he recognized young Gorath, although perhaps young was no longer the case, for it appeared his protégé was undergoing his ordeal.

The thought brought on a moment of panic, for quite possibly, this Orc might stumble across their presence. He had no idea how long Gorath had been out here. Had the young Orc already discovered them? He must find out. Urgon moved closer, staying as quiet as he could. The lean-to looked like it had been patched together in the fading light of day. That likely indicated the young hunter had started out only yesterday.

Urgon thought back to his own ordeal, but the threat of running into another mountain cat was slim. Gorath would likely spend his days hunting and trapping, with little thought to anything else except survival, but what would he do should he find evidence of Urgon and Zhura? Would he turn aside, content to remain apart for the duration of his ordeal, or would he decide to investigate?

The rules were quite clear regarding interference. The youngling must survive on their own wits for a ten-day. That did not preclude meeting others, only prevented them from lending assistance. Urgon, throwing caution to the wind, emerged from behind the tree. Gorath jumped to his feet, his hand going to his knife.

"Did you think me a wild animal?" called out Urgon.

The young hunter relaxed, although surprise showed on his face. "Urgon? I did not expect to see you here, so close to Ord-Dugath."

"I have been here for some time, but what of you?"

Gorath flushed. "I am on my ordeal. By rights, you should not even be talking to me."

"Nonsense. Although I am forbidden to help you in any way, there is nothing that says I am not permitted to talk to you, providing it is about anything other than survival."

"Then speak, for I am in no rush to go hunting."

"How fares the village?" asked Urgon. "Has much happened in my absence?"

"Agrug has kept us all training in weapons."

"And when shall he muster the entire tribe?"

"Soon," said Gorath. "I hope to complete my ordeal before they leave for Eastwood. It is one of the conditions of my accompanying them."

"So they march soon. It is as I feared."

"What will you do?"

"I had thought to confront Agrug," said Urgon, "but to do so with him surrounded by those Humans might prove unwise."

"What if you waited until they march?"

"Will the Humans not be accompanying you?"

"No," said Gorath. "The plan is for the horde to march by themselves."

"The horde?"

"The Human term for the gathering of our people. In any event, he has something special in mind for us."

This intrigued Urgon. "Which would be?"

"I wish I knew. Agrug has few confidants, and I am not counted amongst them. He often speaks of everlasting glory and how we shall play a decisive part in the coming weeks."

"Weeks?"

"A Human measurement of time. A week is a grouping of seven days."

"Seven? Why such an odd number?"

Gorath shrugged. "That is a good question. They all have ten fingers as we do, but maybe their ancestors were not so blessed?"

"It matters little," said Urgon. "This horde of which you speak, will it be the entire tribe?"

"As many as can be mustered. Only the elders will remain, along with the younglings, of course."

"Would that include Maloch?"

"Of course. Why? Is there a message you wish me to convey to her?"

"There is, as a matter of fact. When our people leave for Eastwood, I would be amongst them, but Zhura will need looking after."

"Doubtless Maloch would see to her well-being," said Gorath, "as would Kurghal."

"My sister is not marching with the horde?"

"No, she flat out refused, saying it was not her place to abandon her duty to the elderly."

"Then get word to them both."

"And where should they meet Zhura?"

"Here," said Urgon, "where your shelter now stands. Do you think they could find this spot?"

"Easily."

"Good, then all is settled. It only remains for me to join the tribe when it sets out for Eastwood."

"You mean to challenge Agrug directly?"

"Of course," said Urgon. "How else would I claim the position of chieftain? Why? Is there a problem?"

"He surrounds himself will loyal allies. Getting close might prove difficult. It might be easier if your identity was concealed."

"And how do you propose I do that?"

Gorath grinned. "A helmet would hide your features."

"A helmet? Orcs do not wear such things."

"They do now, although it took a Human smith to craft ones that would fit our heads. Many of our warriors wear them."

Urgon scowled. "We are hunters, not warriors. Fighting in this manner can only lead to disaster."

"Once the tribe is on the warpath, there is little you can do to stop it. Orcs are used to following orders, Urgon. To convince them to do otherwise will prove fruitless."

"But I must, for our very survival demands it."

"Many die in a war. It is only natural."

"It is not the war I oppose so much as the aftermath. Mark my words, Gorath, once this earl has what he wants, he will turn on us. That is the true disaster here."

"How can you be so sure? Perhaps he only has our best interests at heart?"

"Agrug's words swayed many," said Urgon, "but he is in this for his own enrichment. As for the Human earl, I do not trust him."

"Why not?"

"He plots against his chieftain."

"Is that not what you are now proposing?" insisted the young Orc.

Urgon was struck dumb, entirely at a loss for words as the statement sank in, but then reason took over. "You have learned much in your young life," he continued, "but I do this not for personal gain, but for the good of our people. If this earl was not so determined on turning against his own chieftain, I might agree with Agrug's choices, but my gut tells me otherwise."

"So other than take word to Maloch and Kurghal, what do you want me to do?"

"Upon your return, find me a helmet."

"It will be difficult to get it to you."

"Then carry it with you," said Urgon. "When the horde marches, I shall find you amongst their number."

"And then?"

"And then we shall gather our allies and seek out Agrug. I mean to end this once and for all."


The horde was easy enough to spot, for they raced across the terrain like an army of ants. Urgon, despite his misgivings, found the sight inspiring, and he wondered, not for the first time, if what he was doing was right. Before him stretched out more than a thousand Orcs, an assembly seldom seen outside of tribal gatherings. The bulk of them moved in one solid mass, but those more experienced in hunting spread out to the sides, screening the main group's advance. It was towards these hunters Urgon headed.

As he drew closer, he spotted Urzath, running with her bow in hand, strung but not drawn. He wondered why, but then she halted all of a sudden and dropped to one knee as she nocked an arrow. When she let fly, he followed the arrow's path as it disappeared in amongst some trees. Urzath rose and then jogged towards her target. Urgon angled his approach, arriving in time to see her stooping over a fallen deer.

"A clean kill," he said.

She whirled around at the sound of his voice, but then a grin spread across her face. "Urgon! Gorath told me you might be joining us. Where is Zhura?"

"By now, hopefully under the watchful eyes of Maloch." He cast his gaze around. "Where is Agrug?"

"Not here," replied Urzath. "He went on ahead to Eastwood. We are to meet him there."

"And Gorath?"

"In amongst the main force." She knelt and began preparing her kill. "It will take a lot of meat to feed this lot," she said. "Those on the edge are to keep alert for any sign of food."

"Gorath said he would find me a helmet."

"And so he has, but you must wait. Enter the horde now, and someone will notice your arrival. Better to wait until dark, then. When the camp is set, no one will mark your presence."

"How will I find Gorath?" Urgon asked.

"I shall have him camp to the rear of the horde. Will that suffice?"

"It will. Who else stands with us?"

"You remember Skulnug?"

"I do."

"Vulgar is with us as well and, of course, Kraloch," continued Urzath. "We told no one else of your plan, though, for fear of word getting back to Agrug."

"How far do you think you will get by nightfall?"

"Not much farther. They have the energy, but it takes time to cook and feed everyone. Have you your bow?"

"No," said Urgon, "but I have my sword and my armour beneath these rags. I saw no sign of the Humans amongst our people. Does that mean they have abandoned us?"

"Hardly. They left Ord-Dugath right before Gorath started his ordeal. Likely they are in Eastwood by now."

"What is Agrug's plan?"

"That remains to be seen," said Urzath. "We are to rendezvous at Eastwood in three days. Let us hope by then, our glorious leader will reveal what is to come. In the meantime, I suggest you wait here until darkness falls. It should then be a simple matter to follow our trail to the camp."

"I shall do as you suggest."


Urgon looked across the fire to see all the faces staring back at him.

"Are you sure you can beat Agrug?" asked Kraloch. "He bested you before. Who is to say he would not do so again?"

"He surprised me in the middle of the night. And I might remind you he sent others to do his bidding."

"Still," said Vulgar, "he outweighs you by a significant amount."

"Urgon can beat him," said Gorath. "He has right on his side."

"Right?" said Urzath. "Who is to say what is right? Better to trust in his weapons and armour than expect a victory to be handed to him based on his morals."

"I can beat him," insisted Urgon.

Kraloch frowned. "What makes you so sure?"

Urgon met his gaze. "I have no other choice. To fail now would cost the tribe dearly."

"That said, Agrug is not here."

"Who leads the horde in his absence?"

"Tarluk," said Urzath, "but I hesitate to trust him."

"Tarluk is a fool," said Vulgar, "and will agree to anything Agrug suggests. Do you think we should deal with him first?"

"No," said Urgon. "My fight is with Agrug, and he alone. I will not split this tribe over loyalties."

"How do you intend to handle this?" asked Urzath.

"I must find an opportunity to speak with our gallant chieftain, so I can make a challenge."

"You mean to meet him in the circle?"

"Of course," said Urgon. "How else would I deal with him?"

"With a knife in the dark," suggested Vulgar. They all looked at the large Orc in disgust. "What?" he said in reply. "He would only be getting what he deserves."

"Doing that would not make Urgon the chieftain," said Kraloch. "To accomplish that, he must present himself as the alternative."

"Agreed," said Urzath. "And who would trust a leader who stabs someone in the dark? I believe Urgon has the right of it here."

A burst of laughter nearby drew their attention. Another group of Orcs sat around a distant fire, but one of them stood, then headed directly towards Urgon's group.

"Here," said Gorath, tossing a helmet. "Put this on before someone recognizes you."

Urgon pulled on the strange headgear. Despite its appearance to the contrary, it was actually quite comfortable. It consisted of a conical-shaped top with two leather cheek guards attached, the perfect head-gear to hide his face.

"How do I look?" he asked.

"Like any other Orc in this horde," noted Kraloch.

The Orc from the other fire drew closer, her features resolving into a familiar face.

"Greetings, Galur," said Kraloch. "How are things in Ord-Muran?"

"As well as can be expected," she replied. Her eyes wandered over the small group, coming to rest on Urgon. "Who have we here?"

"Who, this?" said Kraloch. "This is Zarug. He hails from the village of Zagral."

Urgon stood, extending his hand. "Greetings, Galur."

She shook it, but her eyes remained locked on his. "You look famil-iar. Have we met before?"

"Not that I know of. Have you ever been to Zagral?"

"Once, when I was still a youngling."

"Then maybe you met my father. We are said to be similar of face."

"Possibly. In any case, I must be off, nature calls."

She left them by the fire, and Urgon breathed a sigh of relief. "That was close."

"You know her?" said Urzath.

"She is one of three Orcs Shuvog suggested I bond with."

"Good thing she failed to recognize you."

"I am not sure she did."

"What are you saying?"

"Merely that she recognized my face," said Urgon. "The real question is whether or not she will tell anyone else of my presence. We must remain alert."

"We are already alert," said Gorath. "In that sense, nothing has changed."

"We must do something," insisted Kraloch, "or her knowledge of your presence here might endanger us all."

Urgon stood. "I shall talk to her."

"Do you judge that a wise idea?"

"I see no alternative, do you?"

"We could kill her," suggested Vulgar.

Again, they turned to the large Orc in shock.

"It was only a suggestion," he mumbled.

"There will be no killing of Galur," said Urgon. "Instead, I will try to reason with her."

"Is that wise?" asked Kraloch. "After all, you refused her offer of bonding."

"Are you suggesting she might hold a grudge?"

"I am suggesting she might not have recognized you at all. Should you approach her now, she will have another chance of recalling your name."

"And if she DID recognize me, leaving her alone might allow her the opportunity to reveal my presence. I have made up my mind. I shall approach her."

Urgon left the campfire, heading in the direction Galur had taken. He waited just beyond the glow of the camp, confident she would soon return.

Sure enough, she reappeared, walking towards him.

"So, Zarug," she said. "It seems we meet again."

"So we have."

She halted before him, looking him over with a critical eye. "Will you continue this game, or will you admit you are Urgon, son of Urdar?"

Urgon removed his helmet. "How did you know it was me?"

"Your eyes, they have an intensity. I heard you were exiled. Is that true?"

"If by exiled you mean chased out of Ord-Dugath, then yes."

"Chased out?"

"Yes. Agrug sent Humans to kill me."

Her look of disgust was easy to see. "Kill you? How barbaric!"

"I thought so too."

"Why would he do such a thing?"

"I dared to object to his plans," said Urgon. "As a consequence, I found myself the object of his scorn."

"Unbelievable."

"Yes, but still, it is true. Tell me, now you know of my presence, will you tell others?"

"It is my duty, but no, I will tell no one, providing you do something for me in return."

"I have little I can promise in return."

"Your friends are strong and vibrant, much like you, would you not agree?"

"I am already bonded, Galur."

She flushed, turning a darker shade of green. "No, you misunderstand my remarks. It is not you who I desire to meet."

Urgon breathed a sigh of relief. "Then tell me how I can help."

"I would like to meet one of your friends."

"Oh? Which one?"

"The tall one."

Urgon looked back at his companions, then met her gaze once more. "You mean Vulgar? By the Ancestors, why would you want to meet him?"

Now it was her turn to stare at the distant fire, although with more longing than he had anticipated. "He is the very definition of muscular." At this point, she appeared to realize her choice of words and flushed again. "Sorry," she said, recovering herself. "I got carried away."

"So let me get this straight," said Urgon. "You promise not to tell anyone of my presence, and in return, I introduce you to Vulgar?"

"Correct, although when you put it that way, it seems so... trivial."

"Not at all, but I have to wonder why you have this sudden interest in Vulgar."

"My village has few un-bonded males."

"Hence your journey to Ord-Dugath," said Urgon. "That I can

understand, but this… horde must contain dozens of Orcs your age, many of them quite strong. Why Vulgar?"

"I first set eyes on him when the horde began its trek westward. Have you ever met someone, and it just felt… right?"

Urgon thought of Zhura. "I have, as a matter of fact."

"So, then, do we have a deal?"

Urgon smiled. "Come," he said. "Let me introduce you to my good friend Vulgar."

# TWENTY-THREE

# The Deerwood

SPRING 960 MC

T he horde made swift progress, and by the third day, it had come within sight of the great city of Eastwood. Urgon had seen it before, but to many of his people, it was a symbol of Human might. Adding to the scene was the large army of several hundred that the earl had assembled. Definitely not as large as the Orc host, but still impressive. Urgon stared at Human warriors as he and his friends marched past.

"They are an imposing sight," noted Urzath.

"Yes," replied Urgon. "Even though they are fewer in number, they make up for it in armour. Had we such protection, we would be unstoppable."

A group of cavalrymen rode past, grabbing their attention, if only for the moment.

"I should not like to meet the likes of those in battle," said Urzath. "I wonder if our Ancestors ever rode horses?"

"According to Zhura, our distant kin rode wolves."

"Then they must have been the size of younglings."

"Not so. In those days, they bred wolves the size of ponies."

"That must have been an impressive sight."

"One would imagine," mused Urgon, "but the Elves defeated us, nonetheless."

"Yet here we are now," continued Urzath, "joining our forces to those of the earl. Surely, there are none who can defeat us? Our army is strong, like a cave bear."

"Yes, but even a cave bear can be brought down by wolves."

"You fear we face defeat?"

"Our numbers are impressive, but we know so little of the Humans. This army of the earl's may be small in comparison to his fellow nobles."

"Nobles? Are you now saying the earl and his friends are worthy of our friendship?"

Urgon frowned. "No, it is merely a term they use to denote their leaders."

"You have learned much of our erstwhile allies."

"Zhura has learned more. The Ancestors have spent lifetimes fighting Humans. There is much to be learned from their experiences."

They passed the city but kept marching until the great forest of the Deerwood appeared on the horizon. Here they halted, making camp as darkness approached. Fires soon flickered to life, lighting the area like a hundred giant fireflies.

Kraloch wore a confused look as he sat by the fire. "All this marching confuses me," he said.

"In what way?" asked Urgon.

"I had thought we intended to march with the earl, but instead, we continue west. Are we to keep moving until the end of time?"

Urgon chuckled. "I think our Human ally is a clever man."

"Why? Because he sent us marching off to nowhere?"

"Not so. Our position is very deliberate."

"Then would you be so kind as to explain it to me?"

"I believe the earl is laying a trap. He will hide us in the Deerwood, allowing us to emerge at a crucial time to take the enemy by surprise."

"And will that work?"

"Hopefully. It largely depends on how intelligent his foe is."

"And how many," added Urzath.

"This horde is the largest ever assembled by our tribe," said Kraloch.

"Yes," Urgon agreed, "and likely numbers close to a thousand hunters. The Humans we passed earlier are much easier to count, formed up as they were in nice, straight lines. I reckon their numbers are roughly half ours, meaning they expect us to be doing the bulk of the fighting." He shook his head. "Yet more proof that we are being used."

"Any news concerning Agrug's whereabouts?" asked Urzath.

"Yes," said Kraloch. "According to Tarluk, he waits for us in the Deerwood."

"That works in our favour," said Urgon. "Amongst the trees, we can get close to him, then I can issue the challenge."

"And if he refuses?"

"He leads us to war. Refusal of a challenge would only put his leadership into question. He will fight. He has to!"

"And you are sure you can defeat him?"

Urgon stared into the fire. "I have no choice. Our people are on the road to ruin. If I do nothing, our days are numbered."

They entered the forest early the next day. Some of their hunters had trod these paths before, and so they led the way, guiding others along the twisted trails, taking them deep into the woods. Kraloch, as a shaman, soon found himself disoriented, unable to tell east from west, but Urgon knew the signs.

"We are turning south," he announced.

"How can you tell?" asked Kraloch.

"The trees show me. Note the moss?"

"There is moss all over the trees."

"On the ground, yes," Urgon said, "but it thrives in dark, moist areas. In these parts, that is mainly on the north side of a tree, but you must look higher than the ground."

"Why is that?"

"The forest floor is damp, promoting its growth. Instead, look higher up the trunk or to the larger branches. Those will guide you northward."

"I can see I am ill-suited to the life of a hunter."

Urgon chuckled. "Then it is a good thing you are a shaman. Lean into your strengths, my friend, and embrace them."

When they finally halted, the tribe scattered amongst the trees, finding small clearings to set up fires. One in ten hunters went foraging for food while the camp was prepared. Urzath soon appeared with a deer over her shoulders which she dropped before their small group and began cutting into. By nightfall, they were well fed and contem-plating their next moves.

"How deep into the woods are we?" asked Kraloch.

"Likely a half-morning's walk," noted Urzath. "Assuming you want the eastern edge."

"Then where is Agrug? Was he not to meet us here?"

"Do not worry," said Urgon. "If he means to attack come morning, he will make his presence known."

"How do you know we attack in the morning?"

"We have little choice. We are too numerous to remain in place for long; we would strip the woods of all the game." He spotted Tarluk wandering the camp. "Something is up."

Urgon rose, pointing at the distant hunter. "He will lead us to Agrug." His companions followed his lead, rising and grabbing their weapons. "Come," said Urgon. "It is time we settle this once and for all."

They followed at a discreet distance, careful to raise no suspicions. Tarluk stopped at every campfire, chatting amiably, sometimes for extended periods. Urgon grew frustrated, wondering if he were ever going to find their elusive chieftain.

Tarluk finally led them to the outskirts of the camp, pausing to chat with a couple of hunters who stood guard. Urgon looked around—there were no fires left to stop at. Surely he must soon lead them to Agrug?

A noise caught the guards' attention, and all turned to the darkness of the woods. Tarluk drew his axe, ordering the two hunters into the woods. He, however, chose not to follow, instead approaching the nearest fire. Urgon drew closer, the better to listen in.

"Get to the woods," ordered Tarluk. "Something is out there."

Five Orcs rose to the challenge, grasping their weapons. Off in the black of night, Urgon heard someone gasp and then the crashing of sticks and leaves as someone fled.

"After them!" he shouted as he tore into the woods, drawing his sword. The clash of metal on metal echoed back at him, and he knew someone was fighting. The big question was who?

Whoever it was, made no attempt at further concealing their loca-tion. A hunter ran towards him, clutching a wound to the stomach. Urgon grabbed him by the arm.

"What is it?" he asked.

"Humans encased in heavy metal armour."

Kraloch began casting, his hands soon glowing with magical energy.

"How many?" asked Urgon.

"Only one—a female by the look of it."

Kraloch placed his hands on the injured Orc, watching as the magical energy seeped into the wound, knitting flesh. Satisfied with the result, he turned to Urgon. "What now?"

Another Orc appeared, clutching a wound to their arm.

"It appears this Human warrior knows her business," said Kraloch.

"We must stop her," urged Urgon, "or she may take word of our presence to our enemy."

Kraloch again invoked his magic, the strange words falling from his lips in a torrent. More Orcs ran past, intent on joining the fray, then came the battle cry, a high-pitched keening taken up by others. Urgon had been on many hunts and knew its meaning—they were closing in for the kill.

He rushed off, leaving Kraloch to finish his spell. Urzath stood a moment in indecision, struggling with her duty to protect the shaman or join Urgon. She finally turned to Vulgar and Gorath. "You two stay here," she commanded, then rushed into the darkness.

Urgon ran forward, seeking the fight, but the canopy of trees blocked out the moon, limiting his night vision. He paused, listening to the sounds around him, eager to pick out any details that might help him ascertain the location of the enemy.

Urzath appeared at his side. He nodded at her, then heard the distant sound of an axe hitting wood.

"This way," he said, tearing off as fast as he could, eager to see this foe who so perplexed them. Twigs snapped beneath his feet; branches tore at his clothes, yet still, he ran, desperate to help.

Finally, he slowed, listening once more, but his breath came in ragged gasps, and he knew he must calm himself if he was to have any hope of hearing the enemy. His breath grew quiet. Orcs advanced in a line now, calling out to each other in their quest to find their prey.

A twig snapped to his front, and then a further clash of steel rang out, echoing off the trees. Again, the hunting cry as the Orcs moved in, closing the trap, but their prey was wily. On and on, they pressed, yet their foe proved too clever. Again and again, the silence was followed by a brief clash of fighting, and Urgon could only wonder if this Human female were a ghost.

It dragged on forever. Urgon found himself caught up in the scene, not as a participant but as an observer, listening for the telltale sounds of his hunters rushing forward for the kill.

"She is clever, this Human," he said. "She knows how to use the darkness to her advantage."

Urzath grinned. "She is a hunter, I have no doubt."

"No, she is a warrior. No hunter would wear metal armour."

"Still, if all are as skilled as her, we will be hard-pressed to defeat them in battle."

"You forget, Urzath, we are here to prevent that very thing."

"Then ignore this attack. Let us concentrate on finding Agrug."

"Not yet," said Urgon. "I would know how this ends."

"We will kill this Human. How else could it end?"

He looked skyward to see light. "Dawn has come," he said, "and with it our last hope."

An ear-piercing whistle sang through the woods.

"What was that?" Urgon asked.

"It seems our Human wants to be found. Why else make such a noise?"

"Indeed. Let us rush forward. I would meet this warrior before she dies."

The noise of combat intensified, and then they came upon the fight itself. A ring of Orcs surrounded the woman, their axes at the ready. The Human was up against a tree to protect her back, but she was clearly worn out.

"Now she is doomed," said Urzath. The woman kept stabbing and slashing, each blow weaker than the last. The Orcs pressed forward, moving in for the kill.

Off to the side, there was a tremendous footfall, the likes of which Urgon had never before heard. Moments later, a massive horse rushed past, almost trampling them to death. Only the quick reaction of Urzath saved him, for she pulled him from its path even as it burst from the underbrush.

Urgon watched, mesmerized as the great beast made its way towards the Human. It slowed as it neared, and she rushed forward, grasping the saddle and hanging on for dear life. The Orcs, unaccustomed to such creatures, dove out of its path. A moment later, it disappeared from sight, although the sound of it crashing through the woods echoed back at them.

"By the Ancestors," said Urzath. "Did you see the size of that thing?"

"It is only a horse, nothing more," said Urgon. "Remember those of the earl?"

"I do, but they were far smaller." She looked at him. "If they have more of those creatures, then we are surely doomed."

Footfalls echoed through the forest, this time behind them. Many Orcs streamed past, armed and ready to fight, and Urgon felt his stomach tighten. It was too late—the battle had begun!

# TWENTY-FOUR

# The Battle of Eastwood

SPRING 960 MC

O ut onto the plain ran the Orcs, their calls for blood carrying far in the crisp, early morning air. Urgon emerged from the trees at the rear, trying to make sense of what was happening.

The earl had deployed his own men some distance away, facing the woods, and now the enemy was trapped between his forces and the tribe. The horde swarmed towards them, one solid mass of green while their foes were formed up in straight lines.

He ran forward, eager to catch up to his kin, but the fight in the forest had put the bloodlust into them. Eager for vengeance, they pressed close and ran fast.

He heard the initial impact as the two forces clashed, a deep thudding noise as axe met shield and sword met flesh. He saw blood spray upward, both black and red, and tried to push forward, eager to do his part, despite his objection to this war.

Suddenly, through the sea of green, he spotted Agrug. The chieftain was behind the main force, urging them on with shouts of encouragement while others fought and died.

Urgon called out his challenge, but his voice was lost amid the din of battle. Rushing forward, he felt the blood pounding through his veins. Agrug was close, and he called again. The mighty chieftain turned, their eyes meeting.

"Stop this now!" shouted Urgon.

Agrug drew his axe. "I will not. This is our destiny."

Urgon came closer until they were only a few paces apart. "You are killing our people."

"No, I am saving them. Would you have our tribe wither and die at the hands of Humans? If we win this battle, there will be none left to oppose us!"

"It is not our way."

"It might not be YOUR way," said Agrug, "but it is the only chance we have to survive as a people."

"At what cost?"

"Cost? Do not talk to me of cost, Urgon. Even your own father gave his life to benefit the tribe. Am I not asking the same of these others?" He swept his hand to indicate the horde.

Urgon pointed at the chieftain's torc. "You are not worthy to wear that."

"Then come and take it from me if you think you can!"

Urgon rushed forward, slashing out with his sword. Agrug, quick to respond, used his axe to block the blow, easily turning it aside.

"Is that the best you can do?" the chieftain taunted.

Urgon struck again, this time using a jabbing motion to hit his foe on the arm. The giant Orc pulled back in time to prevent any serious injury, then immediately counterattacked, although with little force, merely scraping along Urgon's chest and cutting his clothes but deflecting off the chainmail shirt.

"You shall die, Urgon, your name forgotten by our people."

The magic sword sliced out again but whistled through the air. Urgon readied for another attack but was knocked forward as horses surrounded him, forcing the two Orcs to give ground.

Agrug was lost in the chaos. Urgon screamed out in frustration, swinging left and right, his blade cutting into horseflesh and scraping off armour. A rider loomed over him, raising a sword on high just as another Orc leaped onto the saddle behind him, stabbing out with a long knife. Urgon saw the look of triumph on Galur's face even as another warrior plunged a sword into her back. Her eyes glazed over, and she fell to be trampled by yet more horses.

He caught a glimpse of the warrior woman, her great steed rearing up to deliver more death and destruction. A pair of Orcs managed to grab her shield in an attempt to pull her from the saddle, but she simply let go, causing them to fall back. Her horse's hooves came down, crushing bone as she transferred the sword to her left hand and pulled forth a hammer with her right.

Urgon, unable to tear his eyes away, watched, fascinated, as a spear took her in the leg. As she toppled from the saddle and disappeared from view, he tore his gaze away to concentrate on finding Agrug.

The initial charge had spent its momentum, quickly devolving into individual pockets of horsemen surrounded by Orcs. Urgon knew his chieftain must be somewhere near, directing things. He finally spotted him, surrounded by a half dozen of the toughest looking hunters he had ever laid eyes on. Throwing all caution to the wind, he advanced towards his destiny.

An Orc fell in beside him, and he turned to see Vulgar. A few more steps, and then Urzath joined them. Around them, the battle raged, but more and more Orcs left the fight, determined to watch this confrontation.

"Agrug," Urgon called out. "We have unfinished business, you and I."

The chieftain was having none of it. "Tarluk, Ragath. Kill him!"

Urgon took a stance, waiting for the attack to come, but Urzath and Vulgar moved past him, engaging Agrug's bodyguards. The fight was brief but bloody, and after only a moment, the two minions were down, clutching wounds while nursing their egos. Around them, many Orcs formed a circle while still others battled the enemy.

"Time to settle things," said Urgon.

"You will not defeat me," taunted Agrug. "I am far more powerful than you. I shall crush you just as I will crush the Humans who stand against us."

"Look around you, Agrug. Your cause is lost. Even as we speak, the Humans fight back. Do you honestly believe they will let us live in peace?"

"And so you seek to kill me?"

"You brought this upon yourself. You betrayed our people, turned your back on them for your own profit. What did the earl promise you, Agrug? Gold, perhaps?"

"You speak of profit, but it is you, Urgon, who craves power. You seek to become chieftain only to command others."

"No, the chieftain rules by the will of the tribe. It is a sacred duty to do what is best for all our people, not just a select few.

It was a strange sensation, standing here facing off against his own chieftain while the horde battled around him. Agrug rushed forward, his axe swinging in a wide arc to graze Urgon's chest, knocking him from his feet, but the Dwarven steel rings held back the sting. Agrug raised his axe for a second blow, and Urgon stabbed out. The attack was rushed, with barely enough power behind it to do any damage, but it struck his foe in the face, digging into the soft flesh of a cheek.

Agrug roared in pain and then smashed his axe down with all the force he could muster. The blade dug into the dirt as Urgon rolled to the side, then thrust out again, taking his enemy in the arm. As a howl of pain escaped the lips of Agrug, he released his axe, letting it fall to the ground.

"Stop," the large Orc shouted as he stepped back. "You have defeated me."

Urgon stood, not quite believing his ears. Agrug removed his torc, tossing it to Urgon, but as he did, his hand snaked around to his back, and he drew a large knife. Urgon fumbled to catch the torc, his mind distracted, and that was when Agrug rushed him.

The chieftain, substantially larger than his opponent, used his bulk to knock Urgon off his feet, crushing him beneath his weight as they landed on the ground. Barely able to breathe, Urgon tried to use his sword, but so close was the threat that it was impossible to wield.

Agrug's knife stabbed forward. Urgon felt it sink into his shoulder, burning as it dug in, the pain excruciating. He struggled to stay focused on the battle, his life, and the future of the tribe hanging in the balance. Closer pressed Agrug, the knife stabbing out again, this time at Urgon's chest, but the Dwarven links held, preventing further damage. Their faces were now so close he could smell the chieftain's breath.

"Now," hissed Agrug, "you shall die for your interference."

Urgon, pinned by the weight of the chieftain, did the only thing he could think of—used his helmeted head to smash into his foe's face.

Agrug's nose exploded, sending black blood flying, and he rolled to the side, his eyes watering, his vision temporarily impaired. Urgon, quick to react, scrambled on top of him and grasped the chieftain's dagger hand. A test of strength now ensued as each tried to out-muscle the other.

Agrug was stronger, but Urgon had the advantage of position. He leaned in, using his own weight to push the dagger down, finally sinking it into the chieftain's chest. With a final gasp of air from Agrug, all resistance faded as his head rolled to the side.

"It is done," announced Urzath. "You all saw it. Agrug willingly gave the torc to Urgon. Until we can return to Ord-Dugath to select a new leader, it is Urgon we must follow."

Tarluk took a step towards him. "What is your command, my chieftain?"

Urgon looked around. The Orcs still pressed heavily against the Human line while the horsemen were now scattered into small pockets of resistance. He wanted them to pull back, to quit this battle, but it must be justified, or he would lose his grip over the tribe.

Kraloch interrupted his thoughts. "Urgon, you must come," he begged.

"What is it?"

"It is the Human warrior, the same one who fought us last night. We have her surrounded."

Urgon followed his shaman to another ring that had been formed. However, this time, they pointed spears into the middle, to where the armoured woman stood, her weapons thick with black blood.

She shook her head, then tore off her helmet. Red blood ran down her face, while red hair fell to her shoulders. A broken spear was stuck in her knee joint, and she pulled it free, tossing it to the ground. She ran back and forth, striking out at spear tips, but no Orc would take the bait.

"Send in Vulgar," said Urgon.

The ring parted, allowing the massive hunter to enter the fight. He swung his sword left and right, loosening up his muscles. She watched him warily, and then he darted forward, striking out with immense speed. Her sword rose to her defence, deflecting the blow, and then she struck with her hammer, sinking it into the great Orc's knee. Urgon heard the bone break as Vulgar fell to the ground, screaming in agony.

He turned to Kraloch. "You must do something."

Kraloch nodded, then snapped up a nearby spear. The end had broken off in the fight, but it would suffice as a staff.

"What need have you for that?" asked Urgon.

"I do not wish to get too close to that Human. Thus I shall heal Vulgar from a distance."

"Using a staff?"

"It serves to focus my mind, nothing more."

Kraloch stepped into the ring, keeping his eyes on the Human. He chanted, calling up words of power and then touched the end of his staff to the writhing form of Vulgar. The patient ceased his screaming and looked up at his new chieftain. "Shall I continue?"

"No," said Urgon. "Kraloch will choose another to take your place."

Kraloch looked around the ring of Orcs, selecting the largest he could find, a hunter covered in scars. "You, what is your name?"

"Draleth," the Orc replied.

"Care to try your luck?"

Draleth nodded, then made his way into the ring. The hunter carried an axe with a long blade and a short handle, more akin to a cleaver. As he stood watching his opponent, he drew another such blade from behind him and waited, a weapon now held in each hand, ready to fight.

The two combatants rushed towards each other, he with weapons held high, her with a more relaxed grip. They traded blows, back and forth, each blocking the other's attack, performing a deadly dance of life and death. The dance continued, but they were so well matched, neither could score a hit.

Fresh blood poured from the woman's head, and Urgon could tell she was weakening, yet something in her resolve told him the fight was not yet done. Draleth rushed forward, expecting the battle to continue, but then the woman suddenly dropped to the ground, kicking out with her feet to strike the Orc's ankle. Draleth tumbled, falling atop her, but clearly she had been expecting it. Urgon saw the tip of a blade protruding from Draleth's back, and then the woman rolled the body to the side and pushed herself to her feet, swaying unsteadily.

"Do I send another?" asked Kraloch, his voice low.

"No," said Urgon. "I shall see to this myself."

He stepped into the ring, his sword held with the point downward. His intent had been to fight this warrior, but now, seeing her stand before him, he began to have doubts it was the right thing to do. He paused some three paces from his opponent.

"*You fight well,*" he said, using the Human tongue. "*We honour your valour.*"

She stared back, her face betraying her confusion. "*What?*"

He could well understand her bewilderment. He struggled to find the right words, but the Human language was still new to him. *"We will give your life and that of your companions in recognition of your bravery today."*

She said something in reply but far too quickly for him to follow. Still, her hesitation was quite evident. He spoke slowly, hoping she would understand. *"We will withdraw from battle. You have my word as leader of the Black Arrow clan."*

Again, the quick response, although he recognized the word 'battle'.

*"What is your name?"* he asked.

*"I am Dame Beverly Fitzwilliam,"* she replied. *"Knight of the Hound and protector of Princess Anna of Merceria."*

Urgon had no idea what any of that meant. The name was clear enough, although difficult to remember. He looked at her, seeing the warrior for what she was. Blood from her head ran down her arm, dripping from the end of her sword.

He seized on the image. *"To us, you shall be known as Redblade, for your prowess in combat is impressive. Tell your princess that we shall trouble her no more. We wish only to live in harmony."*

Again she spoke—this time enquiring as to why they were here.

*"The Earl of Eastwood promised us land,"* he explained, *"but he is a man without honour. My predecessor was foolish, and now many of my people have died. Even our healers cannot bring back the dead."*

*"I think I can guarantee that the princess will agree to leave your people alone once I explain what has happened."*

Urgon bowed his head. *"Perhaps one day we shall meet again, Redblade. It would be an honour to fight beside you."* He turned to leave, nodding at his companions.

"Order the retreat," shouted Urzath.

*"Wait!"* called out the Human. *"What is your name?"*

Urgon turned, looking at the battle-hardened woman. She had fought well, earning his respect but, even more importantly, had given him the opportunity to save his people. His heart swelled with pride as he spoke the words he had waited so long to say.

*"I am Chief Urgon of the Black Arrows."*

<<<<>>>>

REVIEW HONOUR THY ANCESTORS

∽

CONTINUE WITH WAR OF THE CROWN

∽

If you liked *Mercerian Tales: Honour Thy Ancestors,* then *Ashes,* the first book in The Frozen Flame series awaits.

START ASHES

## A Few Words from Paul

The chronicle of Urgon's rise to power was actually something I conceived of some time ago, back when I was writing Sword of the Crown. In that story, the Orcs fought against the main characters, yet I knew that would change in later stories. Since then, I've built upon Urgon's close friendship with Kraloch as the series progressed, but I still didn't have a concrete idea for his background, other than a few loose concepts.

All that finally fell into place when I came up with the character of Zhura. The idea of ghost-walkers was mentioned back in Defender of the Crown, but now, with time to think over the details, I was ready to introduce their presence. However, I didn't want to side-track War of the Crown by getting into the details, thus Zhura became an essential part of Urgon's story.

At its heart, Honour is about someone bucking the system and righting injustices while at the same time still caring about his people.

Urgon, Kraloch, and Zhura resume their story in War of the Crown and will continue to be important as the series moves forward.

This tale could not have been written had it not been for my wife, Carol, who encouraged me, suggesting several important points during the outlining phase. She is, as usual, my greatest inspiration, and I wouldn't be here without her assistance. I should also like to thank Amanda Bennett, Christie Bennett, and Stephanie Sandrock for their continued support and encouragement.

Alongside them, I must thank Brad Aitken and Steve Brown for their inspiration in getting this series to print, not to mention Jeffrey Parker, who, sadly, passed away this last winter. His legacy, in the form of Arnim Caster, shall live on.

A number of additional people who form my BETA team also

deserve thanks for their wonderful feedback and suggestions, and so my gratitude goes out to: Rachel Deibler, Michael Rhew, Phyllis Simpson, Don Hinckley, James McGinnis, Charles Mohapel, Lisa Hanika, Debra Reeves, David Clark, Michell Schneidkraut, Will Groberg, Wendy Francis, Joanna Smith, Brad Williams, Susan Young, Anna Ostberg, and Keven Hutchinson.

Finally, I must thank you, the reader, without whom there would be no impetus to continue these tales. Your comments have proven to be most inspiring, and I assure you I have plenty more tales to tell.

## About the Author

Paul J Bennett (b. 1961) emigrated from England to Canada in 1967. His father served in the British Royal Navy, and his mother worked for the BBC in London. As a young man, Paul followed in his father's footsteps, joining the Canadian Armed Forces in 1983. He is married to Carol Bennett and has three daughters who are all creative in their own right.

Paul's interest in writing started in his teen years when he discovered the roleplaying game, Dungeons & Dragons (D & D). What attracted him to this new hobby was the creativity it required; the need to create realms, worlds and adventures that pulled the gamers into his stories.

In his 30's, Paul started to dabble in designing his own roleplaying system, using the Peninsular War in Portugal as his backdrop. His regular gaming group were willing victims, er, participants in helping to playtest this new system. A few years later, he added additional settings to his game, including Science Fiction, Post-Apocalyptic, World War II, and the all-important Fantasy Realm where his stories take place.

The beginnings of his first book 'Servant to the Crown' originated over five years ago when he began running a new fantasy campaign. For the world that the Kingdom of Merceria is in, he ran his adventures like a TV show, with seasons that each had twelve episodes, and an overarching plot. When the campaign ended, he knew all the characters, what they had to accomplish, what needed to happen to move the plot along, and it was this that inspired to sit down to write his first novel.

Paul now has four series based in his fantasy world of Eidden-werthe, and is looking forward to sharing many more books with his readers over the coming years.